Little Black River

By
Randall Probert

Life on the Little Black River
by **Randall Probert**

Copyright © 2016 Randall Probert

All rights are reserved. No part of this book may be reproduced or transmitted electronically in any form without written permission from the publisher or author.
For more information, address Randall Enterprises.

www.randallprobertbooks.net

email: randentr@megalink.net

Disclaimer:
This book is a work of fiction. All places and character names are products of the author's imagination.

ISBN: 978-1535366960

Printed in the United States of America

Published by
Randall Enterprises
P.O. Box 862
Bethel, Maine 04217

Acknowledgements

I would like to thank Laura Ashton of Pinellas Park, FL for her help formatting this book for printing. I would also like to thank Warden Lt. Tom Ward at the Ashland Warden Service headquarters, for letting me use his name in the book. I would like to thank Sarah Lane of Bethel Bait and Tackle Shop for the front cover sketch and the map, and Patricia Gott for the author's photograph. The cover's background photograph is from iStockPhoto. And I would like to thank Amy Henley of Newry for her help with typing and the revisions.

More Books by Randall Probert

A Forgotten Legacy

An Eloquent Caper

Courier de Bois

Katrina's Valley

*Mysteries at
   Matagamon Lake*

A Warden's Worry

*A Quandry
   at Knowles Corner*

Paradigm

Trial at Norway Dam

A Grafton Tale

Paradigm II

Train to Barnjum

A Trapper's Legacy

An Esoteric Journey

The Three Day Club

Eben McNinch

Lucien Jandreau

Ekani's Journey

Whiskey Jack Lake

Life on the
Little Black River

Map of Little Black River Area

Prologue

"Ann, I'm hungry enough so I could eat a work horse. When will lunch be ready?" John asked.

Good naturedly and with humor in her voice, Ann replied, "Well, John Wiley, if'n you think you can prepare lunch any faster you're surely welcomed to try."

"No Ann, I didn't mean to ruffle your feathers none. I'm just saying I'm hungry."

"Fix yourself a cup of coffee and go sit on the porch. I'll let you know when it's ready."

John poured himself a cup and asked, "When will lunch be ready Ann?"

"Oh! Twenty or twenty-five minutes. Now go."

As John left the kitchen with his cup of coffee Ann was thinking how forgetful her husband was becoming. She had to keep reminding him to do the same thing and it was, at times, wearing on her nerves. But she loved him and figured his absentmindedness was only his old age. Then she chuckled and said out loud, "He's in pretty good shape for eighty-two." Ann was five years younger. They had met after John had been discharged from the Army. His first weekend home there had been a barn dance in Mapleton where they both lived and when he had asked her to dance, they both had fallen in love.

They had been married for fifty-five years now. Had two sons and a daughter that was the spit'n image of Ann. Coal black hair and eyes that smiled whenever she looked at anyone. She smiled and went back to making lunch.

John sipped his coffee and walked by the porch door and stepped in the living room. He took another sip and wondered what he was doing in the living room. He turned around and walked back to the porch door. He sat down in his wicker rocking chair and set his cup on the railing. He sat there staring out and down on his brother Ralph's potato fields.

John wasn't looking at the fields, nor was he aware of anything immediately around him. He was reliving his life as John Wiley.

John had been drafted into the Army in the spring of '45 and he was on his way across the Pacific in a troop transport ship when the war with Japan ended. The ship was redirected to Tokyo to help maintain military law.

He stayed in the Army and soon was promoted to Sergeant and then to Master Sergeant at the beginning of the Korean War. After serving fifteen months fighting, as Congress classified Korea as a police action and not war, John's opinion of Army life changed and when his enlistment was up in 1952 he left the Army and hitchhiked home from New York.

His dad had a heart attack the year before and upon John's return home he decided to retire. Blayne Wiley had four hundred acres in timber.

His younger brother Ralph didn't know anything but potatoes and he obviously wanted the potato fields and John wanted the timber.

The farm equipment and machinery were in good shape. While all John had was one two-and-a-half ton log truck, a 350 John Deere crawler with arch. John immediately traded the 350 for a new 450 with cable. He had some money he had been saving, but that he was depending on for operating capital. He had to finance the crawler and for now would live at home.

Two years later he and Ann built their own large log house on top of a knoll overlooking the farm. In general the 50s were a tough time, but John had done exceedingly well in the lumber business and after two years he was able to secure large contracts from Great Northern Paper Company on their holdings west of Ashland.

Each year his contract was larger and each year he had to move his operations further west. After thirty years harvesting timber for GNPC he decided to retire and he sold all of his equipment except for a new 450 John Deere crawler. He and his wife Ann had more money than they would ever need, but he just couldn't stop working all together. So at his leisure he cut his own wood on his four-hundred-acre wood lot.

He had seen a lot of changes in the lumbering industry. When he first started in the mid-'50s, most crews were still using work horses to twitch the wood out to the yards. And the two man cross-cut saw was being used by all the crews. Until the advent of the chainsaw. Then came the skidder, big trucks and now mechanical harvesting machines.

At age eighty-two he decided he had to give that up also. He had become so forgetful, Ann had to take over the bookkeeping. He'd forget when the truck was coming to load. And worst of all he could no longer remember how to notch the trees to have them fall and land where he wanted them. These things he kept from Ann, because he was afraid to talk about his forgetfulness.

"John!" Ann hollered from the kitchen. When he didn't show, she opened the porch door and looked around the door jam. John was in his rocking chair. "John. John."

This time he heard her and stood up. "Lunch is ready. I thought you were hungry. Bring your coffee cup in also."

John picked the cup up and emptied it over the railing. "I thought you wanted a cup of coffee. It didn't look as if you had drunk any."

"Oh that. I guess I was day dreaming and forgot it."

"Well come in, before your lunch gets cold."

As they ate Ann asked, "What were you thinking about on the porch, John?"

"I was thinking about this life and when we first met."

She didn't say anything but she was puzzled when he said, 'this life.' It just struck her as odd and she soon forgot about it.

* * *

The next morning at the breakfast table Ann said, "My sister Betty and I are going shopping at Presque Isle. You can come along if you want to."

"That's okay. I think I'll stay here and maybe take a walk in the woods to see how much the trees have grown. This is going to be a nice September day, I think. The best time of the year."

"Didn't you go for a similar walk two days ago—to see how much the trees had grown?"

"Yeah, but that was two days ago. You never know I might see something. Interesting."

"Okay John, just don't you go getting yourself lost," she said with a smile and then they both laughed.

While Ann combed her hair and, as she would say, 'put on her face,' John filled his coffee cup again and sat back at the kitchen bar top. It was always surprising to him how good it always was to feel a hot cup of coffee between your hands. Besides, he liked the taste of coffee.

"Anything I can pick up for you in town, John?"

"Yes, how about some of that good Columbian coffee. We're almost out."

"Okay," she replied and kissed him goodbye.

He got up and stood by the sink and watched as Ann drove out of the driveway. Then he went outside. The sun was bright, the sky was blue and no clouds in sight, no humidity and the temperature was 55°. "Just a perfect day for a walk."

Looking down on the potato fields he could see the men spraying to top kill the plants so growth would stop. A red fox was hunting for mice in the field next to his woods road and a red tail hawk was sitting high in a tree watching and waiting for the fox to scare up a mouse the fox didn't see.

He was surprised to see so much grass was growing in the center of the road. Then again he was surprised to see so much grass every time he was on the road. He just couldn't remember being so surprised before.

He inhaled deeply, enjoying the scent of the spruce and fir. Not far from the edge of the field he saw a cow moose feeding in a marshy area. A few years ago he would have rushed back to the house for his rifle. Now he would rather watch the animals. There was a grunt not too far away, but out of his sight. He knew it was a bull looking for a female and he knew enough about the moose rutting season to keep moving.

Except for being close to his wife Ann, he had always been the happiest when he was in the woods. And it didn't matter if he was working, cruising or strolling through the woods. And he knew that in a past life the forests had been very important to him.

His legs were beginning to tire so he sat on a stump at the edge of the road to rest. No sooner had he sat down, a doe and two lambs walked into the road just ahead of him. There was a slight breeze blowing into John's face, so the deer were not smelling his scent. The two lambs still had their spots, albeit they were faint by now. He was thinking the spots should be gone by now; unless she gave birth late in the spring. Any woods-wise person would say, "When lambs are born late, then deep snow will be late coming."

The three deer fed on clover and other broadleaf weeds along the roadside for a half hour and then went back into the woods. As they disappeared John was thinking how good deer steak and biscuits would be.

He stood and stretched and continued his walk. He saw a couple of two-year-old beaver cutting wood for their winter feed-bed.

"Just don't flood my road, beaver, or I'll have to trap you."

He had been walking on the woods road for more than an hour now and he came to the old log landing at the end. "I'll sit down a minute then start back. Wouldn't want to worry Ann. She gets awful concerned when I go off on my own." He had forgotten his wife had gone to Presque Isle with her sister Betty.

He sat down on an old reject pine log to rest before starting. Everything in his conscious mind was becoming unclear. Like he was trying to walk through a thick fog and not knowing where to go. And this was alarming. He stood up and looked around him. Spinning about slowly. Nothing was looking familiar. And worst of all, he had no idea where he was. He turned around a couple of times in the opposite direction.

Still nothing looked familiar and he was scared now. He had no idea where he was or even how he happened to be there.

Everything that had happened so far that morning wasn't even a blur in his memory. That morning did not exist for John in his memory. John Wiley had never been scared of anything in his life. But now he was frightened. And when anyone is frightened and in the forest they naturally begin to run.

John ran into the woods, not back along the road to his home. To his thinking there was no reason to follow a road that he didn't know where it would lead. Once in the woods he couldn't run, but he kept up a fast pace.

Ann was back at home shortly before twelve noon and when she didn't see John, she simply figured he hadn't got back from his walk in the woods yet. So she prepared a lunch of soup and thick ham sandwiches and coffee.

Ann had everything on the table and still no John and this began to concern her. It had been over four hours since she left for town and John had never taken this long to walk out to the end of the road and back again.

She jumped into his pickup truck and drove out to the end of the road and when she didn't see him, she really became worried. Had something happened to him? Had he fallen and broke a leg? She honked the horn several times and waited. Her concern growing every minute. So far she was refusing to think that he was having a lapse-memory spell. That idea frightened her.

She waited as long as she dared. She knew she had to get help. She honked the horn all the way back.

Once in the house she telephoned Lt. Tom Ward, friend, at the Warden Service Headquarters in Ashland. When a woman answered, "I'd like to speak with Mr. Ward please. This is an emergency."

"Certainly, Ma'am."

"Hello, this is Lieutenant Tom Ward. How can I help you?"

"Tom, this is Ann Wiley."

"Hello, Ann; what's the matter?"

"It's John, Tom. This morning he went for a walk out in the woods and he hasn't come back yet."

"When did he leave, Ann?"

"Betty and I drove to Presque Isle this morning and John was going for a walk. We left the house at 8:30."

"That's only been five hours, Ann."

"Yes, I know, Tom, but John has been having memory problems lately and I'm worried. I drove out to the end of the road and honked the horn. He was nowhere, Tom. And I'm getting so worried."

"I'm kinda holding down the fort today, Ann, but I'll have my secretary start making some calls and I'll head right out. I should be there in fifteen minutes."

"Please hurry, Tom. I'm so worried."

Tom had been friends with the Wileys ever since he and his family moved to the county and he, too, was worried about John. As he drove over the top of Castle Hill in a green streak and down in the hollow on the other side of the hill, he saw John walking along the roadside.

He braked as hard as he could without squealing his tires. He rode by, by a hundred feet, and backed up. By now John's senses had come back and he opened the passenger door.

"Hello, John, you want a ride or are you going to walk home?"

"Hello, Tom." He closed the door without saying anything else.

Tom keyed his radio to the Warden Service repeater and spoke into the mic, "2105, Ashland, disregard that signal 1000. I have him with me now and will be returning to his residence. Please notify everyone." He purposely avoided using John's name on the air or what the emergency was.

"What happened, John? Go for a walk and got turned around?" Tom asked.

"Yeah, something like that, Tom."

In only a few minutes they drove to John's home. Ann came running out crying.

Tom understood that John and Ann had much to talk about and it would probably be easier for them both if he was to leave. He had what he needed for his report. He said goodbye and left.

"What happened, John?" He heard the concern in her voice.

He thought long and hard before answering. When he did he looked square in her eyes and said, "I was really enjoying my walk, I was happy and I was feeling good. When I got to the end of the road I sat down to rest. That's the last I remember until I walked out to the road at Castle Hill. I recognized Tom immediately. That's all I can tell you, Ann."

"Maybe we should go see Dr. Morneau in Presque Isle in the morning."

* * *

After breakfast the next morning they drove to Presque Isle and Dr. Morneau's office. Ann insisted that she drive.

Ann was sure the incident yesterday had to do with John's memory problems that surfaced occasionally. She knew if she kept talking to him about it that that would only make things worse. John had been unusually quiet since yesterday and Ann knew John was worried about what had happened. And she was afraid this was the beginning of a lonesome and difficult road to the end.

But they would not know anything for sure until talking with the doctor.

"Come in, Ann and John. It is good to see you both."

"Good morning, Dr. Morneau."

"Between friends I'd rather you call me Ed. Now what can I do for you?" he asked.

Ann told him about the day before.

"How old are you John?"

"Eighty-two."

"How far is it from your house to the end of the road?" Morneau knew, he and his wife had walked it with John and Ann. But he wanted to see if John could remember.

"It's about two miles."

"How fast did you walk, John?"

"Not fast. I did stop once about halfway and sat on a stump and watched two—no, three deer." He had forgotten the beaver.

"When you started walking again did you experience any dizziness or lightheadedness?"

"No."

"When you sat down in the yard at the end of the road, how were you feeling?"

"My legs were a little tired. That's why I sat down."

"How was your breathing and pulse? Could you tell?"

"I'm not sure. I don't think my heart was working too hard."

"When did things start to change, John?"

"I'm not sure how long I had sat on the log. But before I stood I was getting a little disoriented. When I stood up, it seems it was worse."

"Has this ever happened before, John, where you were disoriented?"

"No."

"I want to check your blood pressure, John."

Ann sat quietly and listening.

"Your blood pressure is a little high, John. Because of your age and the distance you walked, you may have had a minor stroke. I'm going to prescribe a blood thinner, and Ann, if he drinks coffee—decaffeinated coffee only. Exercise, but probably no more two-mile hikes unless someone is with you."

"I want to see you again, John, in one month—unless you have another such spell. Then, Ann, bring him in immediately."

"Thank you, Ed," Ann said.

John stood up and shook hands with Ed and said, "Thank you."

* * *

Ann watched John closely while not trying to be too obvious. And for a week John was his normal self, but Ann began to notice changes. Subtle changes at first. Like he'd make a mistake while talking with Ann and then in mid-sentence correct himself; then she began to notice John sitting more and staring out the window.

He had not shown any disorientation signs, only forgetfulness, so Ann waited until their next appointment with Dr. Morneau.

The morning of the appointment Ann laid out on the bed clean clothes for John and said, "John you put on these clean clothes before breakfast."

"Okay—why?" he asked.

"We have to go see Dr. Morneau in Presque Isle."

"Okay."

John dressed himself and shaved and then walked over to the kitchen. He wasn't sure why he was going there, only this seemed to be routine.

Once in the car and only a few miles from Dr. Morneau's office John asked, "Where are we going?"

"We have an appointment this morning with Dr. Morneau."

"Okay." That seemed to answer his wondering.

As Ann was turning into the parking lot John said, "I recognize this place. Ed Morneau lives here." That was close enough and Ann didn't correct him.

"Let's go in and talk with Ed, John."

"Okay."

The receptionist, Lisa, led them to a small conference room with padded chairs. "Dr. Morneau thought you would be more comfortable here. Dr. Morneau will be with you soon."

"Thank you," Ann said.

Ed was only a brief moment before he joined them. "Good morning, Ann and John."

"Good morning," they both replied.

"Tell me, John, do you know who I am?"

"Of course; you're Ed Morneau," he replied.

Ann and Ed both realized John didn't say Dr. Morneau.

"Do you know where you are, John?"

"Certainly, we're in your house."

"That's close enough. Tell me, Ann, has John had any more difficulties with being disoriented?"

"Not with disorientation, but he has become more forgetful and he sits and stares out the window a lot. There are times when I look at him, really look at him in his eyes, I'm not sure if he knows who I am. Sometimes he has this blank stare as if there is nothing behind those eyes any more. He is here in his physical body, but I'm not sure where his mind is."

"John, I need to ask you some questions. Are you okay with that?"

"Sure, why not?"

"Good. John, how old are you?"

Without hesitating John replied, "Eighty-two."

"What year were you born, John?"

"Eighty-two years ago."

Ed wanted to laugh, but he controlled himself. He noticed Ann smiling. "What year is this, John?"

"I'm not sure—eighty-two?"

"Where do you live, John?"

"In a house."

"What town is this house in, John?"

"I don't know."

"What did you have for breakfast?"

"Don't know."

"What did you do yesterday, John?"

"She says I look out the window."

"John can you count backward from 100 by 10s?"

"100—." That's as far as he could go.

"John, your wife Ann and I are worried about you. About your memory. Can you tell me how you feel?"

Without any hint of emotion John said matter-of-factly, "Scared. I know who I am, I know this is my wife Ann and you are my friend Ed. I know I am in this room, but I don't know what exists on the other side of these walls. I don't remember how I got here. And I know I forget—everything. I know, or think this is the present, but I'm not sure. I seem to be living in two worlds." Dr. Morneau wanted to interrupt, but John was on a roll and he didn't want that to stop. "I look at Ann and sometimes I'm not sure who she is. I know she is my wife. But I can't remember the life we have had together." John hesitated there for a moment and neither Ann nor Dr. Morneau said anything. They were both waiting for John to continue. He was making so much sense.

"I know this is the present—but I have no memories of this present. But memories are of another time. And what I see I know it is in the past. And this past for me is here now—now, in the present. The present and this past are the same. I can't remember anything about this day, but I have very sharp memory images of this past I see."

"I understand John, can you tell me about this past and be explicit?"

Before answering John turned to Ann and said, "You are there."

Chapter 1

On April 14, 1861, two days after the start of the Civil War, news of the war had reached Fort Kent, Maine. Everyone knew war was inevitable, now it had come. This far north and away from the conflict, many people had little interest. But for the Kelley family, they were patriots and breaking up the country was just stupid.

One day while Blair and his Dad Blayne were spraying the potato and apple crops Blayne said, "You have been very quiet all day, son. What's on your mind?"

"I can't stop thinking about that article in the paper yesterday about the war. I hate to think about this country being pulled apart like the south wants to do."

"What are you going to do about it?"

"I'm not sure. I'd like to help to keep the country together, but I don't want to leave you and Peter alone on the farm. Peter's only fourteen and not as big and rugged like you and me, Pa. I'll have to think on it."

* * *

Three years ago Blayne and his two sons Blair and Peter sawed out some cedar boards from Blayne's own saw mill and during the summer when they were not too busy they made an extra long and wide cedar canoe. This was twenty-four feet long. Much longer than a regular canoe. But shorter than the Canadian fur trapper voyager canoe.

Blayne would take his whole family on a week's fishing trip up the Allagash River each summer. There was plenty of room for the five of them and all of their gear.

July and August were the only slow months on the farm, once the crops had been sprayed for bugs. Once the apples were ready to pick they would haul them by wagon to Frenchville, Madawaska and across the St. John River to Edmundston. They would press some apples to make juice and cider and vinegar. The potatoes were hauled by wagon to Madawaska also.

Blayne had a few acres with just wheat also that were sold in Madawaska. The wheat was actually a nice bonus to the farm income.

Blayne sawed only the logs that he harvested on his own land. He was a small operator. Down the road a few miles was a much larger saw mill owned by the McQuale family. They bought logs from other land owners, since the McQuales did not own any timber land. They did quite well with the mill also.

Blayne was very selective about which trees he would take. If it meant felling a larger spruce or pine on top of many nice smaller trees, he would not cut it.

Blayne was a very strong and tough Irishman. He stood 5' 11", a big barrel chest and he weighed 235 pounds. He could lift what four men could and he'd never backed down from anyone.

Blair was an inch taller and 5 pounds heavier, stronger than his father and just as even tempered. He had made a side step on each of the wagons for Blair to stand on and all the driver had to do was drive down a potato row and one handed, Blair would grab the potato barrels and swing them onto the wagon. His dad couldn't do that.

Peter was nowhere as big and strong as his father and brother. And Regina and Faye both were small and petite women.

Everyone liked Blair for he was never in a foul mood. Both Blayne and Blair were aware of their extreme strength and they purposely stayed away from fights.

The fall of 1861 was a good year for the Kelley farm. The apples, potatoes and wheat all had to be harvested at the same time. Some of their usual seasonal help had gone to war and one morning a small, thin young girl came looking for work.

"How old are you, girl?" Blair asked.

"I am fourteen and my name is Monique Lamoureax. And don't let my small size fool you; I can do the work of any of your other hired hands."

Boy, had he been put in his place. "Aren't you the granddaughter of Minnie and Alford Lamoureax?"

"Yes. And yes, I am Indian. Indian and French."

"Would your grandparents want to work also?" Blair asked.

"My grandfather can't and my grandmother is busy making baskets."

"Can you start today? We need apple pickers."

"I can."

Even though Faye was even younger than Monique she was in charge of the apple pickers. Blair and Peter, the potatoes, and Blayne and a hired hand were responsible for harvesting and thrashing the wheat. Regina was in charge of meals and her two hired girls.

Whenever Blair was going past the orchards he would pause long enough to find Monique and see how she was working. She was a skinny younger girl, but there was something about her that intrigued him.

At the supper table one evening Faye said, "Monique is the hardest working picker of all of them. As small as she is I didn't think she would be able to move around the picking ladders. But she never asks for help."

* * *

When the harvesting of all the crops was finished, some of the apples were pressed for cider and then vinegar and by the middle of November everything had been taken to markets. It had been one of the best years on the farm. Blair, Peter and Faye were given a bonus. Blair tucked his away for another day.

The farm was pretty much self-sustaining. They grew their own food crops and exchanged some wheat for flour. There were pigs, chickens and instead of a dairy cow, they had goats for milk and cheese. Once in a while Blayne would buy a bull calf and raise it for beef. They smoked their own ham and bacon. And after the farm and crops were tended, they would shoot a moose. The weather would be cold enough by now so the meat wouldn't spoil. Much of the meat Regina and Faye canned.

During the fall and winter Blair ran a trap line which he did very good with. And every penny he earned, he saved. "I might need it sometime," he would say.

By Christmas the Kelley family were all ready for winter. There was plenty of stove and furnace wood in the sheds, the hams and bacon were smoked and hanging in the root cellar and plenty of goat cheese curing.

The Sunday before Christmas there was a harvest and Christmas celebration at the church. Blair saw Monique early on and asked, "Monique, would you sit with me while we eat?"

"I would like to."

"How are your grandparents?"

"My grandmother is still busy making baskets. My grandfather's health isn't good, but he helps when he can."

Blair noticed the three McQuale brothers watching he and Monique. You never saw just one or two brothers alone, they traveled like a pack of wolves. The three were always together. If you fought one, you fought all three. And they enjoyed ganging up on a lone person when there was no one else around.

All night the three brothers kept watching Monique. Only turning away when Blair would look at them. Blair could tell the three brothers were drinking something more than punch. He wasn't worried about himself, but from the way they had been glaring at Monique he was concerned for her.

When the celebration was over Blair said, "Monique, I don't like how the McQuale brothers have been looking at you. I think you should probably let my family take you home. It'll be a tight squeeze, but we'll make room."

"I would appreciate the ride. I don't like the way those boys have been looking at me."

Blayne Kelley had a big two horse drawn sleigh for the family and there certainly was room for one more.

"If the McQuale brothers ever give you any trouble let me or my Dad know. We'll take care of them for you," Blair said.

* * *

Blair did well fall trapping and he only had a few beaver by year's end. The snow was deep but the second week of January turned off unusually warm. January thaw. And much of the snow melted and Blair trapped long after work, almost every day.

He had held onto his fall fur pelts and would sell them in the spring across the border in Clair, New Brunswick, along with his beaver pelts and castors.

Besides trapping he was also working daily in the woods cutting trees. "Blair," his mother would say, "if you don't slow down you'll eat us out of house and home. You're eating as much now as four men."

"Yes, Ma," as he closed the kitchen door and shouldered his pack basket.

By mid-March Blair had twenty-two nice beaver and two otter. One evening at the supper table, "Dad, I'd like to take tomorrow off if I could, to take my fur to Clair before the ice breaks up in the river. I'll work Saturday to make up for it."

Early the next morning Blair harnessed the team to a smaller sleigh and headed off down the well-snow-packed road to Fort Kent.

Not far beyond the turn to Monique's grandparents home,

Monique was walking. "Would you like a ride Monique?"

"Sure would," and she climbed in and sat down.

"Where are you going?" Blair asked.

"Into town and do a few errands for my grandmother. Where are you going?"

"I'm taking these fur across the river to Clair while the river is still ice."

"Is this what you do in the winter, trap?"

"That and I work in the woods to supply lumber for my Dad's mill."

When they reached Fort Kent Blair asked, "Where would you like to go?"

"The bank and then I have a few things to pick up."

"Would you like a ride back?"

"That would be nice."

"Okay, when I come back I'll wait for you at the bank."

There was a well used crossing across the St. John River and even though it looked safe enough Blair could see pools of open water two hundred yards downstream. This crossing will probably be officially closed the next day or the day after.

Pierre's Furrier was situated on a hill overlooking the river. There were two other trappers there ahead of him. They each had a puny cache of dirty fur and Pierre was arguing that he could not give them top dollar for dirty pelts. After a while Pierre won the argument and the two trappers accepted their money and left.

As they walked by Blair's sleigh loaded with prime looking pieces they stopped and started handling some of the pelts.

"I just as soon you two didn't paw through my fur," Blair said.

"What's the matter, mister? We ain't going to steal none."

Yeah, they were Americans alright. And their appearance was as grubby as their fur pieces. The two kept pawing through the fur and Blair took two steps closer to the larger of the two and grabbed him under his chin and lifted him off his feet. "I said I didn't want you two pawing over my catch," he said in a calm voice.

The smaller guy's eyes were bugging out and he didn't want any more trouble. "Come on, Harry, let's go."

Pierre was watching all of this from the front door and as the two walked off he started laughing. "Huh-huh, I guess they won't bother you no more, young man. Let's see what you have brought me."

Pierre helped Blair carry everything inside and laid them out on the counter. "You sure do take good care of you hides, Blair. You fur always does look more better than other trappers."

"Thank you. But how much will you pay?" Blair asked.

"You have twenty beaver; twelve dollar each." The fall pieces he separated according to species. "One otter, three mink, three fisher, four lynx, ten martin, two raccoon, four ermine, three red fox. I give you $240 for beaver and $160 for rest. You got d'castors?"

"Yes, I forgot, they're in the sleigh. I'll be right back."

Blair laid eight castors on the counter. "Here are eight. I kept two for lure."

"Two dollar each for castor $416.00 total."

"No," Blair said, "I take $425.00 total."

"Okay, only 'cause you take so good care of you fur."

Blair put his money in his pocket and looked at a few things on the shelves, but he didn't buy anything. He left and said, "Thank you, Pierre." Then he rode back across the river to the bank. Monique wasn't there yet, so he went inside and deposited his fur money along with the last fall and winter's wages. He had been saving his money always and now he had almost two thousand dollars.

As he sat and waited for Monique a brisk wind came down the valley and suddenly Blair was cold. He had a heavy quilt and he wrapped that around his shoulders. Monique came walking up a few minutes later carrying two packages. "Hi,

Blair, you cold?"

"That breeze is cold and we'll be riding into it on the way home."

They made one more stop for a newspaper and any earlier copies that might be left over. It had been a month since anyone from the family had been out to town.

It was getting noticeably colder and Blair said, "If you were to slide over closer then this quilt could wrap around both of us. Monique didn't hesitate—whether she was that cold or she wanted to sit closer to Blair. Or maybe a little of both.

The northerly wind had brought with it a bitter cold. "That wind is so cold, Blair."

"Pull the quilt over your head to shield your face."

She did and moved over closer so now Blair could feel her body next to his. It was a good feeling.

* * *

That evening after supper Blair began reading the newspaper. On the front page was an article in bold headlines that caught his attention. "Mom, Dad, there's an article on the front page that an infantry regiment is being formed in this coming August. It'll be commanded by a Colonel Adelbert Ames. The regiment will be called the 20th Maine.

"Mom, Dad, I think it is time for me to do my part in helping to keep this country together."

Blair went on to explain that the 20th would be officially formed on August 29th and all who wanted to volunteer should be at the Bangor Armory on the 26th.

"Are you sure about this, son?" Blayne asked.

"Yes, I have thought a lot about it this winter. I'll be here for spring planting and spraying the crops. Just not for harvest."

"Well I guess that's all settled then. Now, before we lose the road to spring breakup we need to freight all this lumber to market. I'll send four sleds out tomorrow. Blair, you bring back all the cutting crews and all the teams you can. You may have to leave one or two teams to clean up.

"The next day we'll hook up a train of loaded sleds and haul everything out."

* * *

The next morning instead of taking a team into the woods camp, he was up early and walked in. The air was frigid cold again but it didn't bother him. The cold would harden the road surface making it easier for the teams to pull the loaded sleds.

He was noticing a few deer tracks in the woods road this morning. These were the first deer tracks he had seen in winter around the choppings. This was a good sign. He inhaled deeply, smelling the scent of fresh cut pine and spruce. There was only one scent more sweeter than pine and spruce. Balm of Gilead in the spring. Yes this was a good life. He couldn't imagine living anywhere else, except in the woods.

He was there early enough to have breakfast with the cook and foreman.

"Royce I need all the teams taken back to the mill after breakfast. Keep one team here to finish cleaning up. Two if you think you need it. Pa wants to use all the teams tomorrow to freight out all the lumber. When you have everything cleaned up here, you and rest of the crew come out. I'll come in later to close things up for the summer."

There were two teams going out with small sled loads and two teams staying to clean up the remaining logs.

That evening at the supper table Blayne said, "You know, in spite of the war that's going on, we did really well with the lumber. Molsey McGray said he would buy everything we have sawn this winter. And he asked if we could expand a little next season."

"Now you're making me feel guilty about leaving, Dad," Blair said.

"That wasn't my intention. I was only trying to explain how well the lumber business is doing."

* * *

When all the lumber had been freighted to the mill and yard cleaned up and the woods camp closed up, the crews were paid off and they returned to their homes.. Most had signed on for the following winter.

As the weather began to warm, the mill yard and the woods road across the field had turned to mud. Even the main road to town was too soft for either horse and walking on foot.

Once the mill yard had dried up Blayne and his sons began to overhaul and repair the mill equipment, the harnesses and sleds.

Just as the river ice in the St. John began to break up, it rained for two days. Not a heavy rain, but steady. The river rose and finished breaking up the ice. More ice began to flow downstream from above town and soon there was an ice jam and the river rose twenty feet. This was not a yearly occurrence, but Blair had seen it three times before in his life. Explosives were used below town to break up the jam and the river slowly dropped back to a more normal run off.

The ice was all gone a week later and the weather had been so warm even the blocks of ice that had been pushed ashore had melted. The fields were turning green and it was almost time for planting. One evening Blayne, Blair and Peter walked around the potato field and Blayne said, "We should be able to start planting next week."

In the meantime the apple trees were pruned and the brush was burned.

After the first week in May, the sun was high and bright, a little breeze from the west and the ground was ready for planting. While Blayne and Blair turned over and harrowed the soil, Peter was busy cutting seed. A job he really hated. It took all of one day to prepare the field for planting. While Blayne and Peter were busy with the potato seed planter, Blair harrowed the wheat field. They worked from shortly after sunrise to sunset. After four days both crops were planted. Now there was some time for relaxing and to do some fishing.

All five members of the Kelley family, with their camping and fishing gear boarded their larger canoe and with two double ended paddles. Blair in the bow and Blayne in the stern they headed upstream on the St. John River. It was an all day trip to the mouth of the Allagash River.

While Blayne helped Faye and Regina set up camp and the fire, Peter and Blair went fishing. They weren't long before they had two, two-pound brook trout, but it would take several more to feed all five.

"If we don't catch any more trout, Blair, we can always eat blackflies. I have never seen them so bad. All you have to do is open our mouth and suck in and you have a mouth full."

The blackflies were terrible, but Blair couldn't help but laugh at his brother's analogy. "They'll die out, Peter, in another month."

"Yeah, if I have any blood left by then. How can you put up with them so easily?"

"Don't let them bother you. Just ignore them."

"If they were any bigger a swarm of them buggers could carry me off."

Just then Peter's pole dipped to the water and he lost whatever had taken his bait. "There, Peter, maybe you'll stop complaining about the blackflies and concentrate on your fishing."

By the time the sun had set the two had finally caught enough fish for the whole family. Peter was still swatting blackflies and complaining about them. As the air began to cool, the blackflies backed away some.

Everybody was quiet as they ate. Blayne stopped and looked around at his family. He was happy to be here and sharing this moment with those he loved.

He thought he could understand why Blair thought he had to go off to war, and in a way he didn't blame him. But he would miss him on the farm and in the woods. He would have to hire someone to take his place. Peter was not old enough to fill his shoes yet.

* * *

The next day the men caught more fish to have with eggs and coffee for breakfast and then they loaded the canoe and headed upstream again. They canoed through the oxbox and then upstream about another four miles where the river narrowed and a ledge rock along the west shore. Just before the ledges there was a beach of fine gravel and the water was deep, a spring freshlet on the east side. They had camped here before and had had excellent fishing. And besides, there were also plenty of fiddleheads to pick.

Regina had brought a side of ham, beans and flour, but at least one meal a day was fish. The work was always harder and heavier in the winter and now was the time to put back on some of that lost weight. Even Regina and Faye needed a break from the winter work. Their days were always as long and tiring as the men's.

Blayne would spend a lot of the time lying in the sun on the gravely beach, while Blair was always off wandering in the woods. Peter would often tag along, but he was not as interested, nor was his love for feeling serene in the wilderness as keen as his big brother Blair's.

"You never go in the back country or any big woods, Peter, unless you have a compass and know how to use it, a good knife and matches."

"I can use a compass, Blair, but I've noticed you never look at yours."

Blair was so accustomed to the wilderness, a natural,

that he seldom ever had to check his compass. He just always seemed to know where he was going and how to get back again.

In the evenings after everyone had eaten, they'd sit near the fire. Often times sitting there in silence watching the flames. Blayne and Blair would always be the last to call it a day and turn in. It was a happy time and the family looked forward to this trip each year. Peter had even stopped complaining about the blackflies.

The morning came when they knew it was time to go home. With the canoe loaded Blayne said, "Peter you're in the bow on the trip back. Blair, your mother and me are going to cuddle up in the middle. You have the stern. Faye, you fish along the way. Going with the current and two strong boys doing the paddling, we'll probably reach the St. Francis River long before sunset.

* * *

They all had to admit that no matter how much they had enjoyed the trip, it was nice to be home. "I get to sleep in my own bed tonight," Regina said and the rest of the family laughed and agreed. They were all tired.

Until it was time to hull the potatoes, the three men worked on the equipment. Making sure there would be no break downs during harvest. With the equipment overhauled and repaired, Blair began working on winter stovewood.

Peter would try to work at his brother's pace, but before mid-afternoon he had to stop for the day. Even after supper Blair would buck-up what they had hauled in during the day. There was no rush, but Blair needed to keep busy. Besides, he enjoyed the workout. Some days Blayne would have Peter help him instead of Blair and Blair enjoyed this time alone in the woods and he could usually get out almost as much wood.

"How much more wood do you think we need, son?" Blayne asked one day. "You already have enough for two years."

"Well—it'll be nice and dry for year number two." That's all he could say and Blayne walked off shaking his head and laughing.

The town was having a midsummer celebration and Blayne offered a pig to roast. The pig was slaughtered the day before, dressed and skun and wrapped with cheese cloth and put in the root cellar. That night the family ate fresh pig liver and heart with new potatoes, onions and green beans.

Early the next morning Blair and Peter loaded the pig onto a wagon and drove to town. The festival would be on the river bank. Bean-hole beans were already cooking and once Blair and Peter had the pig on the spit, the fire had died down to a hot bed of coals. "You'd better take the team back, Peter, and help with the chores. I'll stay here and watch the pig roast." Peter had wanted to stay also but he knew his father was looking for him to come back and help out.

Even though it was still early, people were setting up tables and making coffee and punch. Blair walked over to one fire and helped himself to a cup of coffee. It was hot and strong. As he was walking back to the roasting pig, he noticed Monique walking towards him and not far behind her were the three brothers McQuale. "Oh, I'm so glad to find you, Blair. Grandmother told me you would be roasting the pig."

"Good morning, Monique." Then he looked squarely at the McQuale brothers. When they saw Blair staring at them, they backed off from following Monique. "Are they bothering you, Monique?"

"They followed me most of the way here. I had to run to stay ahead of them. They're just no good. I wouldn't be so afraid of just one of them, but I've heard how they gang up on someone by herself."

"Well, you stay close to me today Monique and I'll see they don't bother you. You can ride home with us too."

"Oh, thank you; I'd really appreciate it, Blair."

He looked at Monique, thinking, *At fifteen she's still just a little scrawny girl.* But there was something about her that interested him. He just didn't know what it was.

By mid-morning more people were arriving and setting up tables with a wide variety of desserts.

Behind the group, the McQuale brothers were standing together and by themselves and watching Monique. "Monique will you tend the pig for a few minutes? There's something I have to do."

"Sure."

Blair pulled off a small piece of crispy fat and ate it as he made a wide circle around the crowd to come in behind the McQuales. When he was a short distance behind them, they were still watching Monique and did not know Blair was now standing right behind them.

"Hello boys."

All three jumped. "What the hell do you want?" Burl asked. He was the oldest of the three.

The other two were too shaken up to say anything. "What's the attraction with Monique?"

"None of your damned business," Burl replied.

"Why don't we step back here so we can talk," Blair said calmly.

"Go to hell," Boydie said. He was the youngest of the three.

Without saying anything Blair reached out and grabbed Burl and Burk in one arm and he picked Boydie off his feet by his belt and then back away from the celebration. He sat them down but continued holding onto them.

"Now boys, you leave Monique alone. I do not want you three pestering her, following her or hurting her. If I ever hear you have done anything to hurt her—well, I'll take care of you boys myself. I'll hurt you real bad," he said in a calm voice.

"Do you understand me?" When they didn't answer he shook them up some and asked again, "Do you understand me?"

"Yeah. Yeah, we understand you. Now let us go."

Blair released his grip on them and said, "Remember what I have said," and he walked back to the roasting pig and Monique.

"I saw you talking with the McQuale boys. What did you say to them?"

"I told them what would happen to them if they didn't leave you alone. If they ever bother you again, let me know, okay?"

"I sure will. Thank you, Blair. I'm getting hungry." All said in the same breath.

"Nibble on the pork."

"I have been—a little."

The rest of the Kelley family arrived and Blayne and Peter joined Blair, while Regina and Faye joined a small gathering of women.

"How much longer, son?"

"Maybe an hour."

"Hi, Monique."

"Mr. Kelley. Where is Faye?"

"She and her mother are talking with that group of women at the back table."

"Blair, I think I'll go talk with Faye."

"Remember about the ride home, Monique."

The pork and beans were ready to eat at 4 o'clock. It was a good thing too. Everyone was hungry and were asking when the pork would be finished. Two lines were formed and Monique helped Blair serve the pork. It was golden brown on the outside and juicy. And it sure smelled good. Even after everyone had been served, there was pork as well as beans left over. Many people came back for seconds and a few for thirds.

The pork was all cut away from the bone and given to Monique to take home. "I'm sure your grandparents will appreciate this, Monique," Regina said.

"Thank you, I know they will."

The McQuale trio were at the end of the line and they

were too afraid of Blair to even look at Monique. When they had moved on, Monique asked, "What did you say to them, Blair? They wouldn't even look at me."

"I told them to stop bothering you and if they didn't I would take care of them."

On the way home Monique had to sit in Blair's lap. That was okay with her.

After Monique left the carriage at her grandparents and the Kelley's were now heading for their home, Faye said, "She likes you, Blair."

"Oh nonsense. She's just a skinny kid."

"She won't be for long, Blair. Skinny or just a kid," his mother said and smiled.

* * *

Blayne, Blair and Peter were two weeks hand spraying the crops, and the time was getting close when Blair would have to leave. It was on everyone's mind, but no one wanted to talk about it.

One evening as the family were sitting on the porch waiting for the daytime temperature to drop, Blair said, "Dad— Mom, is there any way you could have Monique work on the farm more than just during harvest? Her grandparents don't have much and the only income other than when Monique can pick up some extra work is the baskets she and her grandmother make. She's a good worker and can do almost anything."

Peter spoke up first, "If I spend more time helping out Dad, she can do my chores."

When the sun had set, the temperature dropped where it was more bearable. After the others had gone inside and to bed Blair went for a walk around the farm. The moon wasn't quite full but there was plenty of light to see by.

At the bottom end of the wheat field he could make out a doe and lamb deer. They were so rare this far north, he seldom ever saw one. Maybe a track now and again in mud or snow.

He followed the woods road out to the crew camp and sat on a stump for awhile, not thinking about much at all.

As he sat there listening to all the night sounds, he began thinking it would take probably a day and a half by coach to Mattawamkeag where he could board the train for Bangor. Then from Mattawamkeag to Bangor would probably take twelve hours, depending on how many stops there were. So he figured he'd better leave Fort Kent on the morning of the 25th. Allowing an extra day for just in case.

"Yes sir, Mr. Kelley we have a stage leaving at six o'clock on the morning of the 25th. All the way to Mattawamkeag you say. There's a night stop in Mars Hill. The stage leaves there the next morning at 6 am sharp. No overnight from there to Mattawamkeag. Maybe quite late before you arrive."

Blair paid for his ticket. "I ain't never been below Van Buren before."

"It'll be a long ride, young fella. Guess maybe you joining up with the 20th Maine."

"That's right, Mr. Snow."

Chapter 2

On the morning of the 25th the whole Kelley family was up early and after a hearty breakfast Blayne said, "Peter, would you drive Blair to the stage terminal?"

"Sure, Dad."

"I hope you don't mind, son, but your mother and I have work to do."

"No problem."

"Can I ride with you?" Faye asked.

"Sure you can, as long as Mom doesn't need you."

"I guess it'll be okay. But come right home, you two."

After more coffee, goodbyes were said and Regina started crying when she hugged her son. Blair hugged his father too, and Blayne's eyes were watering also.

Faye kept up an almost constant chatter all the way to town. "Blair, I don't understand why you're going to fight in a war that doesn't seem to concern us."

Blair did the best he could to explain to his sister why he felt it was important for him to fight to keep the country together.

They said their quick goodbyes and Blair climbed on top of the stage with the driver. Peter and Faye stood there watching until the stage was out of sight. "When will he come home, Peter?"

"I don't know; maybe not until the war is over."

"I still don't understand why he has to go, Peter."

"I think it is something he feels he has to do. Come on, Faye, we'd better get home."

* * *

"Glad for the company. What's your name, young fella?"

"Blair Kelley; and yours?"

"French and Irish, good combination. I'm called Holmer T."

"What's the T for?"

"Anything you'd like. You're a big strapping fella, ain't you . Be good in case we lose a wheel and need a lift. How far you going, Blair?"

"I'm joining up with the 20th Maine."

"I'm glad I'm too old to be fight'n in that war. I'd find it some terrible having to shoot at my own kind. Then I don't agree with what the south is doing trying to break the country apart either.

"It can be a hot, rough ride up here. The inside has more spring to the seats than this here board of a seat. But it gets dustier inside too.

"We'll have to change teams at Saint Luce Station. It'll be a quick stop. Passengers will only have time enough to relieve themselves. If they're quick about it. No time for lunches or coffee. I must stay on schedule. Whenever I can, that is."

"You don't say much, young fella."

"Oh, just listening to you, Holmer T."

They left Saint Luce Station and turned to the right just beyond Frenchville. "Where are we going, Holmer T?"

"No need to travel the long route. No passengers today for Madawaska or Grand Isle. This road takes us through the woods and comes out between Lille and Notre Dame."

Blair was surprised why he had never heard of this route. The road was wide and well maintained.

The teams were changed again at the Notre Dame Station and a basket lunch and water was given to the passengers. "Come on, folks. Climb aboard or I leave without you. You have fifteen seconds to get in."

As Holmer T. was slapping the reins the passenger door was being shut. "Are you always in such a hurry, Holmer T?"

"When I have a schedule to keep—yeah."

"We might or might not make Mars Hill before dark. But—we'll be damn close."

* * *

By the time Blair arrived in Mattawamkeag he was exhausted from the long overland trip and could care less if he ever rode on or in another stage coach. He arrived in the mid-afternoon and learned the train would depart at 8 o'clock that evening. This gave him ample time for a good meal. Afterwards he laid on the grass outside the train terminal. And he actually was able to get a few hours sleep.

When the train whistle blew, he jumped up afraid he had overslept and missed the train. But the whistle blast was only a pre-departure warning.

Blair ran to the terminal and boarded the train. Across the aisle was another young man and Blair asked, "Excuse me, are you going to the Armory in Bangor?"

"Yes I am. Are you?"

"Yeah, me too. My name is Blair Kelley."

"I'm Charlie Junkins from Haynesville."

"Hello, Charlie," and they shook hands. "I'm from Fort Kent."

"What made you want to join the 20th Maine?" Charlie asked.

"To stop the south from tearing this country apart. What about you?"

"I was tired of working for my father and needed a good excuse to leave and maybe see some of this country."

"What did you and your father do?"

"He owned a grist mill and in the winter we cut lumber also. I hated the idea that that was all I was ever going to do in this life. What did you do?"

"My folks own a farm and woodlot. We grew potatoes, wheat and apples and in the winter we cut lumber on our own land and my Dad had a saw mill."

"I guess most every young man in northern Maine has spent some time in the woods, and farming."

"It isn't a bad life. I hope I don't live to regret leaving. Of course after the war I'm going back."

Blair was lucky; he was hungry and there was actually a dinner car. He and Charlie chose an empty table and ordered the beef stew with biscuits. "This is apt to be our last good meal for a long time, you realize, Blair."

When they had finished eating they sat there talking. Until they were asked to leave so another party could eat.

Blair was still tired and he leaned against the wall and was soon asleep. But every time the train stopped he awoke.

They arrived in Bangor on the 28th at 4 am. There was a restaurant in the terminal and Blair and Charlie had breakfast before going to the armory. Charlie was amazed how much Blair could eat. But then again, he was a big man.

It was still early when they had finished eating. Blair asked for directions to the armory from the waitress. It was a short walk.

"We aren't suppose to be here until tomorrow. What do you hope to find, Blair?"

"I don't know, maybe others who are early. At least we'll know where it is."

When they found the armory there were two others sitting on the steps waiting. Two brothers, John and Bill Huntley. The brothers were wood cutters from the Princeton area. And like Charlie, they were tired of the woods and were looking for a change.

* * *

After eating breakfast the next morning at the train station the four men walked back to the armory. The front door was open. They went inside and were met by Sgt. Greeley. "Come in, gentlemen. Are you looking to join up with the 20th?"

"Yes Sir," Blair replied.

"That's good. From here on you will not call me Sir. Sir is saved for the officers. I am an enlisted personnel and you'll call me Sergeant Greeley, Sergeant or Sarg."

"Yes Sir—Sergeant."

"I'll ask you to fill out these papers and hand them back to me when you have signed them."

Blair sat down at the table. There were forms requesting his personal information and near the end was an agreement for two years or three. Blair chose the two year agreement and signed his name. He didn't think the war would last any longer than another two years.

Throughout the day more men came to volunteer, but not the numbers Blair had imagined. "At 1800 hours, men, we leave aboard the train, a special train designated for the 20th Maine, for Portland. Where we will pick up more volunteers."

* * *

In Portland there were more volunteers and the Commander of the newly formed 20th Maine, Col. Adelbert Ames from Rockland, and his second in command, Lt. Col. Joshua Chamberlain, a native of Brewer, Maine.

Before leaving Portland they were all outfitted with the union blue uniforms and issued Sharps percussion caps rifles, and every other man was issued a .44 Remington revolver. Blair was one of the lucky ones. The others were told they would receive their revolvers at a later date. Or if during battle you find a dead Union soldier with a revolver to take it—or if a Confederate soldier happened to have one.

Blair was disappointed when the new 20th Regiment left

Life on the Little Black River

Portland, and maybe a little disillusioned. They had no Maine county to claim the regiment, no colors or flag as symbol for the 20th Regiment. And there were no goodbyes or fanfare when the train left. *Is this how much the people of Maine care about keeping the country together?* This was not sitting well with him. He was almost wishing he had stayed home. But then he would be just like all those who didn't seem to care that the 20th Maine Regiment was fighting for a cause for them.

All of the new volunteers had been either wood cutters, farmers and two had been unsuccessful fisherman. And the reason for joining up seemed to be pretty much the same reason. They were tired of the life they had and wanted more.

Before leaving Portland the men were served their evening meal. Beans, ham and bread. Blair ate three helpings. "It's going to take a squad of soldiers, son, just to find you enough food. What's your name and where do you call home?"

"Blair Kelley, Sir, and I'm from Fort Kent."

"You're already a long ways from home, Blair. Why did you choose to volunteer?"

"I don't want to see the south divide the country."

"That's a mighty good reason. Oh, by the way, I'm Lieutenant Colonel Joshua Chamberlain and I'm from Brewer."

As soon as the train began rolling on the rails towards the south, Col. Ames retired to the officers' car while Lt. Col. Chamberlain stayed with the new soldiers trying to answer their many questions. He wanted to get to know each man. The men all took to Col. Chamberlain favorably. They all thought it was strange that a high ranking officer would take the time to get acquainted with his men.

Blair discovered that prior to forming the 20th Maine, Col. Chamberlain had been a professor of modern languages at Bowdoin College, where as Col. Ames was a graduate of West Point and the recipient of the Medal of Honor for his actions in the battle of Bull Run.

Blair decided he was in good hands. And Col.

Chamberlain decided he had a fine group of independent men that would perform well in battle.

* * *

The new 20th Maine Regiment went by rail straight to Washington D.C. and joined up with the Army of the Potomac. There the 20th Maine received some training and what was expected of the men.

Soon after what little training there was, the 20th Maine marched to Antietam Creek in Sharpsburg, Maryland and were held in reserve along with the 5th Corps. The day after they arrived at Sharpsburg, the 17th of September, Robert E. Lee's Confederate Army crossed the Potomac River and attacked. This was the new 20th's first taste of battle. The fighting was furious and halfway through the battle, the squad that Blair had been assigned to found themselves between a rock and a hard spot. The captain was badly wounded, but not fatal, and the lieutenant didn't seem to know what he was doing.

Instinct took over and Blair began organizing the rest of the squad and instead of retreating, he pushed his men forward. He led his men through hell and heavy cannonading. A few men were killed, but the squad kept moving forward and on Blair's command they surrounded the band of Confederate soldiers. But they didn't give up without a fight. There were some intense minutes of hand to hand combat.

Blair, as big and powerful as he was, simply walked through the Confederate soldiers, knocking them to the ground. Two started running away from him and just as Blair caught up to them, they both turned and were now holding long thin knives. One made a swipe at Blair and he grabbed the man's arm and lifted him off the ground and threw the man behind him. He landed on a log and was knocked unconscious. The second man took a swipe at Blair's face. He ducked sideways and brought his booted foot down on the outside of the reb's right knee.

Blair heard the bone snap and the reb started screaming bloody murder.

Blair looked around and the squad had the Confederates' band secured and every one was watching Blair.

"Okay, men, let's get back to our own line. Help the wounded. Get the rebs to help carry their own."

Of the two that had attacked Blair, one was unconscious and the other had a broken knee. He carried each under his arms, with no more effort than if he were carrying two sacks of flour. The rest of the squad was out in front of him and when he came walking back where the captain was, everyone couldn't believe the power that Blair possessed. Instead of just dropping them on the ground, he set them down gently. Then he checked on the captain. "Captain Mayler can you walk back to our lines?"

"With someone to lean on, I think so."

"The Lieutenant is useless soldier. I'm field promoting you to Sergeant. Carry on, Sergeant."

The unconscious reb was awake now and he was rubbing his right arm. "You help your friend. He has a broken knee. Stand up, Captain; I'll help you."

Captain Mayler put his arm over Blair's shoulder taking his weight off his right leg. "You're slowing us down, Captain." Blair put his arm around Mayler's back and under his arms and lifted him off the ground and carrying him, he led the way back.

Part-way back, Blair stopped and looked up towards the knoll on his left. "Captain, will you be okay here for a while?"

"Why?"

"I want to take three men up that knoll. I think there are some rebs there. I'll leave the rest of the squad to look after the wounded and the prisoners."

"This is your show, Sergeant. Be careful."

Blair picked three men and said, "Follow me. We're going up this knoll and see what's happening on the other side."

Captain Mayler laid down leaning against a tree and watched the rest of his squad watch as Blair and the three other men worked their way up the hill. *What did he expect to find up there?*

Blair led the way up the hill. They all could hear sporadic gun fire. Sometimes it sounded muffled, as if in a valley, and other times it seemed close. Blair suspected there might be Confederate soldiers trying to hold the high ground. It may have been Union troops, but since they were behind enemy lines he doubted if the Union troops would be trying to hold onto a high advantage point.

There was plenty of cover on top and firing was now very close. The four worked their way through the bushes on hands and knees. They came out to a small clearing and thirty feet below them were a dozen Confederate soldiers sharp shooting at Union troops passing below. Blair made a hand signal to spread out. When he was satisfied, he made the first shot and then the other three fired. Blair dropped his rifle and withdrew his revolver, stood up screaming and charged down the hill at the remaining eight Confederate soldiers.

They surrendered without firing a shot.

When the eight were secured, Blair hollered down to the Union troops, "The 20th Maine has secured the hill!"

Blair sent two of his men back with the prisoners to rejoin Captain Mayler. "Charlie and I will hold the hill so the confederates can't. John—Bill, if the captain can spare you, you might want to come here and help us hold this hill."

"Yes, Sergeant," John replied. Charlie looked at Blair and smiled.

"Leave it to a county boy to take command of a squad and capture fifteen of the enemy and secure their stronghold. Damn! They'll make you a general, Blair."

When John and Bill returned to the rest of squad with more prisoners, Captain Mayler asked, "Where's Blair and Charlie?"

"They're holding the hill. We killed four and these eight surrendered. They were sharp shooting at passing Union troops below them."

"That's good. Okay, you two go back and assist Blair and Charlie and the rest of us will start back with the prisoners."

"Yes, Sir," John said.

There had not been any more shooting from the hilltop and as John climbed back up he was breathing so hard Blair could hear him coming. "Someone is coming up behind us Charlie."

"I hope it is one of ours." Just then John and Bill stepped into view. Blair had the men spread out some and not bunched up. Most of the firing was off in the distance now and it had been some time since any Union troops had passed by below them.

As Blair sat there watching he couldn't let himself begin thinking about all the killing he had seen that day. The sight of faceless men, arms hanging on by skin and stench of blood. No, he wouldn't let himself think about the casualty of war. If he did, he knew he would not only be jeopardizing his own life, but the lives of his fellow soldiers.

By mid-afternoon the other three men were questioning if they should get back to their unit. Blair would have liked to leave also, but he decided not to, until all the gun shots had stopped. The artillery had been quiet for more than an hour now.

Captain Mayler, realizing Sgt. Kelley and his men had not returned by mid-afternoon, sent two men to the hilltop.

"Sergeant Kelley, Captain Mayler said to return. There is no longer any need to secure this hilltop."[1]

Now as Blair walked back, the dead bodies lying about the battle field made him think about what he had been trying to shut out of his mind all day. This was the 20th Maine Regiment's first

---

1 *The Antietam Creek Battle ended just before dark on the 17th. The total loses from both sides: 22,717 dead, wounded or missing. The Army of the Potomac had successfully stopped Lee's advance to the north, but failed to defeat Lee. General McCellan failed to pursue Lee's Army when it crossed the Potomac to the south. He had been too cautious. It would be considered the bloodiest battle of the war.*

taste of battle and as it was, it was one of the war's major battles.

The first thing Blair did once they were back at camp was to go see Cpt. Mayler.

"Yes, you can see him soldier, Ward B, number six bed."

"Hello, Captain. What did the doctor say?"

"The bullet fractured my femur bone. He put me in a cast and said I'd be out of the fighting for a while. I've been doing a lot of thinking lying here—actually that's all I can do, but anyway—I was impressed how you took control and your foresightedness in checking out that hilltop. I'm going to have a talk with Col. Chamberlain. Now you and your men go eat and get some sleep. Oh and Blair, thank you."

"Yes Sir."

Blair found his men already eating. He helped himself to beef stew with baked beans thrown in. Not bad actually—particularly if you're hungry. And Blair was.

* * *

There were a few skirmishes the next day. McCellan realized he had lost a great tactical advantage the day before when he failed to pursue Lee's Army across the Potomac.

Two days after the battle a Lt. Franklin found Blair drinking coffee with his men and said, "Sergeant Kelley."

Blair stood up and saluted and said, "Yes Sir."

"Follow me, please. Colonel Chamberlain wishes a word with you."

"Yes Sir."

Col. Chamberlain had his headquarters in a tent. Just like the rest of his men. "Go right in, Sergeant. He is expecting you."

"Come in, Sergeant. Sit down. Would you like a drink?"

"If you have coffee, yes Sir."

"Coffee I have. I wanted to see if you expected whiskey. I am glad for your choice."

"Now to get down to business. I had a long conversation

yesterday with Captain Mayler. I'm sorry to lose his expertise for a while and he told me about his lieutenant's failure to take command. He is now requisitioning supplies for the regiment. Mayler also told me how you stepped up and you and your men captured fifteen prisoners, took out a flank in their line and secured a hilltop sniper position. You did this all without guidance or help from a more seasoned officer. This was your first battle, as it was for the 20th. The entire regiment performed so well we are now permanently assigned to the Potomac Army.

"What made you decide to check out the hilltop?"

"I could hear rifle firing that sounded muffled. Like in a valley. Then there was sharper sounding rifle fire that was closer. I assumed there might be some sharp shooters on the hill."

"By securing that hilltop you saved a lot of soldiers lives. Before you secured it, the snipers had killed thirty of our men."

"Because of your leadership ability, Sergeant Kelley, I would like it if you'd take a field commissioned promotion to lieutenant."

Blair was silent for a while thinking about the offer and when he did reply, it wasn't what the Col. was wanting to hear. "I'd rather not, Colonel, Sir. I'm new at this fighting stuff and if it is all the same, Sir, I'd rather stay a Sergeant."

"I respect your honesty, Sergeant. But I am going to promote you to Master Sergeant. Now no arguments."

"No Sir. Thank you."

"Now go to supply and requisition your new Sergeant insignias."

"Yes Sir."

Chapter 3

The 20th Maine Regiment had performed so well in the Battle of Antietam Creek, especially since none of the men had had any experience, they were assigned to the Army of the Potomac and fought in every major battle.

Some of the men that had been on the train from Bangor along with Blair had been shot. Friends of Blair were dying in every battle. Yet the regiment fought on.[1]

Charlie Junkins became Blair's corporal. Cpt. Mayler was well enough to return to the regiment. And in May of 1863, Joshua Chamberlain was promoted to General. General Grant always figured the reason the 20th Maine was such an excellent fighting regiment was due in part to Chamberlain's leadership. His men all liked and respected him. Both as a friend and leader. He seldom stood in the background while his men were fighting.

In June of 1863, General Lee was moving the Confederate Army north and the Union Army was moving into position to stop Lee. On July 2 the two armies met at Gettysburg.

---

1 *Andrew Tozier along with others from the 2nd Maine were mustered into the 20th Maine. Tozier became the Sergeant of Colors. He could see the 20th Regiment taking a beating and the men were dispirited. He stood up in full view of the enemy and raised the regiment's colors. He stood while bullets were buzzing by his head and this inspired the soldiers of the 20th Maine and they began to fight a vicious battle. Chamberlain saw what was happening and ordered bayonets to be attached to their rifles and then he went charging down the hill, his men close behind him.* Wikipedia

General Chamberlain was ordered to secure the left flank on Little Round Top. The 20th Maine had more than they could handle and were taking a terrible beating. They had lost a lot of men.

Blair went charging towards the enemy as well and he could hear bullets buzzing by him. But he was not hit.

Gen. Chamberlain watched as Blair plowed through the enemy lines knocking the men to the sides and over backwards. He was like a bull running through a china shop. He wasn't using his bayoneted rifle to stick the enemy; instead, he was using his rifle as a club. At one point the rifle stock broke and Blair dropped it and began using his tremendous strength. He picked one Confederate soldier up and holding him horizontally used him as a battering ram. Chamberlain wanted to laugh, but fighting was serious business.

The left flank of the Union line was held as was Little Round Top Hill. If not for the actions of the 20th Maine Regiment, in all likelihood the Union Army would have been defeated. But instead, Lee's Army was again defeated and had to retreat.

Later when the battle was finally over and the 20th Maine was back at the regimental center Gen. Chamberlain walked across the compound, limping, to speak with Sergeant Blair Kelley.

Blair stood up and saluted. "What happened, General?"

"I caught a piece of shrapnel in my right foot. It'll be okay in a few days. I saw you, Sergeant, as you went charging into the enemy lines. I wish I had a regiment of men like you, Sergeant."

"Thank you, General."

Blair found some quiet time and he wrote a letter to his family. He hadn't realized just how homesick he was until he started the letter. He even asked how Monique was.

The Potomac Army chased the Confederates back and forth from Pennsylvania, Virginia and Maryland.

Towards the end of that year the Union soldiers were

issued new Henry repeating rifles. The magazine would hold fifteen rounds. This was a big advantage over the musket the Confederates were using. There was one disadvantage. There was no wooden forearm to the rifle and after fifteen shots the barrel was too hot to hold. So the men had to wear gloves. At least on one hand.

Blair marveled at the simplicity of the Henry rifle. It was also easier to carry.

Blair's two year contract was up and he could have gone home. But after being in so many battles and the Union Army had not defeated the Confederates in all of them, he realized even more how important it was to keep the country together. He was offered a $500 bonus if he would contract for another two years. "We can't afford to lose good men like you, Sergeant Kelley. Whether you realize it or not, you are a natural born leader," Gen. Chamberlain said.

So Blair signed another two year contract and the bonus would be held for him for whenever he wanted to withdraw it. He was given a receipt for the $500.00.

He wrote another letter home explaining why he wouldn't be coming home as he had stated in his previous letter. Charles Junkins who had fought in every battle along with Blair also signed a new two year contract. "I can use the bonus money."

General Chamberlain's wounds had healed sufficiently so he went back with his men. General Grant had promoted Chamberlain to Brigadier General. But this did little to keep him on the side lines watching. He was usually fighting with his men.

* * *

After the beginning of the new year there were rumors that the Confederate army was weakening. But they sure were not showing any weakness in their fighting. Many of their soldiers were looking tired and bedraggled, but then so were many of the Union troops. Sherman's march through the south had demoralized much of the south as well as many of the Confederate soldiers. They were now lacking in food supplies.

The winter of '65 was particularly hard on the Confederate soldiers. Their clothes were practically nothing more than rags, they were not as accustomed to the unusually cold winter and they were all hungry.

In April of 1865 after a ten month siege at Petersburg, Virginia, Gen. Grant had sent the Potomac Army between Richmond and Petersburg and prevented Lee's army the security of its capital. Lee turned his army south hoping to join up with the rest of the forces before Gen. Sherman moved up from the south.

Gen. Grant stopped Lee's army in Appomattox, Virginia. Gen. Lee saw little point in fighting. If they lost this battle the south would be defeated in its effort. And lose he knew he would, and he understood it would be pointless to waste so many of these men's lives.

While Gen. Grant was accepting Gen. Lee's surrender in the Appomattox Courthouse, Gen. Chamberlain was in command of the Union Army.

After the surrender was final, Blair sat down and buried his face in his hands and cried. Four years of bloody warfare, the stress and anxiety suddenly all surfaced at the same time. And he wasn't alone either.

For now, what was left of the 20th Maine were on security duty. This was boring, but at least he wasn't killing anyone. He knew this war had changed him, as well as probably everyone on both sides. He hoped he'd be able to put it behind him and some day forget it. He was aware of one significant change though: he was no longer the happy young man. These four years seemed to have aged him greatly. He wrote another letter home telling them the war was over and he wasn't yet sure when he would be coming home.

Weeks following the surrender were boring, routine. Blair had twelve hour security duty each day and twelve hours of rest. This was better than fighting—yet boring as hell. He had put his weight back on. That was one consolation.

June 1st: "Sergeant Kelley?"

"Yes, Lieutenant?"

"General Chamberlain would like to see you in his office."

"Yes Sir."

"Come in, Sergeant, and sit down. I would like to express my thanks, Blair, for doing an excellent job in all of the battles. Have you given any thought as to what you'll do now?"

"Go home and take up where I left off, I suppose."

"The west will be opening up in a hurry now, since the war is over. Thousands of people will be moving west, looking for another chance at life. North, as well as from the south. The Army is going to need men like yourself. Whether you want to acknowledge it or not, Sergeant, you are a leader of men. I have watched you for the most of four years. It is my opinion that you are a natural leader, and you would make an excellent officer. All it would take for your acceptance at West Point would be my signature of approval.

"You don't have to give me your answer now. But I want you to think about it. In two weeks, on June 16th, everybody in the regiment will be mustered out and the 20th Maine will be disbanded. For now though, I wish what I just said about the future of the 20th not leave this room. I'll inform the entire regiment later. All I ask, Sergeant, is to think about it."

"Thank you Sir, I will."

* * *

For the next several days whenever Blair was not on duty, eating or sleeping, he was thinking about Gen. Chamberlain's offer. What an opportunity it would be to attend West Point with the approval of Gen. Chamberlain. But in the end he knew he would not accept the offer.

On June 12th Gen. Chamberlain announced to the entire

20th Maine Regiment that the 20th would be officially disbanded on the 16th and the pay master would be here. "I want to thank you all for your service to this cause. God speed."

Blair followed Chamberlain to his office. "What have you decided, Sergeant?"

"It is a wonderful opportunity and I want to thank you graciously for thinking about me. But I miss the big woods and rivers of home. That's where I'm meant to be, Sir."

CHAPTER 4

On the morning of the 16th, several of the men had already changed back into their civilian clothes. Somehow Blair's had become misplaced. There were long lines of men at the pay master tables. When it was finally Blair's turn, the Sgt. said, "Master Sergeant Blair Kelley: $34.00 a month for 46 months plus your bonus. $2064.00 and sign here."

Blair had had all he wanted of southern living. He boarded the first northbound train. He found a window seat and sat down. He recognized several men of the disbanded 20th also going home.

"Hey, mister, is this seat taken?"

Blair looked up and then smiled, "Sit down, Charlie. It's going to be a long ride back."

"Yeah, but stop and think how much walking and marching we have done in the last four years and I don't care if it takes us a week to get home. Of course, you have to go all the way to Fort Kent."

When the train left the terminal, the car they were in was full. "You have no idea, Charlie, at least I don't think you do, maybe you do, but I am so glad to be heading north again. If I had had to stay in the south one more year—well I don't think I could have taken it."

"Blair, with all the battles we were in you never once was wounded. You usually were in the front of the charge, too. Me, I was hit twice. Just flesh wounds and the doctors wouldn't even take me out of the field even for a day. You're either the luckiest person I have ever known or—there's something that protects you, watches over you."

* * *

They were three days getting to Portland and this train was not an express, so there were many stops on the way to Bangor.

There were tears in both Blair and Charlie's eyes as they said goodbye. They had become good friends and there really wasn't much they could say. It had already been said.

"You take care, Charlie."

"You too, Blair."

There was a two hour delay before the B&A train departed, so Blair had an early breakfast.

"Ma'am, I'd like four eggs over easy, fried potato and how about a thick slab of ham, toast and coffee."

"Are you coming back from the war, Sergeant?"

"Yes, Ma'am."

She came back in a few minutes with a cup of coffee. "To save you from going back and forth, Ma'am, you might as well leave that pot of coffee right here."

She left the pot and returned with—it took two plates to hold his breakfast. "Are you sure you can eat all that, Sergeant?"

"Yes, Ma'am, as good as this smells I probably could eat more."

"I hope you enjoy it, Sergeant."

After he had finished, what he was really needing now as a place to lay down and sleep. But that would have to wait. He went outside in the fresh air to wait.

He found a bench seat in the shade and sat down. It wasn't long before he had fallen asleep. When the train blew its whistle signaling passengers it was time to leave, he awoke.

By the time he arrived in Mattawamkeag he was too exhausted to continue without sleep. Adjacent to the train station was a boarding house.

"The stage coach north leaves promptly at 7 am," the owner of the boarding house told him.

"Would you make sure I'm up at sunrise, please?"

"Certainly, Sergeant. Anything for our boys in blue."

"Thank you."

* * *

Instead of riding inside, Blair asked the driver, "Would it be okay if I rode up there with you?"

"Sure, come on up. Glad to have someone to talk with," the driver said. "My name is Cole Elbert, what are you called?"

"Blair—Blair Kelley."

"Good Irish name. You must be from way up north. I bet your family grows potatoes."

"You're right with both assumptions."

"You must be coming back from the war."

"That I am, Mr. Elbert."

"None of that mister stuff. Call me Cole. Did ya see much action?"

"Too much."

"What outfit were you in?"

"The 20th Maine."

"The 20th under General Chamberlain. Heard you fellas were the damnedest fighting unit in the whole war. There was a story in the newspaper, how the 20th saved the day at Gettysburg. If it hadn't been for the 20th those confoundry rebels would have won that battle and maybe broke the back of the Union Army."

By the time they arrived in Mars Hill, for the night, Cole Elbert had heard all about the battles of the 20th Maine.

The next morning they changed drivers and Mr. Elbert headed back towards Mattawamkeag. The new driver was a nineteen-year-old, big strapping boy, Owen McDonald.

This coach didn't take the cut-off around Long Lake, instead it went to Grand Isle and Madawaska, where Blair spent another night. He didn't care. He was almost home now. By mid-afternoon of the morrow he would be.

After eating supper at the Madawaska House, Blair sat on a park bench overlooking the St. John River. The water level was still high. Either there was a lot of snow during the winter or there had recently been some heavy rain. Either way, this was the prettiest sight that he had seen in the last four years.

He didn't sleep much that night. He was too excited about being this close to home.

The stage coach left promptly at 7 o'clock the next morning. Again Blair rode on top in the fresh air. At 2 pm the stage made its final stop in Fort Kent. "I'm home, by God. I'm home."

It was a five-mile walk to home. One he had made many times growing up at home. Five miles after all the marching he had been doing for four years, now seemed more like child play.

He picked up a handful of dirt and smelled it. And smelled it again. The smell of home. With each mile he picked up his pace until he was almost running. After the fourth mile the land on the left flattened out and there in the distance was home. At least the barn and the peak of the house rooftop. The potatoes were looking good. And Blair began to run. He didn't see anyone until he was between the house and barn. Peter came out of the barn leading two goats. He looked up and saw his big brother walking towards him. He dropped both halter ropes and shouted "Blair! Blair's home." Peter ran over and hugged his big brother.

Regina and Faye came out of the house and they both started crying with joy. They all hugged and hugged. "Where's Dad?" Blair asked.

"He's in the mill. I'll go get him," Peter said, and ran off.

When Blayne heard the news he came running to the yard. He stopped in front of his son, looking him over, head to toe and smiled, "Welcome back, son." Then he hugged him.

"Supper is almost ready, so you men go wash up. Faye, set another place."

"You look good, son. I won't ask you about the war. I know there's probably much of it you'd rather not remember."

While they ate Blair kept talking almost constantly of what he had been doing for the last four years.

His brother Peter had grown and put on some weight and his old clothes became too small, but Regina and Faye made changes with Blair's clothes to fit Peter. "You'll have to go to town and get yourself some new clothes, son, Peter has been wearing your hand-me-downs."

"No problem. I'll need to go to the bank in the morning anyhow."

"I've been talking my fool head off. Tell me about the farm and the mill."

As Faye and Regina were clearing the table Regina said, "Monique has changed some, Blair."

"Yeah, she has boobs now," Faye said.

"Faye!" Regina was shocked that her daughter would talk like that.

That evening the family sat out on the porch and talked. Regina and Faye went in first then Blayne and Peter. Blair said, "I'll be in, in a few minutes." He sat there in the moonlight enjoying the smell of the air, the quietness and being home with his family.

* * *

After breakfast the next morning, Blair hooked up the wagon and drove to Fort Kent. His father and brother had to finish work around the mill. He was still wearing his uniform. These were the only clothes he had.

He stopped first at the men's apparel store and bought everything from socks to shirts and a pair of new leather boots. This was to be his complete wardrobe, so he purchased enough of everything to last him for a long time.

Next he went next door to the woman's dress shop and

bought a new dress, a pretty one too, for his mother and sister. Then he stopped at the general store to see what Mr. Ouelette had for new rifles.

"Good morning, Blair. I saw you walking from the depot yesterday, what is it I can do for you?"

"Hello, Ed. Do you have any of the new repeating rifles?"

"Yes I do. It's just by chance. I saw this new rifle being advertised two months ago and I ordered a dozen. They came in last week. They call it the Yellow Boy, Winchester lever action .44-40 caliber." He handed one to Blair.

He shouldered it and liked how well it fit to his shoulder and he liked the sight and how it handled. "I'll take three rifles Ed."

"Three?"

"Yes, one for my father and brother. And better throw in six boxes of bullets."

"Sure thing, Blair."

"Would you have a Smith-Wesson .22 caliber handgun?"

"I sure do. Only one though."

"That's all I want and two boxes of bullets."

"Anything else, Blair?"

"I can't think of anything right now. If I do I'll be back."

Blair paid Mr. Ouelette and put everything in the wagon. "I sure do like your business, Blair. Come back soon."

Blair next stopped at the bank and deposited the rest of his army pay. He now had $4009.63 in the bank.

He wasn't going to make it home for lunch, so he stopped to eat at Pierre's next to the stage depot.

He ordered a ham and cheese sandwich and coffee. Then the three McQuale brothers entered. They hadn't seen Blair yet. He was sitting at a back corner table. The three sat up at the counter and immediately began pestering Wilma the waitress. She kept trying to push the three back but the McQuales would have nothing of it. They kept up their pestering, "Leave me alone will you," she said.

"Oh come on Wilma, you know you like me and my brothers."

"Burl!" Blair said in an even deep voice. "She said to leave her alone."

"Why don't you mind your own business, mister," Burl said.

Blair stood up and started walking towards the McQuale boys. "She asked you to leave her alone," he said again in that same deep voice.

This time all three stood up away from the counter to face Blair. Burk and Boydie recognized him and they didn't want any part of him. "Hey, Burl, we'd better leave. That's Blair Kelley," Boydie said.

"Come on, Burl, let's leave," Burk pleaded.

"That's a good idea. All three of you leave," and Blair took two steps towards them and they bolted for the door. Burl stopped before closing the door and said, "Some day, Blair, we'll take care of you." Blair started for the door and Burl ran off.

"Thank you. Those three come in here just to pester me. They never order anything. My name is Wilma Knowles."

"Blair Kelley. Those three will hurt someone some day."

"People have complained to Sheriff Tardiff, but it's like talking to a brick wall. Tardiff is an uncle to those three hoodlums."

"They are related?"

"That explains a lot, considering what they get away with."

Blair finished his lunch and when he went to pay for it, Wilma said, "On the house, Blair, and thank you."

Blair had his lunch and forgot about the McQuale brothers. It was a hot day and the road was dusty. But Blair smiled and said out loud, "But this sure is better than dodging bullets."

When Blair was back home he never mentioned the run-in he had had with the McQuale brothers. He pulled the wagon

up in front of the door and hollered, "Hey Faye!"
"What?"
"You and Mom come out here."
They came out and stood near the wagon. "What is it, Blair?" Regina asked.
"Faye go get Dad and Peter. And hurry!" He yelled after her.
"Dad, Blair is home and he wants you and Peter to come up to the house."
"What for?"
"He didn't say, but I think you ought to hurry."
They put their tools down and followed along behind Faye. She was almost running.
"What is it, son?" Blayne asked.
"While I was in town I did some shopping." He gave his mother and sister a wrapped package and waited for them to open them.
They unwrapped the dresses and then held them up. "Oh, these are so beautiful, Blair," Faye said as she held hers next to her body and danced and twirled.
"They are beautiful, son. Thank you."
Then he handed his Dad and brother each a box.
"Oh wow!" Peter exclaimed a new lever action rifle. "It's beautiful, Blair. Thank you."
His father was speechless. He couldn't find the words to express his thanks, so he hugged his son and finally he said, "I have heard about the repeating rifle, but I never thought I would own one. But how could you afford all this son?"
"When I was discharged on the 16th the Army paid me for all of my back wages and a $500.00 bonus when I signed the second two year contract."

* * *

The community picnic that year was held the last Sunday

of July and this meant the bean-hole beans and pig both started cooking at midnight. There was plenty of time, so they were cooked slowly. By noon on Sunday everything was ready to eat. Peter was in charge of the bean-hole beans and Monique helped Blair serve the roasted pork.

Regina and Faye were wearing their new dresses and they both were attractive. There was music to dance by when the eating was finished and many boys Fayes age asked to dance with her. Monique asked Blair. "Blair, would you dance with me?"

He looked at her and smiled and said, "I thought you'd never ask."

"You mean you have been waiting all this time for me to ask you?"

"I wasn't sure if you'd say yes or not," he couldn't think of anything else to say.

They danced well together and Blair decided it was a good feeling holding her in his arms. And he had to agree with his mother and sister Monique had changed.

The McQuale brothers had not been seen in the serving line and as Blair was dancing with Monique he kept looking the crowd over. *Maybe they hadn't come this year.*

Chapter 5

Blair was two months working off the effects of the war. The nightmares of dead soldiers had stopped. He spent several days in the woods trying to get back to some kind of normalcy. He spent many hours walking around in the old choppings. The crew and cook camp were still in good order. Although a porcupine had been chewing on the outhouse. There were the usual mice and squirrels inside the camp, but they really weren't any problem. He could remember hearing one of the workers complaining about mice droppings in the biscuits and the cook telling him it was only seasoning and not to worry about the droppings.

Blayne was happy that his son Blair was back for the fall harvest. Everything went smoothly and there were bumper crops this year. Monique helped out and as usual she proved to be the hardest worker. She didn't go unnoticed to Blair either.

After the harvest and the crops taken to town, Blair and Peter cleared land to expand the wheat field. The wood was chunked up for firewood and the spruce and two pine trees were logged. Blayne cruised his forest for the winter's harvest. When Blair and Peter had the trees all down and worked up they took the wagon to town for black powder to blow the stumps.

One big ole pine stump was giving them some trouble. They had cut with axes all the roots around the stump, but still the black powder wouldn't budge it. "There has to be a big root going straight down from the stump we can't get at."

"How are we going to get it out, Blair?" Peter asked.

"I tell you what, Peter, Dad has some big diameter drill bits. We'll hand bore a hole in the center of the stump as deep as we can make it, then fill it with powder. The blast should split the stump and the main root also."

The biggest bit they could find was four inches. "Maybe this will do. Bring the brace handle, Peter."

It was tough work boring a four inch hole in a pine stump. After a depth of four inches they both had to turn the handle. But evidently they had a four inch hole two and a half feet deep down the center of the stump. Blair filled the hole up to three inches of the top, then he put in the long fuse and packed it off with rags. Then Blair cut out a channel from the hole to the edge of the stump to lay the fuse in.

"Now we need a big rock Peter to put on top of it, so to drive the blast down. They found a heavy one with one flat side. Only it took them both to carry it.

"I hope the blast breaks this rock up so we don't have to carry it back to the stonewall," Peter said.

Blair cut the fuse three feet long, so he would have plenty of time to get clear. "You ready, Peter?"

"Yeah."

Blair lit the fuse and ran behind the hen house with Peter. They waited a few long anxious moments. Blair worrying if he had used too much powder. When it ignited the blast was so loud it reminded Blair of artillery going off. The blast was so powerful it ejected the rock two hundred feet in the air. But not quite straight up. When it came down it landed in the wheat field. "Look at that son of a bitch, Blair!"

"You'd better not let your mother hear you talking like that, Peter."

The smoke was so thick they couldn't tell yet if the center hole blast had worked.

The blast was so loud Regina and Faye came running out. Blayne was almost back to the crew camp when he heard it and began running out, wondering if there had been an accident and a whole keg of powder had gone off by accident.

Blair and Peter walked over and waited for the smoke to clear. When the smoke cleared they couldn't believe what they were seeing. "Where's the stump, Blair?" Peter asked.

Blair looked all around before answering. Then he said, "It would be my guess that those splinters of wood in the hole is all that is left of the stump."

The blast had created a hole five feet deep and about twelve feet across. "It'll be as much work now, brother, to fill this hole, as it was to remove the damn stump in the first place," Peter said.

"You watch your language, young man. You aren't so big I can't still wash your mouth out with soap," Regina said.

"Yes'um."

When Blayne was at the edge of the wood line, he could see his family standing together in the newly cleared ground. His first thought was someone was hurt, so he started running.

Blayne stopped and looked at the hole and then began to laugh, "Hah, hah, hah, my word boys how much powder did you use?"

"Almost a full keg."

"A keg? Why so much?"

Blair told him how much trouble they had had with this one stump and about boring the four inch hole and filling it with powder and he and Peter carrying a bit rock to set on top.

"Well, the stump is gone. Where's the rock?"

Peter pointed toward the wheat fields. "Out there."

"Holy cow, you boys don't fool around do you. Well you two will have your work cut out for you filling this back in. Maybe you can put the rock in for fill."

"That was a good idea about boring the hole—but I think you boys might have used too much powder." Blayne laughed again.

"Well, you three boys," Regina said, "if you're done playing, supper is almost ready."

"This can wait until tomorrow," Blayne said.

* * *

"I'd like to help you two today filling in that hole but I need to finish my survey of the harvest area for the winter."

Blair and Peter harnessed a work horse and hooked it to a rock drag. Peter took the horse out to the field and Blair grabbed two spades. They shoveled enough dirt so the drag was actually below the bottom of the rock. "There, now if we can roll it onto the drag."

They couldn't budge it. So they dug out all around the rock. This loosened it enough so they were able to roll it onto the drag. After it was in the bottom of the hole Peter said, "Too bad we didn't have two more to throw in."

They picked up all the wood splinters and tossed those in. "We'll have to take the dump cart out to the gravel pit."

By the end of the day all they had left to do was cover the top of the gravel with soil. "Well, at least we got the land cleared."

For the next several days the three men worked on breaking up the sod with a special bog harrow. They had to harness two work horses to it to drag it around.

"The winter snow should break up the rest of the sod now, so we can plant in the spring. Good job, boys."

* * *

Regina invited Monique and her grandmother over for Thanksgiving. Blair took the roadster buggy with a top. It was usually made for two people, but Monique and her grandmother were both small women.

Rosa insisted she sit between them. Monique had to hold the biscuits her grandmother had made. It was a tight squeeze and Blair wished Monique was beside him. *Maybe when I bring 'em back*, he thought.

Blayne and Peter had left the house early that morning to go moose hunting out in the choppings. "You make sure you're both back here in time for dinner or you go without," Regina had said. They were anxious to try out their new rifles. Blayne had a strict rule, no calves or cows only bulls. And he preferred a small bull and not something so big that it could spoil before they had it all taken care of.

The air was cool and the sun was banked with thick clouds. Making it good weather for hunting. When they reached the newest chopping they split up. They had followed moose tracks in the road all the way to the crew cabin, before the moose had turned off into the older choppings.

Shortly after splitting up Blayne saw two bulls together. A huge trophy bull and a yearling. He chose the yearling and fired. No sooner had the report died off and Peter shot another slightly larger bull. Blayne hiked over to see what Peter had. "Now we have two moose. I guess that'll more than keep us in winter meat."

They rolled Peter's moose on its back and Blayne held it while Peter pulled the innards out. Except for the liver and heart. They would take care of those once the two were back at the farm. Then they dressed Blayne's moose and went home. "We'll wait until after dinner to come back out for them."

Blair was pulling into the yard just as Blayne and Peter were walking in. "Any luck?" Blair asked.

Peter spoke up, "I'd say! We each got one, Blair. These are some kind of rifle."

Blayne helped Monique and Rosa down from the buggy. "Come in, those biscuits smell good, Rosa."

"Thank you Mr. Kelley."

The men had to eat dinner in a hurry so they would have time to bring the two moose in and hang 'em up in the barn and Blair still had to take Monique and her grandmother home.

This time Monique jumped up in the buggy first and then helped her grandmother up. When Blair sat down, Monique could feel the warmth of his leg on hers. She rested her hand on his leg. Blair was thinking this was feeling kinda good.

* * *

The Kelleys were a week taking care of all the moose meat and then another two days making mincemeat. One hindquarter was left hanging in the root cellar, a few choice steaks had been saved and were now frozen and then in the root cellar and the rest was canned. There was more than enough to see them through the winter so Regina said, "Blair we have more moose meat than we need, take twenty quart jars and four jars of mincemeat over to Monique and her grandmother. I'm sure they could use it."

The wood crews were back to work and Blayne had the mill sawing out lumber. December was a snowy month and all of the crews were afraid the snow might become so deep that they couldn't work. The temperatures were cold which made it good for freezing down twitch trails and the road to the mill.

After the first of the year the weather warmed up unusually warm and most of the snow melted. Then the cold temperatures returned. Which actually made it easier for timber and horse crews.

That winter wasn't completely snowless, but there certainly wasn't the depths that would hinder the cutting crews. It would snow a few inches each week which helped to make sure footing for the horse teams.

The crews had produced more timber than expected and Blayne shut the crews and camps down three weeks early. He kept only enough men to haul the lumber to market. Everyone that year received a good bonus.

By the time the main road to town had softened, Blayne had all the lumber hauled to market.

CHAPTER 6

That winter Monique was able to find work at Ouelette's General Store, three days a week. Twice a week she would carry her grandmother's baskets with her. Mr. Ouelette had a good market for them. On Wednesdays the freight wagon arrived from Presque Isle and she usually worked until sunset taking care of the stock. Mr. Ouelette liked her work and he paid her well.

As soon as the ground had dried up some, Blayne had the boys harrow the new piece again. The soil was dark and rich and by the time they had finished it was ready for planting. They had also harrowed the entire wheat field. The potato field could wait a few more days.

It was the last Wednesday in April and while eating lunch Blayne said, "Blair, just before supper I'd like you to hitch up the wagon and go to town. Mr. Darby at the seed and fertilizer store said our seed and fertilizer will be in today. He said probably not until late. Sometime after 6 o'clock. Peter wanted to do some fishing this afternoon."

"Sure, no problem. Do you need anything, Mom?"
"I don't think so."

* * *

The McQuale brothers had been watching Monique walk back and forth from work all spring and they knew she always stayed late on Wednesdays to put new stock away.

On this particular Wednesday they had been drinking

some of their father's home-brew. Not enough to be drunk, but just enough to make them dangerous.

"Listen, you two," Burl said, "tonight we take Monique."

"Where and when?" Burk asked.

"On Wednesday nights she stays until about dark and then walks home. We wait for her in the bushes on the other side of Quiggley Brook. That's far enough from town and any houses so if she screams no one will hear her. When she comes by we step out and drag her to the grass," Burl said.

"Who gets to do her first? I suppose you do with this one too, Burl?" Boydie asked.

"Don't worry, we'll all have our turn with her," Burl said.

"You know we almost got caught the last time we did this to that Wallis girl."

"But we didn't, did we. Besides the old man will cover for us."

"I still don't know, Burl. What about Blair? He's been sweet on her. And I don't want him after us," Burk said.

"Me neither," Boydie added.

"Look, I think it's time we take care of Blair Kelley. Some night when he isn't expecting it, we take clubs to him. Break a few bones and teach him a lesson."

"Well what about it? Do we do Monique tonight or not?"

"Okay."

"Okay."

* * *

Blair turned his team off the main road onto another road before he went by Ouelette's General Store. When he was loaded and before leaving town he'd swing by the store and give Monique a ride home.

"The freight wagon isn't here yet, Blair. But I'm expecting it any time."

The freight wagons rolled into the yard at 7 o'clock.

"As soon as I inventory the load, Blair, you can start loading."

Two of the freight drivers helped Blair load his wagon with the seed and fertilizer. Most of it was fertilizer. It was a heavy load, but Blayne had told him to use four horses.

He paid Mr. Darby and put the receipt in his pocket. By the time he swung around to the general store it was almost dark. The doors were closed and Monique had already left. "Maybe I'll meet up with her on the road."

* * *

"Okay, you two, shut up. She should be along any minute. Remember how we do this," Burl said.

As Monique crossed the bridge over Quiggley Brook, she paused for a moment to look at the St. John River in the moonlight. She had no idea what was in store for her just seventy-five feet beyond the bridge.

All three brothers jumped out at the same time and grabbed her. She fought them off as well as she could. Even though she was a strong girl, it was three against one. Monique screamed and lashed out and stuck her finger in one of Boydie's eyes. He yowled with pain, but he didn't let go of her. She was dragged to the grass on the side of the road and pushed down on her back. "We're going to do you, you bitch."

Burk and Boydie were holding her down by her arms and Burl grabbed her shirt and ripped it off. Then he grabbed her pants at the waist and tried to rip them off. She kicked up with her foot and caught Burl in the groin. This made him groan in pain and he slapped her in the face as hard as he could. Boydie was more interested in staring at her breasts and he loosened his grip on Monique's arm. She noticed the grip relax some and she broke her arm away from his grip and reached up and clawed the side of Burl's face with her fingernails. Blood was already dripping on her.

Burl reached back to hit her in the face with his closed fist.

Blair had heard her first scream and knew it was Monique and that she wasn't far away. He stopped the wagon and locked the brake and jumped down and began running towards Monique's screams.

He grabbed Burl by the hair in one hand and the back of his pants in the other, just as Burl was about to hit her. Blair picked him up and threw him out into the gravel road. Burk and Boydie had released Monique and she stood up and backed out of the way.

Both Burk and Boydie charged at him at the same time. All Blair had time to do was push them backwards and upside down. By now Burl was on his feet and coming at Blair. Blair grabbed him by the right arm and twisted it until he heard bone snap. Burl screamed with bloody murder. While he was screaming Blair back handed him breaking his jaw and sending him backwards, back on the gravel road.

Burk and Boydie came at Blair with wood they had tripped on and holding it as clubs, they came at Blair. He blocked Burk's swing and Burk dropped the club. Boydie hit Blair across the back of his shoulders and not his head and this didn't even slow Blair. Boydie knew he was in trouble when Blair turned towards him. Blair picked him up in his left arm like he would a sack of flour. And he squeezed until Boydie screamed. He had broken two ribs.

Burk picked himself up and lunged at Blair. Blair knew his strength and knew if he ever hit him with a closed fist he'd probably kill him. He blocked Burk's lunge with his shoulder and grabbed him by the shirt front and slapped him across the face several times. And Burk screaming with each slap. Then Blair drove his heel down on Burk's foot and broke it. He screamed again. Then he let go dropping him.

Monique was crying and her face, Blair could see by the moonlight, was red and swelling where Burl had slapped her. He took his shirt off and wrapped it around Monique and picked her up and carried her back to the wagon.

They rode by the brothers and they were still groaning with pain. "I need to get you home, Monique. Not your grandmothers. My home. This won't be the end of this."

She didn't argue.

Monique stopped crying once they were on their way. When they arrived home Blair left the wagon in front of the porch and he picked Monique up in his arms with no more effort than if she had been a feather pillow. Blayne came out to see why Blair had stopped there.

"What is it, son? What happened?"

Blair didn't say anything until he laid Monique down on the couch in the living room. "The McQuale brothers tried to rape Monique."

"Oh my word no," his mother said. "You men leave us and go out in the kitchen."

"Peter, put the wagon in the barn and unharness the teams," Blayne said.

"Where did this happen, son?"

"Near Quiggley Brook crossing. Burl had ripped her shirt off and had slapped her and was going to punch her in the face when I pulled him off."

"I hurt them pretty bad, Dad. Oh, they'll heal up."

"Did you hit any of them with your fists?"

"No, I knew better."

"What did you do to them?"

"I broke one of Burl's arms and I backhanded him across the face and I think I broke his jaw. I picked Boydie up and squeezed him and I know I broke one rib, maybe two. Burk—I slapped his face back and forth a few times and stomped down on his foot and broke it."

"It'll be a long time before any of the boys are up and around."

"Monique clawed Burl's face with her fingernails and

left some deep gouges."

"What are you going to do now son?"

"We can't stay here. It wouldn't be safe for Monique and you can bet they'll lie to the sheriff and tomorrow afternoon or the next day at the latest, the sheriff will come looking for me. They'll lie about trying to rape her and their ole man will lie for them."

"So what do you want to do?"

"We have to leave, Dad. Monique and I."

Regina had taken a towel and some water into Monique so she could wash up and she brought down some of Faye's clothes for her.

Monique told Regina about what had happened. Faye just listened. After a while the three women joined Blair and Blayne in the kitchen. Then Peter ten minutes later.

Now that the whole family was there, Blayne asked, "What are you going to do, son?"

Blair turned to look at Monique seated beside him and he said, "We can't stay around here, Monique."

"I know and I understand."

"The only place we can go is up river and find a place to homestead."

"Which river?"

"I'm not sure. We'll have to scout around and find a good place."

"You realize to make a homestead legal, you must file on it."

"I know. In a year or two after we are settled we'll come out and make it all legal."

"In order to take the supplies you'll need, you'll have to take the big canoe."

"I was thinking about that also, and Dad? How much money do you have here at the house?"

"I have quite a bit."

"$4,000.00?"

"Yes, I have that much."

"I have over $4,000.00 in my bank account. I can sign my account over to you for the $4,000.00."

"Consider it done."

"Faye can give Monique some of her clothes also."

Monique spoke up. "This is all fine and I want to go, Blair, and I agree it isn't safe for either of us here any longer. But what about my grandmother? She depended on me for what money I could earn."

Regina spoke up so quick it caught everyone by surprise.

"We'll take care of her Monique. She can move in here with us," and she looked at her husband who was showing no surprise or concern.

"Rosa likes to cook, doesn't she?"

"Yes, she's a very good cook."

"She might be interested in being a cook in the crew camps or helping out here. Either way, Monique, don't worry. Besides, there is a spare bedroom and now Blair's will be empty." Blayne sat there nodding his head.

"I don't know what to say. You all are so nice to me. I feel like you are family."

Faye stood up and hugged her and said, "From now on you are family, Monique, and so is your grandmother."

"When do you want to leave?"

"As soon tomorrow morning as we can."

"There'll be a lot of work to do before then, getting everything you'll need and loaded in the canoe."

"I'll be up at least by sunrise."

"Okay, I think we all should get some sleep. We have a big day ahead of us. Monique, you can have the spare room tonight," Regina said.

"I don't mean any disrespect, but I can't sleep alone tonight. I won't feel safe unless I can feel Blair beside me."

"Of course, no problem."

* * *

"You know Blayne, Monique and Blair are good for each other," Regina said.

"I noticed the same thing and I noticed something else."

"What was that?"

"I think Blair is excited about the two of them going off by themselves to carve out a life together in the wilderness."

"But I'll be sorry to see them leave," Regina said.

"Me too."

Blair held Monique in his arms all night. He didn't get much sleep though. He kept going over and over in his mind a list of things they would need.

Blair was out of bed just at the first rays of daylight. Monique started to get up also. "Why don't you get some more rest, Monique. This is going to be a long day."

"I want to be with you, Blair, and help."

How could he refuse. The first thing he did was to make a list of things to take. And most of that was tools to build a cabin.

Blayne and Regina were up soon after. While Regina and Monique fixed breakfast, Blayne and Blair went out to the barn and started loading up the wagon. The canoe was already down by the river.

There were tools, traps, rope, wire. His rifle he wrapped up in a blanket. There were three other blankets. They each took extra clothes and boots, gloves, a 100 pound sack of flour, salt and the only food was a lunch basket prepared by Regina. They would have to fend for themselves, if they were to eat. He took fish line and hooks. He could make an alder fish pole. His hunting knife and compass. Monique packed some cooking cutlery; a pot, a fry pan.

"Do you have any canvas, Blayne?" Monique asked. "We need something for a cover to protect all this from rain and a temporary shelter for us."

"Good point. I have some in the barn."

Peter was up now and he and Blayne went to the barn for the canvas.

"Come in and eat now," Regina said.

There was much conversation while they ate. And no one wanted to be the first to say good-bye.

Blayne excused himself and went to his office to get the money for Blair. "Here's your money son."

When Blair handed his account savings book to his father, Blayne said, "No, you keep that son. I was planning to leave the farm to you three. Consider this your share."

Blair took the money and said, "Only if you hold this book for us. Call it collateral. If we never come back it's yours. I'd feel better if you kept it."

"There's no time to waste," Blair said, "We need to load the canoe and be on our way."

The kitchen and table were left and everyone helped with the loading. Blair and Monique both hugged everyone. Tears in their eyes.

"I'll take care of Bouchard McQuale if he ever shows up and the sheriff. Be careful."

"We'll try to make it out next year. But that's not a guarantee. We'll try."

Blair held the canoe while Monique boarded and Blayne held it for Blair. "You take care of my son, Monique," Blayne said.

"And Blair, you take care of Monique," Regina said.

The Kelleys stood together watching as Blair and Monique canoed out of sight. Before disappearing they both raised their paddle in salute.

Chapter 7

Regina asked Faye to take care of the kitchen and Peter had farm chores. Blayne and Regina took the horse and buggy to see Rosa. When Monique didn't come home after work she figured something had happened. And when Regina asked her to come live with them and maybe be cook at the crew camps she was ecstatic.

Besides her clothes and a few personal things Rosa wanted her tools for making baskets.

When she was shown upstairs to her new room she began to cry. "Will I ever see Monique again?"

"They said they would try to come back next summer for a visit."

* * *

Mid-morning the next day Sheriff Tardiff showed up. Blayne was sitting on the porch. When Tardiff started to climb out of his buggy, Blayne said, "You don't need to climb down Sheriff. You stay right where you are."

"What's the meaning of this?" Tardiff asked.

"It should be clear, Tardiff, I don't want you on my property," Blayne told him.

"I'm here to arrest your son, Blair."

"On what charge?"

"He beat the hell out of Bouchard McQuale's sons."

"Did McQuale say why Blair beat the hell out of them?"

"He said his boys were talking with the Lamoureux girl and I guess Blair is sweet on her and got jealous. Now where is he, Blayne?"

"Blair beat the hell out of your nephews, Tardiff, but they were trying to rape Monique." Tardiff didn't like the association of the McQuale brothers as his nephews. "Did Burl show you his face where Monique clawed his face after he ripped her shirt off and slapped her?"

"Where's Blair, Mr. Kelley?"

"He's gone fishing. Now get off my property, Tardiff, and don't come back. Go arrest your own family." When Tardiff just sat there trying to think of something to say, Blayne stood up and said, "Get!" and he started down off the porch towards Tardiff. Tardiff left.

As Tardiff was leaving Regina came out and asked, "Was he looking for Blair?"

"Yes, I told him what really happened and he didn't like it much."

Blayne and Peter went back to work.

The next morning Bouchard McQuale rode in, in a huff. He was a big man, but no match for Blayne and he knew it and he was always afraid of him.

"Your boy beat the hell out of my sons, Blayne, and I hear you drove the sheriff out of here when he came looking for Blair. It'll be months before my boys can do any work. What am I suppose to do until then? Your boy should be in jail," Bouchard said.

"Now you listen to me, you big sack of worthless dirt." Blayne stepped down off the porch. Bouchard stayed in his buggy. "Did your boys tell you they were trying to rape Monique when Blair came along? Probably not. They probably lied to you. But I'm thinking this isn't the first time they have done the same thing in the past to some other girl, is it Bouchard. Now get off my property and don't come back. Ever."

Mr. McQuale left.

* * *

Because of the lack of usual snow depth during the winter, the St. John River was not at its normal high water level for the end of April. The current was still swift, but with the two of them both using the double ended paddle, even Blair was surprised with their progress. He had decided that this load was not as heavy as when the whole Kelley family went on their family fishing trips.

"How far do you think we'll get today, Blair?" Monique asked.

"We probably could reach the Allagash River by dark, but I think we should stop for the night before we get there. Besides, I think we should stop at the trading post. I have never stopped there before and I think it would be a good idea to see what there is available."

Even paddling against the strong current they were making good time. The temperature started dropping by mid-afternoon and promising to be a very cool night. "It's going to be cold tonight, Monique, so I think we should find a good place to make camp for the night and make a make-shift shelter."

She pointed with her paddle on the right and said, "Over there, Blair, there is a grassy opening and a small stream just above it which should be a good place to catch supper."

"Okay, let's go." Blair turned the canoe to the right. There was a sandy beach there also.

As they were pulling the canoe up on the beach Monique asked, "Have we come far enough from the farm, Blair? I mean—"

He interrupted her and said, "I know what you are thinking Monique. The three of them will be a long time before they can travel—anywhere. The sheriff hasn't got enough gumption to come after us. But there'll be a time in the future when the boys will come looking for us. We'll just have to make sure they don't find us."

They made a lean-to from fir boughs and while Blair was

catching fish for supper Monique was starting a fire in front of the lean-to. Then she spread out the blankets inside.

"Blair, we forgot we still have the food your mother put up for us."

"I forgot all about it. What is there?"

Monique opened the box, "Oh my God, Blair, there's three quart jars of moose meat. One green bean, one corn and two loaves of fresh bread. No butter though." They both laughed.

"Well, the bread will go good with these," and he held up four, two-pound brook trout. He cleaned them and Monique put a stick through two of them for a spit to roast. "These two will keep better in the cold water."

Blair was after more firewood. Afterwards he dragged a dead log out for them to sit on. "I would have helped if you'd asked."

He smiled and said, "No problem."

Blair put a third trout over the fire to roast. "I don't think one trout will fill me up. We haven't eaten since early this morning. What about you?"

"I am hungry. Maybe we can catch a couple more in the morning." He put the last one on to roast then they sat on the ground and leaned back against the log.

"We didn't bring any coffee. I wish I had a cup now."

"Me too, maybe there'll be coffee at the trading post tomorrow."

The first two trout were cooked and they were not long eating them. "I didn't realize I was that hungry," Monique said. "Now I'm glad you decided to cook the other two."

When they had finished eating, "I'm going to get some more wood. We may need the fire during the night."

While Blair was after more wood Monique made sure the canoe was tied off and that the canvas was covering everything inside the canoe.

Blair brought an arm load of wood and said, "I'll get another."

"I'll come with you." The truth being she didn't want to be left alone.

Two more arm loads and they had enough for the night. It was almost dark.

Monique brought out one of the blankets from inside the lean-to and said, "Let's sit down and wrap this around us and watch the fire."

There was no wind and this early in spring there were no blackflies. The tree buds were red waiting to leaf.

Monique leaned into Blair snuggling as close as she could. "I'm sorry Blair, you had to leave your family and run away with me."

He didn't reply at first and Monique first thought he might have some misgivings about what they were doing. "You have nothing to be sorry about, Monique. You were attacked and we left because if we stayed there would be a day when they would come after us both and because of my strength, I have to be careful about getting into fights. I could kill someone if I hit with a closed fist.

"I'm sorry we had to leave before we could talk with your grandmother."

"I feel so sorry for her, Blair."

"Well if it is any consolation she will be with my family now and she will be taken good care of."

"I know she will Blair; your family is so nice."

They both sat in silence for a little and then Blair said, "You know, I actually find all this exciting. We are on a great adventure. You and I will be creating and carving out a new life in the wilderness."

"I feel so safe with you Blair—no matter what lies ahead for us. And I agree with you. I'm excited also."

Then in a more serious note, "Blair, there is something I must tell you." Blair waited for Monique to continue without saying a word. "Before I came to live with my grandparents my mother told me that I would never be able to have a baby." She waited only momentarily before continuing. Blair showed no reaction. "My mother told me that something had been done to me a long time ago. I don't have any memories of what she was talking about. But she said a doctor had told her I would never be able to have a baby."

"Okay, then it'll be just you and me, Monique."

"I have never been with a boy, Blair— I mean I have never had sex. I have never been kissed."

"And I have never been with a girl before."

"Kiss me, Blair." He turned to face her and he brushed her hair back and cupped her cheek in his hand and kissed her. Tenderly at first and then with real passion, desire and fulfillment. They stayed like that for some time. Their lips always touching. Then Monique kissed him with a passion and yearning that she did not know she possessed.

While lips still touching she said, "Kissing you, Blair, has done something to me that I can't explain. Like—almost—kissing you has ignited a fire in my chest and then down between my legs. I have never known this feeling before."

"I can feel the same fire, Monique, and I have never known this before either."

"I want to make love with you Blair—but not tonight, I'm all sweaty and dirty after a long couple of days. Tomorrow night after we wash up good."

They sat up for a while longer. Monique snuggling as close as she could and Blair's arm around her. They sat there in silence, watching the fire until the flames were nothing but coals. "I think it is time for us to go to bed, and I'll put more wood on the fire."

Monique crawled in under the lean-to and took her clothes off. It didn't take long before the flames were flickering high and when Blair turned to look at Monique, the fire was illuminating her naked body as she knelt on the blanket. "Take your clothes off, Blair, and we can put them under the blanket for a pillow."

Looking at Monique in the firelight, he thought he had died and gone to heaven. He couldn't remember anything looking so beautiful.

"I love you, Monique. I think I have for a time now."

"And I love you, Blair. And I have for a few years."

* * *

A flock of geese flying overhead awoke them the next morning. "Our fire burned out and it's cold."

"I'll get the fire going, Blair, and you catch breakfast."

Blair wasn't long and he soon had three nice trout. After they were on spits and roasting, he found his razor in a bag of personals and went to the beach to shave.

Monique was heating some water in the only kettle they had. "It's not coffee, but it'll warm our insides. The trout are cooked," she said.

After eating they packed up. Tore down the lean-to and put the fire out, and soon on the river. "It seems good to be on the river again," Blair said.

It wasn't long before they saw the wharf at Pelletier's Trading Post jutting out into the river. "We were closer than I remembered."

They tied their canoe up to the wharf. There were no other canoes or boats in sight. "Good morning," Mr. Pelletier said, "How can I help you?"

"We need a few items. Coffee for sure, ten pounds. We'll look around."

"Help yourselves."

Monique found tin plates and cups. Blair had a sheath knife, but he would need a smaller one for skinning. Blair saw winter clothes, but he'd wait until later in the season. They found soap, towels and a dish cloth. And Blair found a nice axe. Then he saw a sharpening stone.

"Do you have any canned milk, sir?"

"Yes."

"Have we room, Blair, for a case?"

"We'll make room."

"Two kerosene lanterns, extra wicks and a can of kerosene."

"And now, Mr. Pelletier, what about handguns?"

"Yes sir, right behind here. I don't keep them out front."

"We'll take the two .45 Colts and two boxes of ammunition and these two older belts and holsters. And now I think that'll be enough. How much do we owe you?"

"How does $108.00 sound?"

Blair paid him and asked, "Do you buy everything in fur?"

"Yes."

"Could you package this up."

Monique said, "Blair, I found these green felt hats."

"Good idea." They put them on instead of being packaged with everything else.

There was room for everything and room to spare. They pushed off from the wharf and once beyond the islands, Blair turned the canoe up the St. John River, instead of the Allagash River.

"Why the two handguns, Blair?"

"One for each of us. I don't want you wandering around out here without protection."

The sun was directly overhead when Blair guided the canoe into the mouth of the Little Black River. "You already know where we are going don't you?"

"Roughly."

"How far up this river?"

"I'm not sure exactly. When I was fourteen, my Dad and I went up this river caribou hunting. We found a herd in what he called the oxbows. Some place around there if we can find some good ground and a nice stand of trees. But that was a long time ago and I don't remember how far up the river the oxbows are."

They hadn't traveled very far up the river when Monique whispered, "Blair there's a cabin behind those bushes."

He whispered back, "I can see it now."

"There's a trail there," and Monique pointed with her paddle.

"Do you want to go exploring?" as he turned the canoe towards the trail. Monique jumped out and pulled the bow up on solid ground and held it for Blair.

"This path hasn't been used for a long time and look at all those bushes growing up all around the cabin."

The logs were small and the floor was dirt. "There's a tree down across the roof. I don't think anyone has been here for years."

The tree had broken holes through the roof and the inside was mold and moss.

"You know Monique we have a treasure here."

"How do you mean?"

"There are six unbroken windows. I think I'll get some tools and remove them and we can put them in our cabin." While Blair was after tools, Monique was looking through things inside.

Blair was very careful removing the windows, trying not to break them. Actually none of them were secured very solid. Only tacked in with one nail on either side. He took these to the canoe and tied them on. "What else have you found Monique?'

"Is this stove any good Blair?"

"It looks okay from the outside. It's been protected from the rain sitting where it is, so the top is not all rust." He looked inside at the grates and lining. Everything seemed okay. "It's a smaller version of a cook stove, but it will surely do. Come here, let's see if we can lift it without having to take it apart."

With Monique on one side and Blair on the other they were able to lift it easily. "I wouldn't want to have to carry this very far."

"When the cabin is done we'll come back for it—'course

we won't be able to use it until we get some stove pipe,"

"But I can use the fireplace to cook, can't I?" Monique asked.

"Yes. This will help to heat the cabin also."

"I found these panes of glass on a shelf. I found an old metal bucket that does not leak, two tin cups and plates, knives, forks and spoons, a burlap bag of—I think they are only rags. And I'm not done looking either."

Under the cabin Blair found a keg of nails, some wire and a square point shovel.

Hanging on the back wall was an old calendar from 1855. "No one has been here in eleven years. Looks like it was abandoned. It sure isn't of any use now. Porcupines have been chewing on it and it really smells in here. Are you ready?"

"Yes. I'm beginning to get a creepy feeling about this place."

"Let's make a little distance up river today and find a nice spot for the night."

The river was shallow, but because the canoe was so long and wide it really didn't need as much depth as ordinary canoes to float it. They had only gone maybe a mile and they found another sandy shore and a nice place for a lean-to and fire.

While Monique unloaded what they would need for the night Blair took the axe to cut saplings to erect the frame work for the lean-to and then enough fir boughs to enclose it. He found a mossy spot where there was sandy soil beneath it and figured this would be a good place to sleep.

Monique had everything from the canoe they would need and helped him with the lean-to. When they had finished, Blair went after firewood and Monique fixed their bedding, then she started the fire.

Blair came back carrying an armload of firewood and then went back for more. Before he was done he figured he had close to a wagon load.

Monique took all her clothes off and said, "While you

fish I'm going to wash up. Then when you have enough trout, while I cook you can wash up."

Blair couldn't help but stare at her. She was so beautiful. With towel and soap she walked to the water. Blair decided he had better catch their supper.

He went up stream to get out of Monique's splashing and put the hook baited with a fat grub under some alder bushes and no sooner had the grub hit the water and a huge brook trout took it. Blair was several minutes bringing it in. He figured it was at least four pounds.

He found another grub and in the same spot he caught another trout, a little smaller. He caught two more and decided this was enough for morning also. He cleaned them. Monique was standing beside the fire drying off. "You sure are beautiful to look at."

"Put a spit through them would you Blair, while I get dressed?"

He did, then he took his clothes off and Monique tossed him the towel and soap.

The water was cold and Blair washed up as quick as he could. As he was drying off by the fire he said, "You know even though it's cold, I feel better."

Monique had her clothes back on and she had put some bread close to the fire to warm up. "We have two loaves yet."

"You know, Blair, I was thinking coming up river, yesterday morning a flock of geese flew over. I wonder if they will be nesting close by."

"Okay, what have you in mind?"

"Have you ever eaten a goose egg?"

'Can't say I have."

"Well, they're twice as big as a chicken egg and better eating. If we could find where they're nesting we could get some fresh eggs before the embryos start to grow. Then I could use the egg white with flour and a little can milk to make some bread."

"That sounds good. If I remember correctly up steam

only a little ways from where I think we can find a nice place to build, is a marshy area. As isolated as we are here, it wouldn't surprise me none if they nest there. You know a roasted goose with hot bread would taste pretty good too. All this talking about eating has made me hungry."

"Well, get dressed. I think the trout are ready. At least two of them," Monique said.

They ate those with hot bread and washed it down with water.

"I'm full," Monique said..

"I could eat a little more. Maybe half of one."

When Blair had finished eating he said, "I'm going to get more boughs. I think it's going to be cold tonight too."

While he was after the boughs Monique cleaned up and put the food in the lean-to.

Blair came back with an arm full of fir boughs and he and Monique wove them in the top and sides. "I'd like to put some in front too, but that would block the heat from the fire."

"Well if it doesn't get any colder than last night we'll be alright."

Blair put more wood on the side of the fire so it would not burn as fast. He knew he would have to do it again.

"Are you done?" Monique asked. She was laying on the blankets.

Blair took his boots off and crawled inside and laid beside her. She started undressing him and then she quickly shed her own clothes. "I've been wanting to do this ever since we kissed so passionately last night."

He rolled up on his side looking at her naked body. "You are so beautiful, Monique." He leaned over and kissed her lovingly and then with raw desire. Monique pulled him over on top of her and spread her legs.

They made love over and over and the sun had yet to set.

* * *

Blair didn't get up during the night to tend the fire. They slept intertwined with each other all night and Blair didn't even care if it snowed. He was not going to move away from her even for the little time it would take to put wood on the fire.

When they awoke there was another flock of geese flying upstream and they were much lower this time. They could also see their breath in the cold morning air.

Blair was up first and dressed and he started the fire. There were not even any hot coals left. "Coffee would go good this morning. I'll put some water on to boil."

"I hate to get up. I was so comfortable before you got up."

Playfully Blair pulled the covers off her and she shrieked for the sudden exposure to cold air. They stood around the fire warming themselves while the coffee was brewing. "I'll get the fish so we can warm 'em up."

Blair poured both tin cups and holding his, "Tonight we'll sleep where we will build our home."

"I like that phrase, Blair, our home."

While Monique was packing their things, Blair took down the lean-to and put the poles to one side.

"You ready?" he asked.

"Let's go find our new home. I'm as excited now as I was last night."

Two hours after sun up they pushed off from shore and started upstream. Blair could remember the distance to the oxbows as a crow flies wasn't great, but because of all the corners and zig zags the canoeing distance would be twice as far. So he paddled with the intent of getting somewhere. Monique noticed his urgency and without asking why, she put her shoulder into it also. "This gravel bar on the right where the stream flows through it is about half way to where we want to be. "Look at all this peeled wood in the water."

"Yeah, what does it mean?"

"Beaver eat the bark off and leave the peeled wood. This

means there are beaver upstream on this brook. They are good eating and we can sell the fur at Pelletier's Trading Post.

"We'll have to remember this place. The fishing should be very good where the cold water from the brook flows into the river."

"Look Blair—up there," and she pointed to another flock of geese that were coming down to land up ahead. "You know, if we played our cards right I bet we could have eggs for breakfast tomorrow," Monique said.

Blair didn't answer, but he began paddling faster than ever. Monique tried but she couldn't keep up with him.

Six hours after leaving that morning they arrived at the lower portion of what Blair called the oxbows. "This is just as I remember it. A sandy beach, and behind this there's a shelf-like area." He kicked up some sod and picked up a hand full of dirt.

"Good bottom soil. This will be our garden."

They walked up in the trees and found a beautiful grove of nice spruce trees and mingled in amongst them were tall and straight white maple trees. Blair kept walking farther back scouting. They soon came upon a cedar tree thicket. "We couldn't ask for anything better than this, Monique."

They circled to the west and came to a brook that was flowing towards the river. It joined the river just above where they had put in with the canoe. "Look at this, Blair," she said excitedly.

"What is it?"

"Look at this bluish clay."

"I'll say! There's a whole ribbon of it. We can use this to cement the rocks together for the fireplace and to chink the logs."

"And I can make pottery with it. Oh, Blair, I'm so happy. Someone has been watching out for us. Guiding us to this very spot. Everything we'll need to build is here.

"Let's eat, Blair. I'm hungry. Then we can go after goose eggs."

"Good idea, you get a fire going and I'll catch a couple of trout."

Blair dangled a fat grub in the water where the spring brook flowed into the river and no sooner had the grub hit the water and a fat trout took it. Then another and another. He cleaned them and gave them to Monique to cook and he started unloading the canoe. "We're home, so we might as well unload everything."

"We'll save the bread for breakfast. There's only enough left for one more meal." As they ate, Monique said, "I'll be glad when herbs start to grow. We need more in our diet than meat. But you sure can't beat the taste of these trout."

After they had eaten, they both finished unloading the canoe and the first thing they did was to make a water tight shelter with the canvas. In case of storms or wind they could pull two poles completely closing off the inside.

While Blair was busy securing the canvas Monique was busy unpacking and setting up house. "When are you going to show me how to shoot this gun?"

"Well, I'm all done here; we'll do it now."

He showed her how to pull the hammer back allowing the cylinder to spin. And he had her load each bullet.

Now he gave her the empty gun and showed her how to hold it and aim. "When you are ready to shoot, pull the hammer all the way back. That's good. Now aim like I showed you and when you are ready put your finger lightly on the trigger. Hold the sights on the target and squeeze the trigger. Don't jerk it. Squeeze."

She did as she was told. "Okay, I'll put this quartz rock on that stump." The rock was about the same size as his fist. The rock was about thirty feet away. He handed her the loaded gun. "Okay, now just like I showed you. Hold it with both hands and aim like I showed you and when you're ready squeeze the trigger."

It didn't take long to fix the sights on the rock and she pulled the trigger. The rock shattered into a thousand pieces.

"Wow, I really didn't think you'd hit it with the first try. I guess there's no more need to waste bullets. Now unload that empty shell and put in another bullet." Blair did the same thing with the other handgun. Then they filled the cartridge loops in the belts. Then both buckled them and Blair said, "Let's go get some eggs. We'll take the canoe, but we will have to be quiet."

They were on a hunt and this sharpened Blair's senses, much like the war had done. This wilderness hunting for food and now with Monique— Well, he was finally in his element. He guided the canoe, as big as it was, up through the channel in the river without a sound.

As soon as they found a sandy shore on the left they pulled the canoe ashore. They could already hear the geese honking. As they crept up over the berm two hundred yards at the other end of the marsh was a huge moose. "This is looking good," Blair whispered.

The honking was almost deafening. Twenty feet in front of them—Monique tapped Blair's back and when he turned she pointed to the left. There were two geese sitting on nests.

Blair removed his handgun and knelt below the top of the bushes and indicated to Monique to do the same, then he moved so she had a good view. "You shoot the one on the left and I'll take the one on the right. Just like when you shot the rock. Do the same thing. You shoot first then I will."

Monique held her handgun in both hands like Blair had showed her and when she had the goose's head sitting on top of her front site she squeezed the trigger and then Blair did likewise. There was a sudden roar of geese honking and taking to flight.

"I got it! I got it!" Monique screamed. Blair looked at her and smiled.

"Okay, dead-eye, let's go get our birds."

Monique had hit her goose in the eye and Blair's was in the neck. "Look, Blair, they both have eight eggs."

They took the two geese and the sixteen eggs and went back to camp.

"We're going to need something for cold storage so if you'll pluck the feathers I'll dig a hole for cold storage next to the spring brook."

Blair found a shady spot with thick green moss. He cut the moss into squares and removed it. The soil he discovered was sandy. He dug down two feet before water started to seep through the sand. He went out back and cut down a big cedar tree and used the smaller top and cut to length and laid several pieces in the bottom. Then he cut four slabs off the trunk end for sides and another slab for a lid on top. He had a cool cedar box eighteen inches deep three feet long and two feet wide. He put the square piece of moss on top of the box to insulate it. Then he went back to help Monique with the last goose.

"I'll finish plucking the feathers on this one Blair, if you'll take out the innards of that one."

He took the goose down to the river to dress it and he threw the innards in the water for the fish to eat. He saved the heart and liver. Monique brought the other goose down and watched how Blair dressed it.

"Do you have anything we can put the hearts and liver in? These will be good for supper."

Monique went up and brought down the fry pan. "Before we can use the things we got from the cabin I'll have to scrub them with sand first.

Blair took the two geese to the cold storage box. "Pull that piece of moss off Monique. The lid is under it."

"This will hold a lot of food and it is already cold inside the box."

"Don't close it yet Blair, I'll go get the eggs."

While Monique was preparing supper Blair walked around some more, taking in everything. To the left of the groove of spruce he found a cache of quartz rocks. Just the right size to use for the fireplace.

Back at camp Monique asked, "Find anything interesting?"

"Yeah, and it's a little strange. I found a pile of quartz rocks that look like they were dumped there. We had rock dumps on the farm that look just like this. But no one has ever farmed this land here or picked rocks off. But it'll certainly be good for us when we start building."

"When will we start building?"

"Tomorrow after breakfast. We don't have any time to waste if we want to be in the cabin before winter.

"I think I'll catch us a couple of brook trout to go along with the hearts and liver." It wasn't long before he had two, a couple of pounds each.

"You know, Blair, before winter we should stock up with fish and smoke them. They would taste really good this winter."

"That's a good idea. I have never smoked fish but I have hams and bacon. Speaking of bacon, wouldn't a slab of that taste good right about now."

"Are you always thinking about food?" she asked jokingly.

"Only when I'm hungry."

"I think the heart and liver are done, but the fish need a few more minutes." Blair brought two tin plates and silverware. "This is home, we might as well use these as our fingers."

"I have never eaten goose liver or heart before, but this is very good," Monique said.

"Wait until you roast one of the geese tomorrow."

By the time they had finished eating the hearts and liver, the fish were ready. "You know, as much fish as we have eaten this still tastes pretty good," Blair said.

Before going to sleep that night Blair worked up some kindling for the morning fire plus some deadwood. And instead of trying to keep the fire going all night Blair lowered the canvas flaps like a tent. "That'll keep out some of the cold."

As they were laying together under the blankets, Blair had his arm around Monique.

"Blair?"

"Yes."

"I don't want to sound foolish or anything, but my grandmother didn't teach me anything about sex and making love. Whenever I asked her something she would always say, 'Wait until you have a husband and let him tell you.'"

"What is it you want to know?"

"I would like to know what you call it when I have this yearning inside me and this feeling I get between my legs when I want to make love with you."

"It's called being horny."

"Horny?"

"Yes, are you horny now?"

"No, I was just asking."

"That's good, I'm tired."

* * *

The temperature wasn't as cold when they awoke the next morning to more geese flying overhead and a loon in the river calling for a mate.

Blair started a fire and said, "While you're mixing up that dough I'll catch two more trout."

Monique separated the egg white from the yoke and with only a little water mixed it with flour. She twisted some of the dough around a stick and put it over the fire to bake and then she made three more sticks with dough.

Blair wasn't long coming back with two trout. This time Monique fried them. "How do you want your eggs?"

"Scrambled."

"Me too."

The stick bread was cooked when she finished scrambling four eggs plus the extra yoke. Blair took a bite of the bread and said, "My word Monique this bread is so good. Actually better than my mother's. And these goose eggs are so much richer than chicken eggs."

"Maybe once the cabin is done we can get some chickens, so we can have fresh eggs."

"We can do that. That sure was a good breakfast. Now I have to get to work."

He had already made up his mind which trees he wanted to use for the underpinning. He notched those three with his axe in which direction he wanted them to fall.

"Are you busy Monique?" he hollered.

"No, what do you need?"

"I need you on the other end of the two man crosscut saw."

She had never cut down a tree before, only firewood, but she soon understood what it was all about. That first tree came thundering down and then the two others. They squared off the butt ends and then with the cloth measuring tape they measured off thirty feet and sawed through the meaty wood. "Now what?" Monique asked.

"We have to peel the bark off, or over time the wood will rot."

Using his axe he showed Monique how to cut the bark away from the wood so it would start to peel. She decided she would be of more help if she peeled the bark. She was surprised how easy it was to strip the bark off. "The tree is full of sap right now which loosens the bark from the wood. After July the sap dries up and it becomes very difficult to peel."

Working like a team of draft horses, Blair picked the butt end up and dragged them where they wanted the cabin. It took some time to get all three logs set where he wanted them and leveling them only by eye. "This is going to be awfully big isn't it Blair?"

"I was figuring on a seven foot porch on front. That will make the cabin twenty-four feet long and sixteen feet wide. That should be big enough for two people."

"Okay, now what?"

"We put the floor on."

"You mean it won't have a dirt floor?'
"Not unless you want one."
"No, a wooden floor will do just nicely."
"These tall maple trees mixed in with the spruce?"
"Yeah."

"I'll square off three sides and nail tight against each other and we'll have a strong, solid wood floor. I'll tell you what, why don't you start roasting the goose for supper. And maybe catch a couple of trout to go along with the goose, while I cut some of these down."

The trees were small enough so Blair used only his axe. He cut them to length, a little more than sixteen feet and carried them down to the cabin. By the time Monique had supper ready Blair had twenty piled up beside the cabin.

"While you're working tomorrow, I think I should sneak up and get some more eggs before it's too late. They'll keep for a while in the storage box."

Monique put some wood on the fire, there were still hot coals, then she put the goose on to roast and made her stick bread, with some coffee.

That night as they lay together in bed Blair said, "I hope you aren't horny—I'm exhausted."

* * *

The next morning after breakfast and more hot coffee Blair started decking the floor, starting from the porch end and working back. It was slow work. He first had to cut channels in the two outside logs, cutting the flooring to length and using his draw shave squaring off three sides.

In the meantime, Monique, with the pack basket on her back and the .45 strapped to her waist, said goodbye and walked the shoreline to the marsh. She crawled over the top of the berm at the lower end scanning the marsh for sitting geese. There was a foolish one nesting no more than six feet in front of her. She eased the .45 out and after taking carful aim she squeezed the trigger. Only a few geese had flown off. She waited there on the berm looking to shoot another and after gathering the eggs from both nests she picked the two geese up and laid them on the shore and walked upstream for a ways and looked over the berm again. And again there were two more geese not far away. She now had four geese and twenty-six eggs. She had a pack basket full of food. The eggs were on top of course.

The pack basket was heavy, but she was in her glory, knowing she was a viable contributor to this partnership with Blair. She was not just a tagalong.

Every time Blair heard her shoot he smiled with happiness knowing Monique was doing this on her own without any guidance from him. He knew now he would not have to worry so much about her.

By the time she walked back Blair had the first twenty logs in place and was standing up on them watching Monique walk up from the river. She was smiling so radiantly and this made Blair even happier.

"I heard four shots."

"Four geese and twenty-six more eggs. We could do this every day for a while, but I don't know how long the eggs will still be good. Oh, I saw a nice deer in the marsh too."

"Are you sure it was a deer and not a caribou or moose?"

"Positive. It was alone, but I couldn't tell if it had antlers or not."

"They would still be pretty small and hard to see. But I'm glad there's deer here. If you saw one then there will be others."

"You accomplished a lot today."

"I need to cut down some more trees."

"I'll pluck these and start one roasting and put the others in the cold storage box."

Blair cut and carried several more slim tall trees to the cabin and went back for a few more. He knew before he could complete the floor he would have to carry enough rocks for the fireplace foundation and build that up before finishing the floor, then he could frame around it.

He had another twenty cut and carried back when Monique said, "Supper is ready, Blair. Do you want coffee or water?"

"Coffee."

"It'll be ready soon. Take a break and wash up. That's only a suggestion though." They both laughed good heartedly.

Blair stripped down and jumped in the river. The water was still cold and he didn't stay long. "It was cold, but I feel good now. And I'm hungry."

"We'll have roast goose and bread on a stick."

"I never realized how good roasted goose would be. You know when the chicks are born the flock will probably move on."

"Well maybe by then we will have something else to eat. Blair, I have never had so much to eat in my life, as I have since being with you."

"Hold on to that thought come winter."

"Oh, you're worrying about nothing. We'll be okay."

When they had finished eating, Blair said, "I'm going to carry some rocks from the rock pile."

Blair carried two at a time and made five trips. It was time to call it a day.

He and Monique sat side by each watching the fire, talking and simply enjoying where they were.

* * *

Three days later Blair had finished with the fireplace foundation and building a frame around it to support the floor. The savvy clay was the right consistency to work with cementing the rocks in place. The inside of the rock foundation, he filled with sand from the beach.

"Blair what about the spaces between the floor logs?"

"We'll fill these with clay also. But I want to wait until the roof is water tight."

The next day he spent roughing planks from cedar logs, to frame in the windows and doors.

Whenever they were running low on food, Monique would go hunting. She kept bringing back goose eggs until the embryos became too big. They had quite a supply now in the cold storage box. One day she came with a large beaver in her pack basket.

Herbs were beginning to show in the marsh and along the river and with the beaver she brought back also a big bunch of wood sorrel. The leaves they ate raw and they had a lemony flavor. The roots she washed and put in the kettle along with the skinned beaver tail cut into small pieces and a small bunch of onion grass she found growing beside the river.

Blair showed her how to skin the beaver and flesh the hide at the same time. She was a natural.

When Blair tasted the beaver stew that night he said, "Holy cow, is this stew ever so delicious. How did you get the potato flavor?"

"From the roots of wood sorrel."

"I have never eaten beaver tail, but I have heard it is good. Now I know it is more than just good."

"You are remarkable, Monique. How do you know about all these herbs and such that are good to eat?"

"You have to be an Indian to know these things." They both laughed and continued eating their beaver tail stew.

With the floor finished for now and the window and door frames made, Blair concentrated on felling tall straight spruce trees. And now he needed Monique's help on the other end of the crosscut saw and help peeling.

With each passing day they could see now how this was beginning to look more like a cabin. Their home. There were days when it rained and Blair would spend the day making cedar shakes. "I was wondering what you would use this for."

"I made this when I was a teenager. Most cedar shingles or shakes are made using a saw. With this we can split shakes up to fourteen inches wide and an inch thick. This gauge keeps the cutting edge of the wedge straight and then you just hit both ends of the cutting edge with a hammer and the shake usually pops off before the cutting edge has cut through about four or five inches."

Once in a while he would have to use the draw shave to cut high spots and rough edges.

With each log he set in place, he would use his axe and draw shave and level off any high spots and knots, so each log would sit square on the next. But that's how Blair worked. Everything had to be done just so.

One day while he was setting a log in place on the west side of the cabin, he stopped to listen. There was something splashing in the river and whatever it was was coming downstream. He waited to see what it was. Maybe a moose or caribou, so he went to the canvas shelter and loaded his rifle and went back on the porch where he had a better view of the river. Whatever it was was making more noise now and still coming closer. Maybe it was a beaver dragging a treetop downstream. The noise didn't exactly sound like a moose or caribou walking in the water but he waited.

Eventually he saw some movement but he still couldn't make out what it was. Then he saw the top of Monique's head. What in the world is she doing?

He set his rifle in the corner of the cabin and went down to see what she was doing. When he reached the shore she was just coming by their fish hole and dragging a deer behind her.

She looked up and saw Blair standing there smiling at her. "You've become quite a hunter. Here let me help you."

"Gladly, I'm just about played out."

"You should have gutted it before dragging it back."

"I thought about it, but I need to watch you do one first."

Blair dragged it onto dry sand and rolled the spike horn on its back, "You hold the legs."

Blair started at the anus. "You have to be careful not to go to deep with your knife. Once I have a slit going, I put two fingers in and pull the hide up and run the knife between my fingers like this."

"When you get to his pecker, go around it so not to cut into the tube that has pee in it."

"Then we slit the hide all the way to the chin. Then she watched as he cut around the pecker separating it from the hide. "This will all come out with the innards. Now like the beaver, it is much easier to flesh the hide as you skin."

Blair skun around all four legs and then said, "Okay Monique I'll switch places with you and you skin the deer."

Without any hesitation or saying she couldn't do it, she took the knife and slowly began to skin and flesh the hide.

"Okay, the neck is harder to do because the meat will want to cling to the hide. But go ahead and try it."

She was slower doing the neck and when she was done she had not made any holes through the hide. "That's a good job. Now watch when I quarter it." He cut off the backstraps first and laid them on the clean hide.

"If we're careful we can take each leg off before we pull the innards out." He was being real careful cutting around the hind leg rib socket and tendons. "The front legs come off much easier."

"What will we do with these now?"

"The meat is still warm, so we'll hang 'em in the shade to cool off before we put them in the cold storage box. And we may have to debone the meat so it'll all fit in the box."

"Couldn't we smoke some of it?"

"I think that would be a good idea. I'll start making a rack as soon as we have these hanging and I've removed the heart and liver. There's a lot of meat on the ribs too that we can roast over the fire.

They hung the four legs up and Blair said, "I'll need something to put the heart and liver in."

"We can use that big pain I found in the camp. I scrubbed it with sand and it's clean."

Blair removed the innards and put them in the river. They would soon be eaten by the fish, otters and minks. It wouldn't go to waste. He washed the heart and liver in the river.

Monique took the full pan back up and Blair began cutting alder trees to make the smoking rack. It didn't take long before he had finished and propped up over the fire. Monique had often at times had to smoke meat at her grandparents and she didn't have to ask how to do it. She knew not to have much of a fire. Let the heat in the smoke cure the meat.

Meanwhile she built another fire and began roasting the ribcage and heart.

While they ate supper that night of stick bread, deer heart and picking meat off the ribs Monique said, "Oh I forgot to tell you, earlier I found a rock that to me looks like slate. There were big slabs of it."

"Where was it?"

"I went further up the river than usual and there was a small open marsh and on one side of it was the slate."

"We'll take the canoe up tomorrow. If it is slate we can use some of it in the fireplace. I need to finish that now before starting the roof."

Monique said as she poured some kind of broth in the tin cups and handed one to Blair, "Try this and see if you like it."

Blair took a sip and smacked his lips and said, "It tastes like potato soup." He took another sip.

"I made a soup from wood sorrel roots. Do you like it?"

"I sure do. You know for being in the wilderness without much, you sure do manage to fix delicious meals. I hope we don't get fat from eating so good."

* * *

That evening after all the food and dishes were taken

care of both Blair and Monique carried more rocks down to the cabin. "I can't wait to see this fireplace when you have it done. I think these quartz rocks are going to make a beautiful fireplace."

Blair pretty much wore himself out during each day working on the cabin, so Monique would get up every couple of hours or so and check the curing meat and add more wood if needed.

Before leaving the next morning to look at the slate, Monique made sure the fire and meat were okay. "We shouldn't be gone for long, Blair. We need to keep an even heat in the fire. Maybe I should stay here and watch it. I'd hate for it to spoil."

"Okay, I'll try not to be long." He carried his hammer, axe and spade down to the canoe.

The water level was beginning to drop and they wouldn't be able to use the canoe if it dropped too low.

He found the small marsh Monique had described and sure enough there was a vein of slate sticking up out of the ground on edge.

Using the claw of his hammer he loosened a slab and was able to pull it free. Then he did the same again and again. It wasn't long before he had all he wanted for a load in the canoe and probably more then he needed to finish the fireplace.

"I didn't expect you back so soon. How'd it go?"

"I have a canoe load. I loosened each piece with the hammer claw and then it pulled free."

She helped him carry the pieces up. "How is the meat doing?"

"I turned it over, but it'll take another couple of days."

Blair started work back on the fireplace. About a foot above the floor he made a twelve inch wide hearth from slate the length of the fireplace.

Then he worked on making the firebox and once he had that he stopped. "I can only go so high with this and then I have to let the clay harden for two days." He used more slate for a mantle above the fireplace.

"I like how that looks Blair. We have us a palace." They both laughed.

While he waited for the clay to harden he started the gable ends. He built up both ends at the same time. With each log set on the ends, he tied them together with a long spruce purling. With a two foot overhang in the back and three feet in the front so the purlings had to be long. With Monique's help they lifted one end up on the end wall and then pushed and pulled it along to the other end.

There wasn't much more he could do until he had the fireplace chimney up through the roof. After another two days, he was a foot below the outside wall. In the meantime he cut more long purlings to length and peeled the bark.

With the stone work above the roof level he had to make a support hole on either side of the stone chimney to support the ends of the purlings. And he had to frame around the chimney. This took another day.

He set the two bottom purlings in place on the chimney and then finished the chimney to the top. He made it high enough above the ridge of the roof so there would be a good draft in the fireplace.

Two more days and he had both gable ends up with the purlings tying it together from end to end. He had spaced the purlings about eighteen inches apart to give strength and support for the cedar shakes. These would go on quick.

That night as Blair and Monique were lying on top of their bedding Blair said, "I'm almost worn out and I never supposed we could have it up so soon. When we first started, I actually expected we would be living in the canvas shelter this winter. Now we'll soon be in our own home. But God, am I tired."

* * *

They slept in late the next morning. Monique knew Blair needed his rest, so she lay beside him not moving or making a sound. When he finally woke up the sun had already been up for two hours. "You needed rest, Blair, so I decided to let you sleep."

After eating breakfast and several cups of coffee, Blair went to work nailing the shakes to the roof. He was nailing them in place almost as fast as Monique could carry them from the pile. By noon there was only one more course to nail down. "This can wait until after lunch," he said.

He had more coffee and was actually feeling better than he had all morning.

They started on the other side and it was slow work fitting the shakes around the chimney. But by supper time that side was half enclosed. He wanted to go back to work afterwards but Monique wouldn't let him. "No, Blair. This isn't a race. You don't need to keep driving yourself so hard." She won out and he relaxed for the evening.

They were resting on the sandy beach and Monique rolled over so she was resting on his chest and she smiled at him and said, "There's something I have been wanting to say to you for many days, but I was afraid, you were always so tired—I'm horny."

Chapter 8

Seven weeks after they started to build, their cabin now stood with walls, roof and fireplace complete. "The blackflies were bad enough, now we have mosquitos also," Blair said.

"When will you put the windows and doors in?" Monique asked.

"I'd like to leave the windows out for a while so the inside will dry. I'll get to work on the doors, then a bed, shelves, a countertop, a table and chairs. And a barn to corral these mosquitos in."

"I thought you were being serious."

While Blair worked on the doors, Monique went for a walk up the river following the shoreline. She came back, in a little more than an hour, with her arms full of some kind of green plant. "What have you there, Monique, more greens?"

"Not exactly. These plants repel biting insects. I have an idea."

She built another small fire in front of the cabin where Blair was working and she put some of the plants on the fire. The atmosphere filled with a smoky fog. "Hey! You know there aren't any bugs flying around me now. What's that plant called?"

"Tansy. You can rub the leaves on your skin also, and the bugs won't even land on you."

"How long have you known about this plant?"

"Oh, for years. I was waiting for the leaves to fill out."

Almost every day Monique would go out hunting for herbs. On one forage she found many shaggy mane mushrooms.

She picked only the large ones.

"These are good raw or cooked."

Before Blair continued finishing work inside the cabin, he wanted to build a roof over the porch. Once he had all of the materials and more split shakes it only took a day. Then he built a bed. While he was working on that Monique would take a piece of canvas out in the softwoods and brush, dried pine and spruce and fir needles on the canvas. When she had it bundled up it filled the bed, for a soft mattress. She spread a blanket over the needles and laid down. "Blair lay down beside me. This is pretty comfortable."

"Yeah, but I think the needle bed should be thicker. At least to support me."

"Okay, I'll get more."

Monique added more pine needles. For those she had to go further behind the cabin. While Blair was building a table, shelves and a countertop, Monique went looking for some reed grass with thick stalks that she could bundle together and make a broom to sweep the inside of the cabin.

When Blair had finished the last shelf he said, "I think it is time to start grouting, filling in the cracks in the floor."

Monique already had the floor swept clean.

Blair made two trowels from cedar, to smooth the clay in the cracks. He was surprised how much of the floor they could cover with one pail full. It was slow work and it took the two of them all of one day. "We'll have to let the clay harden now before we can walk on it. As soon as the floor is dry I don't see any reason why we can't more in."

"What about filling the cracks between the logs?"

"I'd like to wait until later. Let the logs dry more. As the wood dries it will shrink and the cracks will widen. We'll probably have to do some chinking next summer also."

The next morning as they were finishing their coffee, Blair said, "I think we should try to float down to the other cabin and bring the cook stove up, before the water level drops anymore."

The river was shallow but the extra long and wide canoe didn't need deep water. They floated downstream with ease, "We might have to wade in a few spots going back."

With the green leaves on the trees and bushes the porch and cabin were not now visible from the river. In fact they had floated beyond it and had to come back.

Blair took off all the doors, the top and lids and the grates to make it lighter for Monique. They were able to carry it out to the canoe with no difficulty. But getting it in without punching a hole through the canoe was another question. Finally Blair said, "Maybe I should do it alone." He picked the stove up without any problem, but when he started to walk out in the water beside the canoe, the extra weight was making him sink in the mud.

He managed to get back on solid ground and he set the stove down. "Blair, couldn't we drag the canoe ashore then put the stove in."

Blair turned and looked at Monique and at first he didn't say anything. Monique was afraid Blair might think she was thinking he was being stupid. But when he started to smile her worries went away.

"I'm glad one of us is thinking. "They both laughed then.

Once Blair had the stove in the canoe it laid surprisingly flat on the bottom.

Before leaving they went through the whole cabin again to see if there was anything else they could use. Blair was looking outside and under the cabin. Under the front of the cabin where there was more clearance Blair saw a wooden crate about three feet long and eight or nine inches square. He pulled it out, stamped in the wood on top of the box was New England Stove Company.

"Hey Monique."

"What?"

"I think I just found a box of stove pipe."

She came over to see just as Blair was opening the box. He popped the lid up and there were four lengths of piping, a damper and one flexible elbow that had been straightened out to fit in the box. "Well I'll be to-go-to-hell. This is all new, never been used." He put that in the canoe also.

"All I could find was this dish pan. There was some garbage laying on it. That's why we didn't see it before," Monique said.

"If we hurry we can get back before supper."

* * *

With the little extra weight there were several little rips that Blair had to get out and pull the canoe behind him. Monique was alright inside the canoe, but she insisted on wading if Blair had to.

Even having to drag the canoe some, they were still back earlier than they had first supposed. They unloaded it onto the shore. "While you fix something to eat I'm going to give this a good cleaning."

Monique was making a stew with brook trout, potato flavored wood sorrel roots, mushrooms, and onion grass, with stick bread.

Blair could smell the stew cooking. As he cleaned the stove, he was actually surprised to see it was in remarkable condition. The oven was so clean he didn't think it had ever been used.

He left the doors and etc. on shore and picked it up; it wasn't that heavy just awkward, and starting carrying it up to the cabin.

Monique saw what he was doing and hollered down to him. "Blair! I can help you, you know. We're a team, we work together."

Blair stopped in his tracks. And he waited for Monique to come help. It was even more awkward with the two of them carrying it, but he surely wasn't going to tell her that. "Let's put it on the porch for now. It'll be out of the weather."

They went back down to the river and brought up all the parts.

Monique served up their supper. Blair took one spoonful of stew and said, "Anyone eating this would naturally think you had put potato in it. I'm surprised these sorrel roots have such a strong potato flavor. What will you surprise me with next, Monique?"

"Oh, how about some corn on the cob?"

"You're joking right?"

She shrugged her shoulders and kept eating.

After supper Blair began picking up wood scraps around the cabin. Stacking the log short ends up under the huge pine tree to dry. Many of his tools, for now, he stored under the porch. The cookware and dishes Monique put on the porch.

Blair put the kegs of nails, for now, on the porch. When the inside floor had thoroughly dried, he would keep those inside. "You know, Monique, our building isn't finished yet."

"How do you mean?"

"Well, we need storage space for food. A root cellar and a shed to keep tools and things that don't belong in the cabin. With a roof attached to the shed to store wood."

"Which is more important?"

"I think probably the root cellar."

"Where would you build it?"

"Let's go for a walk." Not far, about fifty feet from the cabin there was a knoll. "If this is sandy soil it wouldn't take long to dig a hole big enough to build it."

"Okay, what about the shed?"

"What about right where our canvas shelter is?"

"Now let's go for that walk."

"Where?"

"Well coming up the river in the canoe I've noticed an outcropping of rock or ledge not far below here."

It was a beautiful evening for a walk. Something they had not had a lot of time to do since leaving home in Fort Kent.

They had always been so busy with this new life.

It was about a half mile hike then an easy gradual climb up ledge rock dotted with bushes growing out of cracks and crevasses in the ledge. At the top was a deep carpet of dark green moss and a huge spruce tree growing from one of the crevasses. "Look at that view, Blair. Isn't that beautiful?"

"It sure is. We can almost see downstream to that old cabin. Look," and he pointed, "there's a huge bull moose."

"His antlers are still in velvet," Monique said.

"So this can't be September. Do you have any idea of the date?"

"I started keeping track of the number of days, but when I was busy I forgot. I don't think it's August yet."

"No, not August. Maybe late in July though. I never for a moment would have believed we'd have the cabin done this year. Let alone so soon. We still have work to do, but the cabin is more or less done."

Monique sat down on the moss and leaned back against the tree. Blair did also and put his arm around her. They didn't do much talking. They both were comfortable enough just sitting there in each other's company.

They sat there watching the sunset. "Maybe we should leave, Monique, while there is still some daylight."

On the way back Monique said, "I wish we could sleep in the cabin tonight."

* * *

The next day while Blair was digging a hole for the root cellar, Monique strapped on her .45, shouldered the backpack, kissed Blair and said, "I'll be back by noon."

They still had some smoked deer meat left and there were still brook trout in the river, Monique was after herbs. Specifically cattails.

After Blair had removed the thin layer of sod on top of

the knoll, digging in the sand was easy. It was a hot day and he had to stop often to wipe sweat from his face and have a drink of water. He realized then that some day they would need a well and pump. The spring brook, where they had been getting their water, would freeze solid in winter and he didn't know if he wanted to have to chop ice in the river each time they needed water.

He'd worry about that later. Right now he had to finish digging this hole.

As Monique walked along the shore she kept seeing pieces of peeled beaver wood. Then she started thinking how good the other beaver tail stew tasted. Maybe she could get lucky again.

She had earlier seen cattails growing on the upper end of the marsh, on the right. But before leaving the river she saw a new beaver dam across the river. She walked up slowly trying to be quiet. When she was about ten feet below the dam a beaver with a piece of wood in its mouth to add to the dam climbed up on the dam. Not the least aware that Monique had her sights on it. She squeezed the trigger and the beaver dropped.

She put it in her pack basket and went after the cattails. She cut the tops off. They were just developing and Monique knew they would be good. Then she cut the stalks off at the bottom of the plant and kept the bottom few inches of the stalk. Only the white portion.

Her pack basket was full now and she still wanted the wood sorrel and root. She went to the same place where she had been getting it all summer. She took her pack basket off and then her shirt and filled it with sorrel. Then she shouldered her pack again and headed for home.

Blair took another break for a drink of water and he saw Monique, bare breasted, wearing her green felt hat, with her pack basket on her back, walking along the shore. He walked down to the river to meet her. He was grinning when she looked up at him. "Well, I didn't have room in my pack for the sorrel."

That's all she said.

Blair helped her take the pack off, then she pulled out the cattails and then he pulled the beaver out. She took the sorrel and cattails up and Blair skun the beaver, and cleaned out the innards. He washed it out before taking it up to Monique. "I left the heart and liver in. I'll take this hide to the pine tree to dry like we did the other hide. Then I want to finish digging that hole." He didn't know if summer beaver with short guard hair would be worth anything or not, but he couldn't just throw it away.

He wasn't long digging down as deep as he wanted. Now he had to dig out an entrance for the doors.

Monique was busy cutting all the meat off the beaver and storing it in the cold box. She skun the tail and cut it into small pieces and put it on the fire to simmer for awhile before she added the cattail and sorrel roots.

Before the stew was done, this time Monique put in a half of a can of canned milk, and then left it to simmer for only a little. "Supper is ready, Blair."

She filled their bowls and put the stick bread on their makeshift table. Blair took one sip of the stew and exclaimed, "Not only do I taste potato from the sorrel roots, but now I can taste corn. This is so delicious Monique. Where did you get the corn?"

She handed him one of the cattail female flowers and said, "Eat it like you would corn on the cob."

"Raw?"

"Yes, go ahead," she waited for his reaction.

"It tastes like corn on the cob too."

"Okay, now try the white stalk raw. It's good boiled also."

He tried the white stalk and it was full of juices and also good.

"I wish we had enough mason jars so I could can some of these herbs before they go by. The sorrel, cattails and onion grass would keep for a while in the storage box, but not all winter."

"This winter we won't be able to go out and pick what we want for vegetables. We'll have to put some up." Monique didn't have to say anything else. She knew Blair well enough to know he was already thinking on it.

After eating, Monique walked with Blair over to the hole he had been digging. She was surprised how long it was. "How big is the root cellar going to be, Blair?"

"Oh, I figured on eight feet by six feet and seven feet tall so I don't have to duck every time I come in."

"But why such a big hole?"

"Well, we'll need room to walk in."

"I guess I can understand that. Now I want to see if the floor has dried enough so we can walk on it and sleep in our new bed tonight."

They walked over to the cabin holding hands. Something they had not done too much of. "It looks like dried cement, Blair."

He knelt down to feel of it. "It's just as hard as cement also. We'll still have to be careful and not drop anything on the floor or drag anything across it. We're bound to get some flaking, but the floor seems pretty sturdy. There's no bounce when I walk on it."

"I'll go get our bedding and you can help me make the bed."

As they were making the bed Blair said, "You know a nice moose hide to lay on top of the needles would be nice."

"Do you plan on shooting one?"

"Yes, but not until cold weather."

"A bear rug on both sides of the bed would be good too. To step on after getting out of a warm bed. I would like a bear too, so I can render the fat down to cooking lard."

"Okay the bear will have to come first, 'cause they hibernate."

"I'm surprised we haven't seen one yet," Monique said.

"We've been too busy to look."

"We don't have any soap left, but now we're going down to the river and wash up, we can wash these clothes we're wearing at the same time."

The water was relatively warm compared to what it was in early May. They took their clothes off and waded over to the opposite side where the water was deeper. Up to their waist.

"You need your hair cut, Blair. You wash our clothes and I'll run up and get a razor."

Instead of washing the clothes, he turned to watch Monique run naked up to the canvas shelter. He never tired of looking at her beautiful body.

As she was coming back she said," What are you looking at?"

"Oh, I was just watching you run naked."

"Sit down so I can reach your head."

"Do you know what you're doing?"

"Don't worry. I used to cut my grandparents' hair with grandfather's razor. He never complained."

When she had finished he was covered in hair and had to wash off again. They took their wet clothes and hung 'em over the porch railing.

Blair turned and picked Monique up in his arms and carried her inside and lay her down softly on the bed. "I was hoping you were reading my mind."

CHAPTER 9

They slept in the next morning and their new bed was so comfortable they hated to get up. "This is so much better than sleeping on the ground," Blair said.

"It is, isn't it."

While drinking their coffee on the porch, sitting on blocks of wood, Monique said, "I'll make some more bread dough this morning and that'll be the last of the goose eggs."

"We need some laying hens, don't we?"

Blair went to work building the root cellar. Monique joined him when she had the bread dough made and put away in the storage box.

"You aren't going to peel these logs?" she asked.

"The wood is drying out and the bark isn't peeling off good now and it would take too much time. Besides these will all be underground."

With Monique's help the project went along much faster. Plus he didn't have to be so fussy about spaces between the logs.

After two and a half days the root cellar was finished. The top, shelves on the inside and two doors. All that remained was to backfill around it. While he was doing that Monique filled the cracks on top with clay.

As Blair was shoveling sand on the top Monique went inside the root cellar and was surprised how much cooler it was than the air outside.

When Blair had thrown the last spade full of sand, Monique said, "Blair, now I want that cook stove inside."

They carried it, being careful not to scrape it along the floor. He packed clay around the stove pipe where it went through the wall. When he added the other sections of pipe, he wired it back to the cabin to brace it against the wind.

Monique was busy putting the grates, lids and doors back on. "You know this is beginning to look like a house now. I don't suppose I can use the stove right off, huh?"

"Yeah, that clay will have to set up first. A day or two at most."

That night it rained heavy all night and then it turned into a steady rain all the next day and night. The water level in the river had returned to the early summer level. As they lay in bed the last morning, listening to the rain on the roof and waiting for it stop, Blair said, "The river is up and I think we should take a trip down river to the folks and get some things we will need for the winter." Monique hugged him as tight as she could. She would like to see her grandmother and get the things they would need for the cold winter.

"So today, you make a list of things you can think of that we need and I'll do the same. We'll leave first thing tomorrow morning, if the rain has stopped."

"We don't have any paper or pencils."

"I have my carpenter pencil. I guess we'll have to make do with that. I'll find some smooth birch bark we can write on."

The rain soon stopped and this was signal enough to get up. After coffee and breakfast Blair went in search of some smooth white birch. He didn't have far to go.

Monique checked the clay around the stovepipe and it had dried solid. She built a fire in the stove to heat some water. While she waited for Blair to return she was making a mental list in her head of food stores they would be needing. She was so excited about the trip out she found it difficult to stay in one spot for long.

Blair came in with bark and gave it to Monique and his carpenter pencil. "I'm going to see if the trout have returned with the high water."

Monique sat at the table and began her list:

squash	*large dish pan*	*cabbage*	*potatoes*
vinegar	*onions*	*flour*	*2 pillows*
sugar	*salt*	*sheets*	*beans*
eggs	*2 blankets*	*canned milk*	*matches*
quilt	*paper & pencils*	*calendar*	*apples*

As she thought about the list she was watching Blair through the window. He was already coming back with several.

"I'll put these in the cold storage box for now. Then I think I'd better get those windows in since we'll be gone for a few days."

That evening Monique made a fish chowder, using up the last of her sorrel roots and onion grass. While Monique was fixing supper Blair toe-nailed the root cellar door closed to keep bear out and he would do the same to the cabin doors in the morning. He nailed slates across the porch window. Then he checked the storage box to make sure no meat was left in it.

"You know Blair we still have the six jars of canned meat your mother gave us."

"I had forgotten about those," Blair said.

"Where's your list, Monique?"

"On the table."

Blair went over it and the only things he added were tools, stovepipe and cap, kerosene, winter clothes and old newspapers to read.

"You have about everything I had in mind."

When they had finished eating there was enough fish chowder and bread left for morning. They took their coffee out on the porch and sat on the blocks of wood, leaning back against the cabin wall.

"When we get back I need to build an outhouse and two chairs for inside. This winter I can build more furnishings, but we really could use the two chairs."

"Are you anxious to leave, Blair?"

"It will be exciting to see our families and to pick up more food stores, but there is a part of me that hates to leave. This may sound foolish, but what we have built here seems more like home than the farm."

"I have that same feeling, Blair, and I agree, it will be good to see family and let them know we are doing okay."

The sun was setting. The rays were displaying a magnificent sunset. Bright crimson reds and orange, tinged with a halo of yellow. Blair stood and reached out to Monique with both hands. She grasped his hands and he pulled her to her feet. They stood there looking at each other. She was much shorter than he, so he put his arms under her butt and lifted her up to him.

Monique wrapped her legs around his waist. Still looking into his eyes. They kissed and Blair said, "I love you, Monique."

"And I love you, Blair."

"We love each other, Monique, and we live as man and wife—I think we should get married while we are at the farm. Have a minister come out to the farm."

"I would be happy," and she kissed him again.

He carried her inside. Closed the door, lay her softly on their bed, teasingly removed her clothes, then his and lay down beside her.

* * *

While Monique was warming up the fish chowder and bread, Blair got the canoe ready to go. They weren't taking much. Blankets if they had to sleep out, a piece of canvas to cover everything on the trip back, fish line and hooks, some smoked deer meat and coffee. He put his money in the pack basket along with the blankets and towel. He already had the back door nailed shut.

They donned their green felt hats and Blair said, "Take

your handgun, Monique," she didn't argue and she understood his concern. He left his in the cabin. "You ready?" he asked.

"Sure am; let's go."

The water was still high and they made surprisingly good time down to the St. John River. The current was swift and they were riding high.

It was late morning as they canoed by Pelletier's Trading Post. He was standing on his wharf and waved as they paddled by. "At this rate we'll be at the farm long before dark."

Monique was noticing Blair was not calling the farm home anymore. It was the farm.

By mid-afternoon they met two other canoes coming down the St. Frances River. They waved and kept paddling. With their double ended paddles they could go much faster than the two behind them.

"I never have made this trip this fast. But then again the current is strong now."

As they were nearing the farm they could see someone standing on the wharf. Whoever it was had not seen them yet. "Isn't that your sister Faye?"

"Yes, I think so."

Faye turned her head and at first she didn't recognize them, although the canoe held some familiarity. Then she suddenly jumped up and started screaming their names over and over. Blair brought the canoe along side the wharf and Monique got out. By now Peter had heard his sister screaming and he came running and ran even faster when he saw Blair and Monique.

Faye and then Peter both looked at Monique. With her green felt hat and wearing a .45 handgun on her waist. It was Peter who spoke first. "You two with your green hats certainly look homey. And Monique, with your handgun around your waist you even look alluring."

Monique took her gun belt off and handed it to Blair and he put it in their pack. Monique then hugged Faye and Peter and so did Blair.

"You're just in time for supper. Boy are the folks going to be surprised. Come on, everyone is in the house."

Blayne looked out the window just as Monique was walking up the steps. "Oh my God. It's Blair and Monique!"

He went out on the porch to greet them and Regina with serving spoon in hand was right behind him and then Rosa. Blayne was smiling and Regina and Rosa were crying.

"Hello, Grandmother."

"Oh, Monique, I so have missed you. I have been afraid for you, Monique."

"There is no need to be afraid, Grandmother. Blair is a good man and we have a good life together. How have you been?"

"The Kelleys are so good to me. Treat me like family. I am happy to be here."

Regina and Rosa had roasted pork with baked potato and green beans. "You both look like you have been eating well," Regina said.

"Monique is a marvelous cook. If it wasn't for the cabin keeping us so busy, we both would be fat."

Monique asked, "What day is this?"

Everyone laughed, good heartedly. "This is Thursday," Peter answered.

"The date?" Blair asked.

"August 10th."

"Okay, today is Thursday. Saturday, Monique and I wish to be married here in this house. Not in town. Then we'll have to leave Sunday morning before the river drops."

They talked and ate pork and then for dessert they had hot apple pie with strong cheese.

Everyone had so many questions. "Where did you build?" Blayne asked.

"Do you remember the oxbows on the Little Black River?"

"Yes."

"We're at the bottom end."

After dessert Regina said, "Why don't you men move into the living room and we'll join you as soon as we have the dishes done and the kitchen picked up." Monique stayed to help.

In the kitchen, the women were as interested about Monique and Blair's new life as the men were. And they asked Monique many questions.

With the four women working together they were not long before they joined the men. Once everyone was seated Blair and Monique told them all about their new life and how happy they both were.

"It is a great adventure. We don't have all the niceties you have, but we are very comfortable and happy."

They told their family about finding the rundown cabin and salvaging the cook stove.

"What do you eat?" Regina asked, "If you are always working."

"You would be surprised. I shot one goose, Monique has shot eight, two beaver, and a deer. She is an excellent shot. And she uses a .45 colt handgun and not the rifle."

"My Monique is a hunter?" Rosa asked.

"She is a great hunter," Blair said.

"The only problem I foresee is firewood. We built a fireplace, and we're going to need a way to haul the wood to the cabin, or we are going to have to carry every piece. A horse or mule would be good, but that's out of the question. We'll work on it."

"There are so many things we would like to pick up, so when we go to town tomorrow to see the minister, we'll have some shopping to do."

"Anything we can help you out with here?" Blair gave him a list of things. "We can help you out with almost everything food wise except milk, salt and sugar."

"How many eggs do you have?"

"We could let you have three dozen."

Life on the Little Black River

Blair looked at Monique, "We should have at least five or more."

"Okay, we'll pick up a couple dozen in town.

"When we come out next spring we would like to buy two goats and a dozen hens and one rooster."

"That won't be a problem"

Regina and Rosa went to bed and the others stayed up to midnight talking. It was mostly Blair and Monique doing the talking. Blayne, Peter and Faye were alright with that. They wanted to know all about their wilderness experience. Faye was amazed how Monique had always seemed like a timed little mouse, never standing up for herself and yet here she was just as much a part of this wilderness couple as Blair. Sometimes she led and sometimes she followed. It seemed as though she now had an equal say in everything the two of them did. And her expertise with the .45 handgun was simply shocking.

Faye said, "Monique, I can understand how you and Blair share everything, but I find it astonishing that you go off for miles from the cabin and Blair, by yourself and of all things armed with a handgun and that you are able to shoot the eye of a goose and a deer with it. And you, Blair, letting Monique go off on her own like that. I'd be too afraid. I don't even like going out in our own woods alone. Monique, you are some kind of a super woman, you know."

"Thank you, Faye."

"Yes," they all agreed.

"Yes, you are," and Blair looked straight at Monique.

Finally everyone went to bed except for Blair and his dad. There had always been a special relationship between the two and Monique understood this and she was happy to let Blair have some time alone with his dad.

After everyone had left the living room Blair asked, "Has there been any repercussions from the McQuales or the sheriff?"

"Sheriff Tardiff showed up the day after you left. I told him you had gone fishing. Apparently he wasn't told the whole story. I told him not to come back. Bouchard McQuale showed up the next day looking for a fight. But he knows better than to start one. His boys lied to him about trying to rape Monique. I set him straight—whether he'll believe me or not I don't know. But I told him what would happen if he or his boys bothered you and Monique or my family. And I told him not to come back.

"I've heard rumors that none of the boys have been able to go back to work yet. This might give them time enough to think things through and cool off. They might realize that three together are no match for you."

"I understand that, Dad, but some time they'll come looking for us."

"I know you'll be careful, caution was always so easy for you. I want you to be honest with me, son. Are you and Monique really this happy living in the wilderness?"

"Yes, Dad, we are. So far everything has been a lot of hard work. And I expect it is apt to be even more difficult this first winter. But that isn't how Monique and I look at it. This is a great adventure we are on. The two of us carving life out of the wilderness. I have always loved this farm, Dad, don't take me wrong there. But this is different. Monique and I have grown so close, we no longer think or act by our self. Everything we do we do together. You must see the changes in Monique, how this has been so good for her."

"That's what I wanted to hear, son. Not that you two were running away from anything."

"I think we would have been happy here on the farm also, Dad. But here there would be trouble with the McQuales and I think you understand this."

"Yes I do. I'm happy for you both son. And if there is ever anything you need, you know all you have to do is ask."

"Yes, Dad, I know."

* * *

Everyone was up early the next morning and Blair helped his brother Peter with the morning chores, while Monique helped with breakfast.

Blayne set aside the squash, cabbage, potatoes, apples, flour, three dozen eggs and bean, pea, corn and tomato seed. He wished he could do more for them.

He was by himself in the egg room thinking about Blair and Monique and what his son had said the night before about living a great adventure. In an odd sort of a way, he wished it was he and Regina doing what Blair and Monique were doing. He was so proud of them both.

After eating, Peter and Blair finished their barn chores and then it was time to go to town.

"Blair, is it okay if Faye rides to town with us? Mom has a few errands for her."

"Sure, no problem."

Monique came downstairs wearing her green felt hat and wearing her handgun. No one asked why. She gave Blair his green hat. "You two ready?" he asked.

Peter had helped Blair earlier to harness a team to the wagon. "Thank you for your help, Peter," Blair said.

Monique was a little apprehensive about going to town. Having Blair and Faye with her helped, and of course the .45 Colt. It was a nice day for a drive to town. The air was still cool and not too humid.

People they met recognized Faye and she waved to them, but they were not too sure about the two with the green hats. Blair pulled up in front of the Ouelette's General Store and secured the team. "You have your list Monique and here's $100.00. I don't know if I'll be back before you have finished or not. While you and Faye are shopping, I'll go see the minister." He kissed her and said, "Be careful."

The Community Church was only two blocks away. Blair knocked on the minister's door and his wife answered the door. "Yes, may I help you?"

"Yes please, I'd like to see Reverend Scohill, Mrs. Scohill."

"Won't you come in, Blair?"

"Thank you."

"He is in the kitchen having a cup of coffee. Would you like a cup, Blair?"

"Yes please."

"Hello, Blair. I haven't seen you around much."

"No sir, I moved away."

"Where to, son?"

"I'm sure you have heard about the trouble with the McQuales and that is why I'd rather not say where Monique and I are living."

"Well, what is it I can do for you?"

"Monique and I would like to get married tomorrow and we'd like to have you perform the ceremony."

"I'd be happy too."

"We would like you and your wife to come to the farm and marry us there. Someone will come after you and then take you home later."

"What time?"

"10 o'clock tomorrow morning."

"We can do that."

"Fine, someone will be here at 9 o'clock then. We would also like to invite you and Mrs. Scohill to stay for dinner."

"We will plan on it."

"Thank you. This coffee is very good, Mrs. Scohill.

"Before I leave, Reverend, would you know where I could buy two wedding rings?"

"I carry a few here. Mrs. Scohill will you find the ring case for Mr. Kelley."

Mrs. Scohill came back and opened a finely crafted wooden box. "You'll have to have a large one Blair. Maybe a size eleven. Here try this."

"It fits perfectly."

Life on the Little Black River

"Now for Monique, if I remember correctly she is a petit girl, here's a size five and a size six."

"I'm only guessing, but I'd say a six. How much for the two?"

"$30.00. I'll bring the size five with me just in case she needs a smaller one."

"Thank you, and someone will be here with the carriage at 9 o'clock."

From the Reverend's house Blair walked back to Ouelette's General Store. Outside the store he was confronted by Bouchard McQuale. McQuale stepped in front of Blair blocking the path. "Do you have any idea the damage you did to my boys!?" he roared.

"Did your little boys tell you the truth why I beat the hell out of them? Probably not. They wouldn't know the truth if it hit them on the end of their noses. And I doubt if you would either. Now, Mr. McQuale, are you looking to square things?"

McQuale knew he could not beat Blayne Kelley and his son was bigger and stronger.

"You tell your boys, McQuale, that if either one of them ever comes after us, I'll hurt them much worse the next time. And that goes for my sister Faye and my whole family. You McQuales stay clear of the Kelley and Lamoureux families. Now, McQuale, you get out of my way or I'll tell the whole town what your boys tried to do to Monique and why I beat them. Move!"

Bouchard McQuale turned around and walked off.

Blair went inside and Monique and Faye were about ready to leave. "Before we go there are some things I want to pick up that aren't on your list. Did you get a calendar?"

"Yes."

"Mr. Ouelette I'll need two lengths of stovepipe and a cap. A bit brace and a set of bits, a keyhole saw, two buckets, a cold chisel, a set of wood chisels and a pair of pliers" He also picked up an assortment of small wrenches in case he ever had to work on the cook stove. Everything Blair picked up he could put in the two buckets.

Blair paid Ouelette and then the three went to the mercantile store. "Hello, Mr. Oliver, we need two pairs of wool pants for my wife and I. Two heavy winter shirts apiece and two sets of long underwear apiece and winter boots."

"You know, Monique, before next summer we both will be needing leather boots and a wool coat for each of us."

"Blair could we afford to buy my grandmother a warm winter coat?"

"Sure, did you see something she would like?"

"Yes, it isn't as heavy as ours but it'll be just right for her."

"Will you wrap everything in one package except for this coat?"

"Certainly, Mr. Kelley."

"Faye, what about your errands for Mom?"

"All taken care of."

Blair had enough confidence in Monique so he knew he wouldn't have to check if she had filled the list. Everything was put in the wagon and they were on their way home. "What did the Reverend say?" Monique asked.

"He'd be happy to marry us tomorrow. Someone has to be at his house at 9 o'clock tomorrow morning. I invited he and his wife for lunch."

"Okay, Blair, I saw you talking with Mr. McQuale. What was it all about?"

"Oh, he was just blustering actually. I told him what would happen to his boys if they ever bother you again or if I hear they have bothered you, Faye, or anyone in the family. He didn't like what I had to say, but I think he understood."

* * *

After his encounter with Blair Kelley, Bouchard McQuale forgot about his business in town and drove home, full of anger and contempt towards his three sons. They were like a pack of wolves that hunt together on weaker prey and not one of them had the backbone of a mouse. But they were his boys.

When he arrived home, he didn't even unharness the team. He dropped the reins and went inside. "I just had a talk with Blair Kelley—"

"He's back in town, Pa? Where?" Burl asked.

"You never mind. He told me that if you three idiots ever bother Monique again, his sister Faye or any one of the Kelley family he'll give each of you a worse beating than before."

Burl started to say something and Bouchard said, "Shut up, Burl! I don't want to hear one word from any of you. And you three have lollygagged for almost five months now. That stops now. Now get your asses out to the barn and get to work." When they didn't move Bouchard said, "Now damn you! Move!"

* * *

Mr. Ouelette had packed the eggs in clean dry sawdust and that box was put in the root cellar. Everything else was set in the shed along with what Blayne had gathered. When Monique gave the winter coat to her grandmother she burst into tears, and she hugged and kissed both Monique and Blair. After lunch Blair said, "I'm going to walk out to the junkyard, Dad."

"What are you looking for?"

"Seems as though I can remember two old iron wheels about eighteen inches across. I think I can make a hand cart to carry firewood."

"They're still there."

Monique was trying on one of Faye's dresses for the wedding, so he and Peter walked out back. "Blair, do you really like living out in the wilderness, just the two of you?"

"Yes, I do, Peter. It's an exciting life. I always enjoyed the farm and working in the woods, but this is different. I can't explain it better than that. Maybe you can come visit some time and see how we live. I do know one thing though. What I have learned to do here on the farm has helped me greatly; to build a new home and life. I hope you and Faye will stay with the farm."

"I know I will."

The two iron wheels were right where Blair had last seen them. "Now all I need is two bolts that'll go through the center."

"We have those in the tool shed."

Saturday morning started off just like any other day. Blair helped Peter with the morning chores before breakfast. "Peter I would like you to take the carriage in to town and bring Reverend Scohill and his wife to the farm. You are supposed to be there at 9 o'clock."

"Okay, will you hitch the team while I change clothes and clean up?"

"Sure."

Blayne helped Blair with the team. "You know, son, in a way I wish it was your mother and I doing what you and Monique are doing."

"You'll have to come out some time, Dad, to visit. You can't miss the cabin on the Little Black River."

"We will some time, son."

* * *

When Blair saw Monique wearing one of Faye's dresses, he couldn't believe the transformation. He took her hands in his and smiled. "You are so beautiful, Monique."

When Reverend Scohill pronounced them man and wife, Monique started crying—then her grandmother, Regina and Faye.

Blayne and Regina congratulated them, hugged them and Blayne said, "We both are so proud of both of you. We know you will take care of each other."

Regina and Rosa had prepared a pork roast. When everyone had eaten their fill there was very little left over.

When it was time for the Scohills to leave, Peter and his sister Faye offered to drive them back to town.

Blayne and Regina were sitting on the porch with Blair, Monique and Rosa. "After seeing and talking with you two, we know you'll be okay living in the wilderness by yourselves. I'm not saying that we won't miss you—'cause we will—but I think I speak for all of us when I say we know you'll be alright. Watch out for thin ice, angry bear and wolverines."[1]

* * *

The next morning Blayne and Peter helped Blair load the canoe. "Do you have everything, son?"

"I think so. I think this load will be as heavy as the first one. But the current isn't as swift. I hope there'll be plenty of water in the Little Black."

Everyone was quiet while they ate breakfast. No one really knowing what to say.

And like last time Regina gave them a basket of food to enjoy on their trip up river.

"How long will it take you, Blair?" Faye asked.

"We had to camp out two nights. But then we were in a hurry to put some distance between us and the McQuales."

The family walked with Blair and Monique to the river. "Blair and Monique, we all are so proud of you," Blayne said again.

Peter held the canoe while they got seated and then he pushed them out into the current. "We'll be out in the spring after the water drops."

They all stood there watching until they were out of sight.

---

[1] *In September of 2010 my brother Dave and I were on motorcycles on Rt. 204 in Quebec Province and just south of Daaquam we saw a road killed wolverine. So if they are that close to the Maine border it is reasonable to believe they are also in the big woods of northern Maine.*

Monique was paddling fast and hard. "Why are you paddling so vigorously?'

"I really enjoyed spending time with our family, but now I can't wait to get home."

"Okay, so you'd like me to paddle a little faster too, huh?"

She splashed him with her paddle, "I get the picture, Mrs. Kelley." And he began paddling trying to outdo Monique. The current not so swift, they were making fantastic time.

They went by Pelletier's Trading Post shortly after noon, and made camp where they had on their second day originally.

That night they enjoyed some of Regina's put up food with coffee. There was still an hour or so of daylight left, but they both had worked hard all day to get this far. There was no hurry, but it became more of a game to them.

"I want you to be honest with me, Blair."

"Yes."

"Do you think the brothers will come looking for us out here?"

"When I talked to Bouchard by Ouelette's store I had the feeling that would be the end of it. I think he probably went home and read the riot act at his sons. But I think some time they'll try to find us."

"Me too. So we can't be careless then."

The temperature rose during the night and when Blair awoke at dawn he was already sweating. "Look at the water level Monique."

"It dropped during the night."

"I guess the heavy rain has drained off from this country now. We're apt to have to drag the canoe up behind us today, at least some of the way."

"Well, I'm glad we left when we did then."

After breakfast they pushed the canoe into the river and started upstream. Only they hadn't gone far at all before they had to get out and pull the canoe along. They were seeing more and more peeled beaver wood in the water and along the shore.

"The peeled wood sure is a good sign for beaver trapping this winter."

Two hours later they found a dam across the river. "Well this might explain why the water level has dropped. Maybe we can get back in on the other side of the dam."

"It's amazing how beaver can build a dam like this in only a few short days."

The temperature kept getting hotter and hotter with each passing hour. "I feel so sweaty and dirty," Monique said. "When we get home and everything unloaded I'm going to sit in the river for a while and cool off."

"I think I might join you."

"We're getting close to home now. See that ledge up there."

"Oh, I can't wait," Monique said.

They were able to sit in the canoe and paddle it from the dam to home. They pulled the canoe ashore. "I'll have to pull the nails in the doors." He carried an armload up with him.

They were an hour unloading the canoe and taking care of everything. "We done?"

"I think so."

They took a towel and some soap to the river, stripped and sat in the cool water up to the neck. "This is nice."

They washed and washed their sweaty clothes and then lay in the evening sunshine to dry.

"I'm hungry, but I'm too tired to cook."

"We can finish up what Mom gave us."

Before going to bed Monique insisted they put the new sheets on their bed and the pillows. They had to spread a blanket over the needles first then the sheet.

As they were lying in bed Blair said, "You know wife, it's good to be home."

Chapter 10

While eating breakfast the next morning of smoked deer, bread and coffee, Monique said, "We have sixty hen eggs. If we have eggs for breakfast once a week that's five eggs. That's twelve weeks. At that rate the eggs will be gone before winter. Plus whatever I use to cook with."

"So are you saying eggs for breakfast only once in a while?'

"I think so. They'll keep for a long time in which ever is colder. The cold storage box or the root cellar."

"While I'm working on the outhouse today, you can take care of the food stuff. Sometime soon I want to shoot a bear and try smoking the sides for bacon."

First off, Blair had to dig a deep hole, so he wouldn't have to move the outhouse for a couple of years. The location he chose was sandy soil and the digging was easy. By mid-morning the hole was five feet deep.

Surprisingly, Monique found the root cellar was colder and she moved all of the food there except for the flour, salt and sugar. They would have to stay inside the cabin. Afterwards she began fishing and much to her surprise the water was black with brook trout. By noon she had fourteen beautiful trout.

"Blair I can clean and split these trout to smoke. Do you want to save the innards for bear bait?"

"That would be a good idea. You can use that old pail we found at the cabin."

After lunch Monique started the outdoor fire and put on

some green maple wood to create smoke. Then she positioned the rack over the fire and laid out the trout she had so far. When she was done there was still room for a few more. She went back to fishing.

Blair had the four walls of the outhouse up and was working on the roof. The seat and door would have to wait until tomorrow.

When Monique stopped fishing she laid out to smoke six more nice trout and had six to eat fresh.

Before Blair cleaned up for supper he had an idea how to improve the smoker. He started making a skeleton frame from poles around the meat rack and then he wrapped a piece of canvas around it, making a cone. "This will hold the heat and smoke in and the fish will cure faster."

"Are you done? Supper is getting cold."

"Yeah, I guess I was a little carried away."

"Fried brook trout, fried cabbage and the last of Mom's bread."

"What did you do with the fish guts?"

"They're in the root cellar."

"Oh good. They'll keep there until I can finish this outhouse. Then I'll take 'em across the river and clear a patch so we can see when a bear comes to 'em."

They sat out on the porch watching the sunset. The whole sky was a fiery red and orange. "It'll be a nice day tomorrow," Monique said.

Before going inside for the night they both walked over to the smoker to check. Monique stirred the coals and put on another piece of maple. "How are the fish doing?" Monique asked.

"You know they may be all cured by morning. Having this canvas has really made the process work faster."

"It won't be too long before the night air has a chill in it," Blair said.

"Which means we need to gather food and firewood."

"I guess we'll be busy, huh."

There still was a faint red glow in the sky long after the last sunrays had disappeared.

* * *

The next morning before eating Blair checked the smoker. The fish were almost cured and he added another piece of wood.

"The fish should be cured by mid-morning."

"We have twenty trout on the rack now; do you want me to catch many more?"

"You might catch enough to fill the rack again. This will give us more bear bait."

While Blair was finishing the outhouse, Monique took the cured fish off the rack and put them in the root cellar. Then she went fishing. The mouth of the small spring brook was again black with brook trout. She caught twenty before lunch.

"I'll have the outhouse done in another couple of hours. Then I'll go across the river and clear out a shooting lane."

"By then I'll have the fish cleaned that I caught this morning and in the smoker. That's a pretty good contraption you made."

"I hope it'll work trying to make bacon from bear."

While Blair finished the outhouse Monique took care of the fish and said, "I'm going up to the marsh to see what I can find for herbs."

"Okay."

When the outhouse was done Blair took the pail of fish guts, some wire, his axe and pushed across the river in the canoe. Clearing the alders on shore near the water was difficult, then as he moved back the alders turned to small trees. He kept checking behind him making sure he had a straight line of sight from the porch.

Fifty feet from the river he wired the pail of fish guts to a tree about five feet above the ground. He picked up all the brush and cut a few overhanging limbs. From the bait he could see a clear shooting lane back to the porch.

Monique wasn't back yet so he started to pick up a lot of the wood debris around the cabin. Anything that could be burned in the cook stove, for now he stacked on the porch. The brush from the treetops and branches he put in a pile to burn once the ground was covered with snow.

He checked the smoker and the fire wouldn't need more wood until later.

When Monique was back she had a pack basket full of edible herbs. Her favorite, the shaggy mane mushroom.

The female blossoms on the cattails had gone by, but the white section or the lower stalk was still very good. She and her grandmother had once tried the root, which was supposed to be good. But it was awful bitter tasting.

After she had put the herbs away Blair showed her the shooting lane he had cleared out and said, "The pail of fish guts is hanging from a tree about fifty feet from the river."

"I see it."

"If you see the bear and I'm not here go ahead and shoot it. Use the rifle and not your handgun. Sight it in just as you would your handgun."

"Where do I aim on the bear?"

"Well, a head shot is always good, but from this distance you'd take an awful chance of missing—right behind the forward shoulders. Aim just under the backbone to hit the heart from here. If the bear is a sow with cubs, don't shoot."

"Are you busy?"

"Not right now. What do you need?"

"I'll make a fish chowder if you catch us a nice big trout."

"Okay, I think the rest of the fish could come off the smoker before dark."

The brook trout were schooled up again at the mouth of the spring brook. Probably for the cooler water. Where they can't go downstream to the big river because of the beaver dam. Well, it worked out well for the Kelleys. Blair caught three that were small and on his next try, he hooked one that was bigger than anything they had caught so far.

While Monique made the chowder, Blair looked for a good spot to make the shed. There was a small level place behind and to the right of the cabin. He wanted it near enough to the cabin so during winter storms they would not have to go far for wood. He checked on the smoker fire and added only a little bark. He sampled one of the trout on the top rack and it was almost cured. He took another piece and ate it and then took a piece in for Monique.

"That is good. You can actually taste the maple. As good as this is I think we should smoke cure another twenty."

"Okay, but after we have smoke the bear bacon."

* * *

Blair started cutting the trees he would need for the shed. Half of the shed would have the four walls and roof—'cause this is where he would keep his tools. The other half would be post with a roof to store firewood under.

Monique kept busy making jars, crocks, pitchers, urns and vases from the clay and baking them in the outside fire pit.

The third morning after Blair had put out the bear bait pail, Monique was setting the coffee pot on the table when she looked out the front window. "Blair." No answer. "Blair—bear."

Blair went to the window. It was a lone bear and no cubs. The rifle was standing in the corner and already loaded. He eased the door opened trying to be quiet. The bear's attention was on the now smelly fish guts in the bucket that he couldn't reach. He climbed the tree and jumped out at the bait and missed. But he had come close. He climbed the tree again and Blair had a perfect shot at the throat, just blow the bear's chin. He pulled the trigger and the bear fell.

Monique held the legs on his back, while Blair skun and fleshed it. "How old would you say?" Monique asked.

"I'm thinking he'd only weigh two—maybe two hundred and fifty pounds. Probably three years old. This one has plenty of fat."

He cut the hide high around the head, then he made the slit up the belly and pulled the innards out. Then he picked the carcass up so the blood would drain and away from the hide. "This hide will surely make a nice rug for the floor," Monique said.

"Can you carry the hide to the canoe and spread it out on the bottom? Then I'll lay this on it."

Once on the other side of the river Blair quartered the bear and said, "We probably should hang these a couple of days in the root cellar before we take care of the meat. I'll cut the sides off for bacon."

"What about roasting the ribs today for supper?"

"That would be okay."

After the meat was hung up Blair mixed up a salt brine solution in two pails and put the sides of bacon in to soak.

"How long will they have to soak?"

"Two days." He cut off some shavings with the draw shave from a stick of maple and added those to the brine also, for flavoring.

Monique started a fire in the pit and set the ribs to roasting. It would take several hours.

Then she asked, "Blair, will you help me nail this hide to the side of the cabin, to stretch it?"

It was already fleshed, so all she had to do now was stretch it and let it dry and once every day she would rub hemlock bark on the fleshed side. The oil in the hemlock would give it a nice tan color and soften the hide.

Blair went back to work building the shed. During the day, every time he would look at Monique she was acting so happy. A remarkable change with her had taken place since that night of the attack five months earlier. She was always smiling and there seemed to be a golden glow that was surrounding her. He would only see it when he would first glance her way. Then it was gone. But he knew from her happiness, the glow was always there whether he could see it or not.

"The ribs are going to be done before supper. I hope that'll be okay."

"I've been smelling those ribs roast all day and I'm so hungry, I could eat a bear."

They each took one bite of the roasted meat and said together at the same time, "This is so good."

"It's been a long time since I have had bear, I had forgotten how good it is."

"This is better than any bear meat I have ever eaten," Monique said.

She had boiled some cattail stalks and fried potato in bear fat with an onion.

"Man! This whole meal is so good, Monique."

"Tomorrow I want to melt down some of the fat for lard. Now that we have an oven, you wait until you taste my biscuits with bear lard.

"Did your grandmother teach you how to cook like this?"

"Almost everything I ever learned was from my grandparents."

"You know something I have had a hankering for?"

"What?"

"Beans."

"I remember how good those bean-hole beans were at the festival. I'll make some. But first there is another meal I want to make for you."

"What's that?"

"I'll surprise you. But tomorrow after breakfast you must promise me to stay out of the cabin—unless it won't be a surprise."

"Okay, I promise. Now you have me wondering."

"Good."

The next day Blair had the shed done except for the roof shakes. The roof pitched sharply from the front to the back side. One flat surface. He already had many of the shakes made.

All day Monique kept him from going inside. Whenever he would need something, she would get it for him. He had no idea what to expect for supper. She had walked out back and found some mushrooms she had found earlier and was waiting until they were full grown.

Monique rendered some bear fat to lard and put it in mason jars and then put them in the root cellar.

"Blair."

"Yes."

"Go wash up, supper is ready."

When he opened the front door he was met by the most delicious smell he could imagine. "A boiled dinner? Are you kidding me?"

"I hoped you'd like it. It isn't ham, but I took some of the loin instead."

"What else is there?"

"Potato, cabbage, onions, mushrooms and loin. The meat is real tender. I sampled some while it was cooking and it is good."

Monique filled his plate and he waited until she had filled hers. They both took a bite. "Wow! Is this ever so good. Just think a delicious boiled supper out here in the wilderness."

"It is good isn't it?" Monique said.

"You're really spoiling me with your cooking."

"I'm glad you like it. I wasn't sure how the boiled dinner would be with bear meat instead of the traditional ham."

"I like ham, but this certainly has more flavor."

Blair ate so much his belly was bulging.

"Oh my word Blair, you look like you are pregnant."

"Well—it was all so good I just couldn't stop eating."

It had been an early supper and they didn't feel like

doing any more work for the day. "Blair, let's walk up on top of the ledge and watch the sun set from there."

It wasn't a long walk and the incline was so gradual it was deceiving as they stood on the open ledge looking back at the cabin—their home.

Blair sat with his back against the tree and Monique between his legs leaning back against him. "We are so lucky, Blair. I hope you realize this. I have never felt so content and happy in all my life."

Blair held her tight against him and said, "Monique, I am just happy being with you."

* * *

The next day Blair finished the roof over the shed. The door was hung and he made a work bench and shelves. He only wished the other part was full of firewood. He still had almost three months to do that.

The next day he put the sides of bacon on the smoker rack and closed the canvas cone. "This will take longer than the fish. Now I need to work on firewood."

There were many dead and drying hardwood trees on the shelf between the cabin and the river. But he wanted to save those in case they would need more wood during the winter. So he and Monique went out back and to the left to a beautiful stand of hardwood. "I need your help on the other end of this saw. After we have several down you can go do what you had planned."

Blair was very selective which trees to take. If they were growing together, he took one and left the other. He stayed away from white birch for now. There was too much creosote in the wood, it would plug the chimney. He wouldn't mind burning it, if first it dried during the summer.

After they had felled several hardwood trees Monique said, "I'm going to make a circle through the woods back home to look for more mushrooms."

"Okay."

He would lift up a butt end and swing it onto another tree, lifting the butt end up so he wouldn't have to bend over so far. When he came to the smaller tops he stopped and selected another tree. He would have to make a saw horse to hold the smaller pieces.

He worked effortlessly, enjoying what he was doing and being in the wilderness. By noon he had worked up all the trees he and Monique had felled. Split the blocks and stacked the wood in rows, until he could make his hand cart with the two small iron wheels he had found at the junk yard.

Monique found a few edible mushrooms and in a low wet wallow she found a bunch of ferns growing. There were only the fern plants she was familiar with. And the white roots were succulent, cooked or eaten raw.

The soil was black, wet and loose and she was able to pull the plant up roots and all and break the pulpy white root off. She had not thought to bring a basket so once again she had used her shirt to carry the mushrooms and now she filled her shirt with fern roots.

When Monique returned to check on the curing bacon the fire was almost out. She made a few chips with the axe from a maple stick of wood. She would have to continue adding the chips until there were sufficient coals to put on a bigger piece of wood.

When Blair came back to make a couple of sawhorses, Monique had not yet put her shirt back on. "My, I do like that look."

She turned to look at him, with both hands on her hips and her feet spread just a little, she gave him a tantalizing pose and smile. "Are you done already?"

"I need to make a couple of saw horses before I can finish the tops and limbs."

With Monique's help it didn't take long to make two sawhorses. "Before I go back to work, I need something to eat."

"What would you like?"

"Oh, maybe a little smoked venison and bread and raw cattail stalks with coffee."

While Monique was preparing something to eat Blair checked the bacon. It was curing well, but had a long ways to go. He went down to the river to wash up and when he kneeled down to splash water in his face he saw a big bobcat track.

"Monique!" No answer. "Monique!" he hollered a little louder.

"What is it?"

"Come here, I want to show you something."

She stopped what she was doing and walked down to see what he was hollering about.

He pointed to the track and said, "Look."

"Is that a cat track?"

"Yes, a big bobcat. He probably could smell the bear bait, which I need to empty, and the bacon in the smoker."

"How fresh is it?"

"I'd say since daylight this morning. I bet he was here in the yard when you came back and spooked it."

"What do we do with the smoker?"

"I think some time we'll have to build one from wood. But for now we have to keep this one going. I think I'll set some traps and catch it."

They ate lunch on the porch. "Someone is going to have to stay around the cabin until the bobcat either leaves or we catch it in a trap."

After eating he took one trap across the river and dug a cubby hole in the soft soil and set a trap and then he set pieces of wood around the trap forcing the cat to step on the trip pan when it came after the fish guts.

He set another trap close to the river and he used a piece of smoked trout for bait. Then he set another trap close to the smoker and another near the little spring stream, near the storage box. He cut off the head of one of the larger smoked brook trout, for bait.

When he had finished, he showed Monique where the traps were.

"If you can stay around the cabin this afternoon I'll go back to my firewood."

"Go ahead, I'll find things to keep me busy here."

Blair carried the two saw horses out back and set them up about six feet apart so he could lay the long tops level. This was even better than before. He didn't have to bend over so far. He wasn't long sawing up all the tops and some of the bigger limbs. He stacked the limb wood and fell two more trees.

He chunked up the trees and split the bigger blocks. The smaller round wood he left. They would make for good fire at night.

He cut another tree and had that all worked up, split and piled. It was time to go home. He was thirsty, hungry and tired.

"Have I time for a bath in the river before supper?"

"Make it a quick one."

He stayed away from the trap. He didn't want any more human scent around it than necessary. He could smell the fish guts now. He should have taken care of it much sooner. It would attract a lot of meat eaters to it. Maybe they'd get lucky tonight.

Blair went in the river clothes and all. He figured to wash them also. When he had finished he drooped his clothes over the porch railing and went inside to get dressed and eat.

Later as they were sitting on the porch Monique asked, "Can bobcats swim?"

"They will if they have to. Actually all cats are good swimmers."

"I hope we get it tonight."

"I'm counting on the trap across the river. Those fish guts are really smelling bad now. I could smell them at the river."

"When are we going to chink the logs in the walls?"

"I'd like to wait a little longer. Give the wood more time to dry and shrink."

"These clay pots I'm making I can store things in, in the root cellar. They're nothing fancy, but they come in handy."

"I have an idea about something you can make that will come in useful this winter."

"What's that?"

"A commode."

"That would be a good idea. I don't know if I'll want to go out to the outhouse at night this winter. I'll get on it."

"What's to say that bobcat won't go for the smoker and not the traps?"

"I'm hoping it'll go for the tidbits at each trap, not wanting to go after the bacon above the fire."

"Are bobcat hides worth anything?" Monique asked.

"I used to get $25.00 to $30.00 for one. I don't know what they're worth now.

"How long have we been back?"

"This is August 22nd."

"What day of the week?"

"Wednesday."

"Feels like Saturday."

Monique burst out laughing then and asked, "What exactly is it about today that makes you think of Saturday?"

"It was a guess."

Before going to bed, Blair checked the smoker and added wood. Yep, this is the end of August, the night air is cooling off."

"I sure like this bed better than sleeping on the ground," Monique said.

"It is nice."

* * *

Some time after midnight a bobcat was caught in the trap across the river and yowled a blood curdling scream and Monique sat up in bed. Her heart beating rapidly in her chest. She elbowed Blair several times before he woke up.

"What is it, Monique?"

"Listen, I think you have the bobcat in one of your traps."

They were silent then listening. Everything was all quiet. "I don't hear anything. Maybe you were only dreaming."

"I was not dreaming. Listen."

He laid back on the bed and started to roll over on his side when the bobcat let out another screaming yowl. Blair jolted upright and said, "Damn, I guess you weren't dreaming," and he got up out of bed.

"What are you going to do?"

"Can't leave him in the trap all night. He'll scream all night and neither one of us will get any sleep."

"Well, I'm coming with you."

Blair lit the lantern and the two pulled on their clothes and Blair put his .22 handgun in his pocket. "We'll leave this lantern lit and take the other one." He lit that while Monique was pulling on her boots.

Before crossing the river they checked the other three traps around the cabin first. Nothing had been near any of them. "Let me get in first Monique then you push us out."

Blair used his paddle like a set pole and pushed them the rest of the way across. The cat was making a lot of noise now thrashing in the bushes. He was snarling and growling. His eyes were green in the light of the lantern.

Blair knew he had to have a good clean shot with the .22. He tried to get around behind it so he could shoot it in the ear. Monique saw what he was trying to do and she started around the other side of the cat. This distracted the bobcat just long enough so he was able to get a good clean kill shot. The cat dropped to the ground and stopped struggling. Monique stepped over closer and held the lantern while Blair took the trap off. "Look at this, Monique," and he held up the trap so she could see, "he was only held by two toes. I don't think he would still be in the trap come daylight."

"What are you going to do with it now?"

"I'll hang it in the wood shed and skin it tomorrow."

"What about the other three traps?" Monique asked.

"I think we'd better leave them until the bacon is cured."

"I'll check the smoker, then I'm going back in the cabin," she said.

"Okay."

She added only a small piece of wood and then closed it up again. The bacon was beginning to smell good.

When Blair climbed back in bed with Monique he said, "That was exciting. Now if we can get back to sleep."

"I put some more wood on the fire. The bacon is beginning to smell good. We'll have to be careful of animals now trying to get at it."

"I think you're right. Next year I'll build a smoking shack. Now let's go back to sleep."

It didn't take long before they both were asleep. Just before daylight rain drops started making a soothing, quieting music on the roof. Blair rolled on his back and put his arm around Monique. They were both awake, laying there in their total love for each other listening to heaven's music.

"You know—we have to get up some time," Blair said.

"I know, but isn't this great?"

"Yes it is, but while you get breakfast I need to look at the smoker, especially with this rain."

Blair made the opening in the top of the smoker smaller, to keep out the rain, letting the smoke inside cure the bacon. He added some more chips and then a piece of wood.

As they were eating breakfast the rain became steady. "I guess I don't work on firewood today. That's okay really. I need to make a cart to haul the wood in."

"And that must be what the small wagon wheels are for," Monique said.

"I need to skin the bobcat first and put it on a stretcher to dry."

Once he had the hind legs skun, he peeled the rest of the hide like a banana. Then he skun the front legs and the head. He had only brought two stretchers with him from the farm.

When he had finished Blair went out to his tool shed and began working on the cart. First he would need two small ash trees about three inches across. He knew of a few just like that on the shelf between the cabin and the river. He took his axe and had both down in quick order. He cut the tops off and carried the two poles back to the open woodshed where he would have more working room. His shoulders were wet but he didn't care.

While he was building his push cart, Monique was tending the smoker. "Blair, is it alright to can the rest of the bear meat now?"

"It should be okay."

Monique was all day taking care of the bear meat and canning it. If the outside fire was not being used to smoke-cure the bacon, she would have used the fire pit for the canner. In this warm weather the fire in the cook stove was keeping the cabin interior warmer than comfortable.

It rained all night and the temperature dropped making for better sleeping. The bear meat was all canned and put away in the root cellar. Monique kept two pieces to roast over the open fire. Blair had his push cart almost done. Securing both iron wheels to the main frame took a little ingenuity, but he eventually found a way to do it. That's what took him so long.

The next morning it was still raining and he used the time to finish his cart. When he was done, he stood back looking at it and was satisfied. It had two handles like a wheelbarrow. He could probably carry five or six arm loads of wood in it.

"Would you look at the bacon, Blair, and see what you think."

He sliced off a small piece and chewed on it. "It certainly has a good flavor, but I think it could stand another twelve hours. Maybe this evening we can take it off."

The bacon was taken off the smoking rack and hung up in the root cellar and Blair removed the rack and for now put it behind the woodshed.

The next morning for breakfast they ate bear bacon, eggs, warmed up bread and coffee.

"This bacon is delicious. I was, I admit, a little skeptical when you said we could make bacon from bear. But this is better than pork bacon. It has a deep maple flavor."

"I like the smoky taste also," Blair added.

The river was full with water, so each day Monique went looking for herbs in the woods. Sometimes circling to the northwest towards the marsh. While she was gathering herbs Blair worked steady on firewood. He worked until noon and then filled the cart and brought that back to the woodshed and after lunch he'd work all afternoon and then bring another cart full back to the woodshed. He figured he now had three cords of firewood piled up in the woods plus what he had put in the shed.

He wasn't sure how much wood it would take to heat the cabin during the winter, so when the woodshed was full (about four cord) he piled down two more cord along the front side of the woodshed. Now he needed some of the dry standing hardwood that was on the shelf beside the riverbank. He worked up two cord of that for the cook stove and piled that beside the woodshed also. "There, we have eight cord cut, split and in the woodshed and piled along the side."

"Maybe we need a bigger woodshed," Monique said.

The bobcat hide had dried and was put with the two beaver hides in the root cellar.

The foliage was beginning to turn color. The piss maple in the wet areas always were the first to turn. The nights were getting cooler and Blair said one morning, "I think we can chink the cracks between the logs now."

The four corners where the end of the logs overlapped took longer to seal. The two of them working together were two days before everything was sealed. "Now the wind can't blow through the logs on us when we sleep."

The cook stove kept the cabin warm during the day preparing meals and after supper Blair would start a fire in the fireplace. The wooden walls and the stone fireplace would heat up and keep the cabin comfortable, even after the fire had burned itself out.

"I'm surprised how much the fireplace illuminates the cabin," Blair said.

"It is a comforting feeling isn't it? Sitting here in the glow of the fire. And I like the bear rug in the morning. You need one on your side now."

"Well, the next bear. Or if we can get a moose this fall."

* * *

As they were eating breakfast the next morning a flock of geese flew low over the cabin. "Flying that low they must have taken off from the marsh. We might try a hunt later this afternoon, if you haven't anything else you want to do."

"I'll go, for a roast goose."

"How good are you with that handgun with a goose on the wing?

"Don't know if I could."

"Me neither. I think we'd have to have them on the ground."

While they waited for the afternoon goose hunt, Monique went in search of more herbs.

"Where are you going to look?"

"I thought I'd follow the river downstream today. I have never looked for edibles that way. What are you going to do?"

"I'm going to use those boughs that we trimmed off the spruce trees and put them around the bottom of the cabin to keep the wind out."

Monique shouldered her pack basket and with her .45 on her hip and carrying a pail she started out following the river downstream. There hadn't been any frost yet, so she was hoping to fill the pack and pail.

Not too far below the ledge that they like to sit on and

watch the sunset, she found an area with many hazelnut bushes. And all the bushes were heavy with nuts. She wasn't long filling the pail.

She left the pail there for now and continued on. As she was stepping over an old rotten maple log a bee came out of a hole in the wood and stung her on the inside of her leg. And then another one stung her.

She moved away from the log and waited for the bees to calm down. She was hoping they might be honeybees and not wasps. She could see several walking around the entrance hole and some flying around above it. These were honeybees. But she would need Blair's help to get the honey.

A quarter of a mile below the honey bees she found a meadow that was not visible from the river. She was like the hunter. Her curiosity getting the better of her, she had to go see. There was a game trail going up through the meadow from the river. There were large deer like tracks in the soft soil, but she didn't think there were moose tracks.

In one corner of the meadow she could see a lot of small white blossoms. There were so many blossoms, it looked a little like snow. It had been a long time since she had seen plants like this and she was sure it was field pennycress. She picked a hand full and chewed on it. It tasted like she remembered. She could remember her grandmother warning her not to eat pennycress if it was growing near a mature pile and or outhouse, as the plant sucked up many minerals from the soil or contaminants. But there were no contaminants here. She filled her pack basket and headed for home.

Blair had finished putting the boughs around the cabin and was sitting on the porch when Monique returned home.

Monique was as excited as a child on Christmas morning as she told Blair about her discovery of the honeybees, getting stung, the meadow and the tracks in the game trail. Now it was time to go goose hunting. "I sure wish we had a shotgun," Blair said.

"Maybe we should get one."

"Good idea."

Blair already had the canoe in the water. Monique pushed off and they silently started upstream. Just below the beaver dam they could hear geese honking to their left. Blair guided the canoe to shore and they stepped out being careful not to make any noise. They crawled on their stomachs up to the top of the berm and looked over. Staying below the alder bush cover. There were geese there but nothing close enough for the handguns. "We wait," Blair whispered.

As it was getting closer towards evening more geese were coming in from the north. To spend the night or perhaps for a day or two of rest. They waited and waited, then just as Blair was going to call it quits, three geese waddled in from the right; they were only ten feet away. Without saying a word they both took careful aim on two separate geese and they fired at the same time. Both geese had been hit in the head.

"There, now can we go home?"

Blair began laughing and said, "Yeah, I'm hungry."

* * *

After supper they sat outside and plucked the feathers off of each bird. "When you clean these, Blair, save the gizzards and hearts and I'll make a giblet gravy to go with roast goose. If you hang these up in the root cellar, how long will they stay good and not spoil?"

"Well, I think the temperature is going to drop probably around freezing. So I'd say we leave the geese in a pan in the shed. Let them cool off nice and in the morning put them in the root cellar. They should stay good that way for three, four, maybe five days. Have you something planned?"

"Yeah, I'd like to get honey tomorrow and then the next day roast both geese and I'd like to make a stuffing for them too."

The sun had set but before going to bed Monique wanted to crack open and shell the hazel nuts.

After two hours they were ready for bed and there was still more to shell than what they had done. "Boy, don't these nuts smell good."

"Have you ever taken honey from a live beehive?" Monique asked.

"When I was too young to help I watched my father and uncle once."

"Did they get stung?"

"Oh yes."

"Before we go, I want to go up river and pick a lot of the tansy weed."

"That just might work."

The next morning Blair went up river with her to pick the tansy. They soon had filled the pack basket, plus what Monique could carry.

Monique washed out one of the pails and armed with axe and matches she led the way to the beehive. "At least it isn't hot and humid," Blair said.

"There," Monique pointed, "that old log there. The entrance to the hive is about three feet from the left end."

Blair checked the other end of the old log, it appeared to be hollow. "Let's start a fire at both ends and put on some tansy and then a fire on either side next to the entrance hole and add more tansy. Once we have a good smoke going I'll try to open the log. It looks old and maybe just rotten enough so I can pull it apart without using the axe."

Once the fires were going Blair peeled some loose birch bark off a nearby tree and twisted it into a cone and put some tansy inside. He looked at Monique and said, "A torch. If the bees come swarming out light the torch and see if you can fan it to keep the bees back."

"It's smoky enough now so my eyes are watering."

"Mine too."

Blair tested the left end and part of the log tore away easily. But the bees didn't like it. And they were rebuffed by the tansy smoke. Blair was stung on his arm and he tried to ignore it. Monique put her torch down close to the angry bees and Blair broke away more of the wood. More angry bees came out. And this time both Monique and Blair were stung.

They could see some of the honeycomb but he needed to remove more of the wood. The bees were becoming angrier and angrier. But thanks to the tansy smoke Blair and Monique were only stung once in a while. The next piece of wood Blair ripped off exposed all of the honeycomb.

Monique had the pail ready. Blair reached in and broke away the comb as quick as he could. "There's more honey here than I thought there would be."

"The pail is almost full," Monique said.

"I'll take a little more." But while they were busy getting the honey, they forgot to add more tansy to the fires and there was less smoke and the bees were beginning to fly around them.

"Blair, I have had enough of being stung. We have enough."

They backed off and the bees left them alone. "When they have calmed down some I'll have to make sure the fires are out."

A half hour later the bees had quieted down enough for Blair to put the fires out, what was left of them. Monique was rubbing mud on her stings. Blair's hands had received most of the stings. His right hand was a bit swollen.

"Let's get home," he said. "I don't know if I ever want to go through that again. Maybe if we had the right equipment."

"Yeah, but think how good it'll taste this winter."

They left the axe and pail of honey on the porch and then went down to the river to wash the mud off. "You know this cold water takes some of the pain out of my hands."

"Let me look at them," Monique said. "Oh, they are swollen. Do they hurt?"

"They kinda feel numb and stiff when I move my fingers. What about you?"

"I didn't get stung as many times as you did. My arms feel like they're on fire. That's why the cold water feels so good."

They both began to laugh then. "We make quite a pair."

"I hope this honey will be worth it. And it lasts for a long time. I'm not so sure I'd want to go through that again."

"Well, I tell you what; I'll bake an apple pie and you tell me then if it was worth it," Monique laughed.

Blair put the honey in the root cellar and Monique went inside to fix supper. His hands were still swollen so he tried putting some of the savvy clay on them. He could immediately feel some relief. They no longer had any numbness to them and he could flex his fingers without any difficulty. He took some clay in for Monique to try.

She too could feel some immediate relief in her arms. "What made you think of using the clay?" she asked.

"I don't know. Just an idea."

"I'm surprised how well it works. Maybe next time we should carry along some clay."

* * *

The next morning the redness, swelling and pain were gone from their arms and hands. "I'm going to mark out a trap line for fall trapping."

"I think I'll stay home and roast both geese with a special surprise."

Blair took a smoked trout to nibble on when he was hungry, his compass and axe. From the cabin he headed north, occasionally scarfing a tree for an indicator. Sometimes cutting limbs out of the way and bushes, so he would have a clear travel lane. He came to an open meadow without water and found a game trail going up the center of the meadow. There were fresh tracks and he recognized them as caribou tracks, traveling a little west of north.

After he crossed the meadow and about a mile north of the cabin he scarfed more trees to indicate the trail was now heading east. Not quite a mile east from the corner, he figured, he came to the little spring brook that flowed beside the cabin.

He followed the brook south and the brook abruptly turned southwest, he kept going south in the direction of the Little Black River. Before leaving the spring brook he sat down on a blow down and ate some smoked fish and drank some water. So far, everywhere he had been looked like excellent trapping habitat.

He knew this leg would be a long one and he tried to hurry along so he wouldn't be late for Monique's surprise.

As soon as Blair had left, Monique brought in both geese from the root cellar. Put wood in the stove so the oven would be hot enough and then she began making a stuffing for inside the geese. She crumpled up some bread, crushed a few hazel nuts, stirred in some sorrel roots and leaves. Then she cut up the hearts and gizzard into small pieces and fried them slowly. She figured she needed more meat for the giblet gravy so she diced one kidney and added that to the fry pan with just a little bear fat. After the meat was cooked she added some flour mixed with cold water and stirred that in the fry pan. It was already smelling delicious, and her stomach was growling.

When the gravy was ready she put two spoonfuls in the stuffing mix and stirred it and tasted it. It was lacking something. She chopped up some onion grass into a powder and added that and tasted it. It was better.

She filled both geese and put them in the oven. Then she transferred the honey and wax from the pail into one of her clay crocks with a cover. She filled another small clay container for them to use. The crock was set back in the root cellar.

The last mile of the south leg to the river was somewhat easier. There was less brush that he had to work through. When he reached the river he knew there was no time to waste. He ate the last of the smoked trout as he was walking, following the river back to the cabin. In most places all he had to do was scarf trees here and there.

He found the meadow Monique had found earlier and the game trail went down to the river, but he could see where the trail had crossed the river onto the other side. But he did find an active beaver colony in a cove just above the game trail.

A little ways further and he came to the beehive in the log. Something else had definitely been ripping away the wood to get the rest of the honey. There were a few bees flying around, but they were not bothering him. His first thought was bear, but he wasn't sure.

From there he followed the trail he and Monique had made. Now he cleared the bushes and limbs and this close to home he didn't bother scarfing trees.

He could smell roast goose as he put his axe in the shed. Inside the cabin, he said, "I could smell roasted goose at the shed. Boy does that ever smell good."

"Before you get too comfortable," she tossed him a washcloth, and soap, "go wash up. I already did."

He wasn't happy about having to wash up in a cold river. But Monique had gone to work and fixed a special surprise for him for supper. So the least he could do was clean up. He left his boots and socks inside and walked barefoot down to the shore. Even the sand was cold. He removed his clothes and washed up as fast as he could. Even his hair. Then he grabbed his clothes and ran back inside and stood beside the stove to towel dry.

"You know it wouldn't take much work to put in a sunken tub in the floor in front of the fireplace."

"Wouldn't it take up too much room?" Monique asked.

"Probably would. But wouldn't it be nice."

"You finish drying off and I'll get you some clean clothes."

Monique already had the table set. "As soon as you're dressed, sit down. Supper is ready."

Life on the Little Black River

"All except for potatoes this is a wilderness meal. Roast goose—and might I add with stuffing and giblet gravy—some pennycress weeds, mushrooms and hazelnuts. All we're lacking is the wine. You get to carve the goose and I'll dish out everything else. There is a little vinegar you might try on your greens."

"I don't know what to say, Monique. This is better than Thanksgiving dinner."

They both heaped their plates with a little of everything. Even as petite as Monique was, she was eating her share. "All this, Monique, is all so delicious. And to think except for the potatoes everything else is nature's bounty. You keep surprising me all the time how well you can prepare food."

"I learned it all from my grandmother. We never had much, but we never went hungry either."

"The skin on this goose is golden brown and although the stuffing is different I have never had any that was any better."

There was so much to eat they had only eaten one goose. "This one will keep just fine in the root cellar."

While Monique cleaned up the kitchen Blair took everything else out to the root cellar. The sun had set hours ago and the temperature was dropping. He took in an armload of wood for the fireplace. "It's going to be cold tonight, I think, so I'll start the fireplace. We won't need it all night, so when we go to bed we can just let it burn out. It'll heat up the cabin, so we'll stay warm all night."

Monique turned the kerosene lantern down and blew out the flame and the fireplace gave the cabin a warm glow and she stood in front of the fireplace and took her clothes off and said, "I've been wanting this all day."

Later, as they lay in each other's embrace, Blair told her all about what he had seen that day, and she was as interested as Blair had been.

"What do you suppose it was that tore the log apart for the rest of the honey?"

"I'm not sure. Raccoon, martin—don't think so. Maybe

a fisher. I don't know if a bobcat or lynx would go after honey like that or not. But I think I'll set a trap there and maybe bait it with some honeycomb."

"When will you start trapping?"

"What's the date?"

Monique laughed and then said, "The only way I know is because of the calendar. Every day seems just like the next. Today is September 20th."

"Well, probably the middle of October. The animals should have their winter fur by then."

* * *

The next morning while Blair was starting the cook stove Monique ran out to the root cellar and brought breakfast back. "What have you there, Monique?"

"Breakfast. I made an apple pie yesterday and I used the honey instead of sugar. I hope it'll be good.

"It's cold outside this morning."

"Winter is coming."

"Are you still planning to shoot a moose or caribou before winter?"

"Yes. Why?"

"Well—I'd hate to run out of meat this winter if for some reason we don't get a moose or caribou."

"What are you thinking?"

"Well, if you're going to make another trap line, I think I'll catch more brook trout to smoke. What do you think?"

"That might be a good idea. Better to have too much than run out."

"Coffee is ready and I've had the pie warming on the stovetop."

"I would have thought the apples would still be too green," Blair said.

"They make the best pie. I put a glaze of honey and flour

on the top."

    Blair took a bite of pie." Holy cow!"

    "Do you like?"

    "Oh yes. It is delicious just like everything else you cook."

    Monique took a bite and said, "If I have to say so myself, it is very good. This makes for a pretty good breakfast."

    "Indeed. I wish we had some cheese to go with it."

    "Well, if we get goats next year I'll be able to make goat cheese and butter."

    "What are you going to do today?"

    "I want to make another trap line across the river and follow the brook on the left side of the river to the oxbows. I'd like to see if there are any beaver on that brook also. I'll take another smoked fish with me."

    "Before you go would you set up the smoking frame over the outside pit and wrap the piece of canvas around it. I'll start the fire before I start fishing."

    "Would you save the fish guts and cut the heads off? This will make for good trapping bait."

    In the shade where the sun couldn't shine Blair found frost on the ground. Especially behind the woodshed. He set the smoker frame up and wrapped the canvas around it, picked up his axe and pushed himself in the canoe to the other side of the river.

    It was a short hike to the brook. There were only a few limbs to clear. He saw an otter swim down the brook to the river. And he found some peeled beaver wood on the bottom of the brook.

    This brook was looking like good water for both mink and otter, let alone for beaver. The further he hiked the more peeled wood he was finding. And about a half mile upstream he began finding very active beaver workings. There were trees chewed down. Some with tops and branches gone. He even startled one beaver chewing on a small birch tree.

Upstream a little further he found the dam and behind that a large area had been turned into a pond. He could see four beaver in the water dragging popple branches to their winter feed bed next to the house. It was a huge house, which would mean several beaver. Blair was truly in his natural element.

At the upper end of the pond he turned south. This leg of the trap line was looking good also. The ground was mostly flat with a thick moss cover with tall spruce and fir trees.

After a mile he turned east to hit the river again. He left the softwood cover and now he was in a nice stand of hardwood. Mostly rock maple, ash, beech and some birch. He made sure he left a well scarfed trail so he would not have to hunt for it later.

Back on the river, he sat down to rest and eat the smoked trout. He knew where he was on the river. He was in a cove that was also an active beaver colony and almost directly across the river was the beehive log.

He started to make his way back to the canoe. There was more work here than anywhere else on this line, but he found some good sets. After a half mile he came to a spring brook that flowed into the river. He had not crossed this on the south leg. There was fine sand on the bottom and he could see mink and otter scats.

From what he had seen along both trap lines he was anxious to start trapping. But he would wait until the middle of October.

* * *

Monique had started a small fire for the smoker and when she went to her usual fish hole she was surprised to find so many brook trout. The spring brook was also black with trout. Once in a while one would roll and she would see the bright orange belly. She walked up the spring brook to see what the fish were doing, and decided they were spawning.

She wouldn't bother the trout in the spring brook. She

fished in the river, with great success. Putting back the females with eggs.

She stopped fishing at forty. She cut the heads off and put them in the pail with the guts. She split them leaving a hinge at the tail end to hang them on the rack.

She put half of them on the smoking rack, then she mixed up a salt brine and the last twenty she dipped in the brine before hanging them on the rack."

The pail of heads and guts, she put in the root cellar with a lid on the pail.

Before Blair was back to the canoe he could smell smoke and fish waffling in the air.

Monique could hear him scarfing trees and went down to the river to meet him.

She held the canoe while Blair stepped out. "How'd it go?"

"I found two nice beaver colonies, saw an otter and found where mink are in a small spring brook. All along the line looks prime for trapping."

"Come over here, I want to show you something."

He followed her up from the river and to the spring brook. She pointed and said, "Look at that."

"They're spawning. I wonder how long they have been in this cold stream."

"It's like food in our pantry."

"How many trout do you have smoking?"

"Forty. I figured that will see us through along with what we already have."

For supper that evening they had the other roasted goose and trimmings; with a slice of apple pie for dessert. There was no floor show tonight and after Blair checked the smoker and added some maple wood chips and a green block of wood, they both went to bed.

"You have been unusually quiet this evening. Is something bothering you?"

"Not bothering me actually, but I think we should start

trapping on the other side of the river. As cold as the nights are getting, the river could freeze over and then we couldn't get across until much later when it would hold our weight. I think tomorrow I'll boil the traps and get everything ready to set traps the day after."

"I have about all the edible herbs that I can get, except for maybe some more hazelnuts if the squirrels haven't gotten them all."

CHAPTER 11

The next morning after eating breakfast Blair built a small fire outside and started boiling the traps to remove the scent and rust. He checked each trap over carefully making any repairs necessary.

He went over his list of things he needed: traps of course, bait, wire, nails, axe, pliers, hammer and nails.

"What do you want to eat tomorrow?"

"We'll catch a beaver and roast it."

He put four #4 Blake & Lambs in his pack basket, three #3s and ten #2s. With everything else his pack was full. They'd have to carry the pail of bait and the axe.

Wearing an extra shirt and not a jacket, green hat and both carrying their .45s they crossed the river and Blair wanted the first trap where the bear bait had been. There was a covey in the roots of the spruce tree and Monique watched as Blair nailed a fish head just above the ground at the backend of the covey. Then he hollowed out enough duff and soil so the #3 trap would sit flush with the ground. Then he covered the trap with a fir bough. "I used the #3 thinking something bigger than a fisher might have taken the bear bait. Where we caught one bobcat there may be more around here."

When he had finished he broke off a spruce branch and swept the ground where they had been standing.

They made another land set about fifty feet from the marsh in the oxbows. At each set, so they wouldn't have to hunt for the traps, he double scarfed a tree near the set. Monique had broken off a branch to sweep the ground, as Blair set the trap.

As Blair was finishing the set he noticed Monique drop her pants and squat down to pee. "Hey. Don't pee here."

"Why not, I really have to go."

"The smell of human urine—well the animals won't come near the trap. You peeing right here is like an animal marking his territory. Go off to the side about fifty feet."

Their next three sets were for mink and otter in the small stream. He made a covey with rocks and staked the fish head to the bank at the back of the covey with a stick thrust through the head to the bank. The trap was set so the pan was just below the water surface.

At the next set he said, "Okay, Monique, you saw how I did that last set; do the same thing here. You find the spot for the set." She chose a natural sandy covey and she dug out a hole in the sand bank about two inches above the water. She carefully set the trap and placed about a foot in front of the bait hole. Blair handed her a fish head. After she placed the bait she set rocks to guide the mink or otter to the trap.

"Very well done."

"I would think when the jaws close around the animal's leg, the force of the jaws would very easily cut the leg off."

Blair didn't say anything. He took a #3 from his pack and set the jaws and put the trap on a flat rock and put his fingers on the trip pan springing the jaws closed on his fingers.

Monique was startled and said, "Are you foolish? Why did you do that for?" her voice a little louder than normal.

Blair held his hand up with the trap still clamped to his fingers. "See, the jaws didn't even cut my skin. It doesn't hurt anywhere near what some people think. There's only one problem now though."

"What's that?"

"There are two springs and I only have one free hand."

Monique started laughing then and jokingly, she said, "You fool, you need my help don't you?"

"Yeah, you compress this spring and I'll do the other."

When his hand was free she said, "What would you have done if I wasn't here?"

"Step on the springs with my feet. Of course that isn't easy to do when you have your hand caught in the jaws."

They set one more water set in the brook and moved up to the beaver colony. There was already a big beaver packing mud on the dam. Blair motioned for her to step behind a tree and whispered, "As soon as that beaver leaves we'll set a trap on the dam." Monique helped him to remove the back pack from his shoulder and then they waited. But they didn't have long to wait. In the meantime Blair took out a trap. Monique whispered, "The beaver just swam off."

Monique followed him out on the dam where the beaver had been working and he made a trough across the top so water would drain through it. Then he placed the trap in the trough and anchored the chain to a live alder sticking up through the dam. Then they went ashore.

Blair explained, "Beaver check their dam several times in the run of a day to see if there is any leaks. When they see the trough they'll naturally check it out and will step in the trap. When the trap closes the beaver will naturally swim off. But only the length of the chain. It'll struggle against the tethered chain and will soon drown. And that, my dear, will be lunch. If you'll start a fire. I'll set a land trap."

He took a #2 trap and made a set under a hardwood tree, using its root system for a cove, about a hundred feet away from the flowage.

Monique heard the trap on the dam spring and beaver splashing in the water as it swam off and she excitedly hollered, "We got one! Blair, we have a beaver!" Then she walked out on the dam and grabbed the chain to pull the beaver in.

Blair saw what she was doing and said, "You'd better wait and make sure it's dead before you try to pull it in."

"I don't feel him tugging on the chain. I think he's dead already."

"Okay, pull it in slowly."

She began pulling the chain in. "I don't feel anything on the chain. I wonder if he got away."

Just then she screamed. The beaver surfaced right in front of her and he was swimming towards her. She screamed again and dropped the chain and lost her balance and sat down on the wet muddy dam. She scared the beaver as much as he did her, and made a somersault in the water and swam off again.

Blair was laughing and trying to talk at the same time. Finally he managed to say. "Better let him go and swim off and drown. You'd better come off that dam before you fall in the water," and he started laughing again.

"Not on your life! This beaver isn't going to make a fool out of me." Blair was still laughing and at the same time he was proud of her tenacity.

"Do you want some help?'

"No!" The chain was pulled out tight and the beaver didn't seem to be struggling. But she waited another five minutes to make sure this time.

She pulled on the chain and there seemed to be only a dead weight she was dragging, so she brought it in and she couldn't believe how big it was. She was so excited she lost her footing again and sat down on the wet mud. This time she laughed along with Blair.

"I'm going to need your help to get this trap off his leg. And it's too heavy for me to carry across this dam without falling in again," and she laughed at herself again.

Blair took the beaver out of the trap and reset it in the trough again and carried the beaver to shore. "This must weigh fifty pounds."

"And you'd better take your wet clothes off and hang 'em up near the fire to dry. I'll skin this brute."

"Are your feet wet?"

"No, they're okay."

Blair watched as she took her pants off and then her

underpants and hung them up near the fire to dry. He took off his shirt-jacket for her to wrap around her.

He wasn't long skinning and fleshing the beaver. He had already cut two sticks to roast small pieces of meat and he put a piece on one and gave it to Monique and then he did the same with another roasting for himself. It didn't take long to roast small pieces like this and they were soon roasting another.

"Are you warm enough?"

"My butt is a little cold, cause I was wet there. I'll be alright as soon as my clothes are dry."

They ate their fill of roasted beaver meat. Then Blair cut off the four legs and tail and wrapped them in the hide and put that in his pack basket. He had also cut out the castors. These he put in the bait pail.

"While your clothes are drying, I'm going to hike around to the inlet of the pond and set a trap or two."

Just then the trap on the dam snapped closed again and another beaver swam off with it. "Do you want this?" he asked Monique.

"In bare feet and bare butt—no you go."

He took the pack back off and by the time he was at the trough the beaver had stopped struggling and he pulled it in. "Same size as yours." He reset the trap again and carried that ashore.

Monique watched as Blair skun and fleshed that beaver. Helping to hold it. He passed her his knife and she knew what this meant. She cut off the legs and tail. "This fur is in good shape. Look at the guard hairs. This is prime fur."

He shouldered his pack and with axe in hand he walked around the flowage to the inlet. Something had killed a beaver in one of the beaver trails to the hardwood trees. Whatever it was had eaten most of it. He checked for tracks and scat and didn't find either. He decided this would be a good place for a #3.

He found a natural setting in the roots of a huge yellow birch tree. He nailed a fish head to the tree and tucked some fish guts under the wood at the back of the covey. He made sure the trap was level with the ground and then he used dry leaves to cover it. He then spread some of the castor on the tree near the fish head, then he brushed the ground where he had been working.

He made another otter set in the inlet and called it good for now, there at the flowage.

Before starting back he looked down the flowage. Monique was out on the dam without her pants on—probably pulling in another beaver.

She pulled it onto the dam and took the trap off and reset it and then stood up, stretching her back. The beaver was heavier then she wanted to carry back across the dam with bare feet.

When Blair got back she was standing with her butt to the fire trying to get warm. While Blair skun and fleshed that beaver Monique put her clothes back on, "There I feel better now. The pants are really warm."

With that hide and meat rolled up and in his pack basket, he had a load. "You know we probably should head for home. There isn't enough daylight left now to finish setting up the rest of this line. Besides, we now have three hides to stretch and the meat to take care of."

* * *

There were only ashes left in the cook stove, but the cabin was not cold. While Monique fixed something to eat, Blair nailed the three beaver hides to the sides of the shed. The castors he hung up to dry in the woodshed.

As they lay in bed that night Monique was glad they were able to take care of everything. After supper the fish were fully smoke-cured and in the root cellar. She didn't want to have to stay home the next day and do what they had managed to take care of.

Monique strapped on her .45, but she noticed Blair was only taking the .22 revolver. Then it occurred to her that they would only need a .22 to dispatch any animal in their traps.

"The air doesn't feel as cold this morning," Monique said.

"Are you planning on going swimming again today?" he gestured.

"If I do I'm pulling you in also."

When they pulled the canoe on shore they heard a familiar yowl coming from the bait tree.

"It's a bobcat," Monique said, "And ain't he some ugly."

The bobcat had the chain wrapped around a bush and he was now on a short tether. Blair was able to get in behind the bobcat and shoot it in the head. "Ordinarily, I wouldn't bother resetting this trap, after we have taken two bobcats, but this close to the cabin and food stores, I think it will be wise to reset.

They left the bobcat with the canoe and continued on. In the next set they actually had a large otter. The bait was gone and Blair added another fish head with some castor. The next set was empty. The land set just below the beaver pond produced a male fisher. "The males aren't worth as much as the females."

"Why is that?"

"The males have coarser hair."

They actually had another otter in the trap on top of the dam and beaver had filled in the trough.

"While you're skinning the otter, I'll reset the trap after I dig out the trough."

Blair decided to wait until they broke for lunch before skinning the other otter.

"I can hear something Blair up in the hardwoods where you set that trap."

"Have you finished with this trap?"

"Yes."

"Let's go see what is making the noise."

The dry leaves were making a lot of noise and this was

disturbing whatever was in the trap. It was trashing about more, the closer they came.

"It's another cat, and bigger," Monique said.

"Bigger all right! That's a lynx and worth more than a bobcat."

"He has some free chain and this isn't going to be as easy as the bobcat. You take this," and he handed her the .22, "I'm going to move over here hoping he'll focus his attention on me. Take aim at the back of his head. The first shot may only knock him down and daze him, so be ready to come up quick like and put the barrel in his ear and shoot him again, okay?"

"Okay."

Blair got down on his hands and knees and started crawling to the side. The lynx sure enough was fixated on Blair and not paying any attention to Monique. She didn't have a good shot at the back of its head, but she did just below the ear. She pulled the trigger and the cat dropped. Monique moved in quickly and stood there looking at it. "I don't think I'll have to shoot it again."

Blair stood up and stepped closer and said, "Good shooting."

They had a beaver in the trail set and a mink in the otter set. "We have done pretty good today. Six pieces of fur. You know, again I think we should call it a day here and go home and take care of what we have."

"Aren't we going to eat first?" Monique asked. "I'm hungry."

"Yeah, me too. Do you want to skin this beaver?" It was as big as those they had caught the day before.

"I'll try."

"I'll build a fire." But he helped her get started first though.

When he was satisfied that she was doing it right, he let her be.

The trap on the dam snapped again and Blair looked up in

time to see a beaver swim off and then submerge. He walked out on the dam and watched the water boil as the beaver struggled. Soon all was quiet and he pulled in another beaver not quite as big as the other three they had taken from the flowage. He reset the trap and took that one ashore and began skinning.

Monique was almost finished with her beaver. "How many beaver do you think are in this colony?"

"I would think a dozen or a few more, by the size of that house and the feed bed."

"I'm finished here. Do you want me to cut off the legs and start roasting the meat?"

"Yes, I'll get the castors if you would prefer."

Blair wasn't long skinning his beaver and with the legs cut off he removed the castors from both beaver. He also cut off both heads and put them in the bait pail. The carcasses he put in the water, so any furbearing animal would be lured to the traps and not the carcasses.

"This is a great way of life isn't it Blair? I'm really enjoying being out here and helping."

"Yes, it is a good way to live. I wouldn't dream of doing anything else. And I'm glad you like being out here also."

They had taken four beaver from this one colony in two days and there were more adult beaver here. They finished eating and picked up and started back for the canoe.

When they got back the bobcat was still warm which meant the hide would still come off easy.

There was still daylight left and after Monique put some wood in the stove she went out to the shed to help Blair. These animals were skinned differently. It was more like peeling a banana. He hung up the bobcat and he watched as she split the tail and peeled the hide away from the bone. She was being very careful and he went back to his otter. They had six hides to skin.

When they were finished, she watched as Blair put them on the stretchers. Monique nailed the beaver hide to the cabin wall to stretch and dry.

"The air is cooling off even before the sun has set. I think this is going to be a cold night," Blair said.

As the temperature dropped during the right the moisture on the cedar shakes would freeze and expand and sometimes snap so loud it would sound like a .22 being fired inside the cabin.

In the shallow pools where there was no current the water had iced over. In some places there was a half inch of ice. They made their trek up to their last trap by the beaver flowage and picked up two pine martins, a red fox and one more adult beaver on the dam.

This day they had the time to set up the rest of that line and back to the river and upstream to the canoe. By the end of that line they had set six more traps. All being land sets.

"I don't know how long we'll be able to trap on this side of the river. But we'll keep trapping until there's too much ice on the river."

On the new half of that line they only picked up five more pine martin. One more beaver and one more otter. "I think it's time to pick up and set up the other line now. I don't want to take any more beaver from this colony or trap the inland route until it's dry. I think we have left enough for seed."

Two days later they started laying traps on the line that started behind the cabin. They set one trap on the north line, one at the corner, one halfway to the next corner, one at the corner or east and south line. This south line was over two miles long and they set five traps. The one at the river was an otter set and a hundred yards up stream they made a mink set. Monique was now setting traps without Blair's help and the work went much faster.

While Monique was setting up a beaver trap on the dam in the cove near the meadow she had found, Blair followed the game trail into the meadow and found a nice spot for a bobcat or lynx. He used a #3 trap. When he got back to the dam Monique was just finishing.

"We might as well take a beaver home with us. Would you just as soon we wait a few minutes?"

"I could use a rest."

"Truthfully, so could I. Let's sit over there out of view."

They were sitting enjoying a rest and talking with each other with low voices, so not to spook a beaver if it came to investigate why water was running over the dam. Just then a terrible blood curdling shriek came from the meadow where Blair had just set a trap. "What was that Blair? It didn't sound anything like a bobcat or lynx we have caught."

"I don't know. I have never heard anything like it."

There was not another sound. "Maybe we should have a look at the trap."

Monique followed him, ready to draw her .45 if she had to.

They walked up the game trail in silence. And everything else was also silent. There were no birds flying and no red squirrels scolding and chattering. "Something isn't right Monique. There isn't a sound to be heard."

They were close now to the trap and still no sound. Blair withdrew his .45, just to be on the safe side. So did Monique. A little further and Blair could see where the set was, but there was no animal. "Something doesn't look right with the set."

Still being cautious they walked up to the set. The trap was lying off to one side and it was sprung. The ground had not been disturbed at all. "Something sprung that trap, or it wouldn't be lying off to the side. But I have never heard a screech like that."

Blair picked the trap up and there were two toes clamped in between the jaws. "Well, we had something," He released the tension on the springs and dropped the toes in Monique's hand.

"What is it Blair? It isn't bear is it?"

"No, but look at these claws. They have a rugged structure. I bet whatever it is, is the animal that tore the honey log apart."

"What is your best guess?"

"Well, that track I saw earlier had me puzzled, but with these two claws, I'd say a wolverine."

"Are there any in Maine?"

"Yes, but not many."

"There's something bothering you, Blair. What is it?"

"The wolverine is suppose to be the most feared animal in North America. It's pure meanness. I hope we can catch it in one of our traps."

"Are you going to reset this trap?"

"Yes, you never know, it may be back. It knows there is a morsel of food here."

Blair reset that trap and when they returned to the beaver flowage they had a beaver. He pulled it in and while he was skinning, Monique reset the trap. "Monique, will you finish cutting off the legs and castors. I want to look around. I won't be far away."

He was looking for a hollow long and on top of a hardwood knoll he found the old remains of a once huge maple tree. And the center was hollow. He found a rock and plugged off the other end and went back to join Monique.

"What did you find?"

"A perfect hollow log for another set. We'll use the entire beaver carcass, or what's left of it."

He shouldered his pack and Monique carried the axe. He pushed the carcass in the hollow log about three feet. Then, using the axe, he cut out enough of the log on the bottom so a #3 trap would set level and then he placed bits of old pulpy wood on the trap to hide it. The he spread some castor on the front of the log for a lure.

Monique had gone off to one side and had gathered an armful of dry leaves and she spread those over the ground in front of the log. "That's a good idea."

They left there and set only one more trap at the honey log.

"Where do you want the honey?"

"Smear it on the inside of the log where the honeycomb was."

Blair set the trap in amongst the pulpy wood that had been torn away. And here he decided not to use castor as a lure. "I'm hoping the smell of honey will be lure enough. And I now think it was a wolverine that tore at this log to get at the honey. If it scents the honey, it'll be back and since it got some honey here once, it won't be as cautious as the other set and who knows, maybe we'll get two."

From there they were back home in a few minutes. "You've been quiet all the way back, Blair. What's bothering you?"

"I was just thinking about that wolverine that lost two toes. I've heard stories about wolverines, which makes me worry about you."

"You think that wolverine will hunt us, because it lost two toes?"

"I don't know. And I don't know if there is any truth to the stories I've heard."

"Well, we are just going to have to be careful until we catch that one."

Blair went to work nailing the beaver hide up and taking down those that were ready.

Blair laid awake on his back long into the night thinking about the wolverine. Then after a few hours of sleep he was feeling better and not as worried.

"I think this morning we'll check traps in reverse direction from yesterday. I'm particularly interested in the two wolverine sets." He only took one extra trap this morning and the bait pail and axe. They each strapped on their .45s and he put the .22 in his pack. The first trap to check was at the honey log and before they could even see the log they could hear an animal growling and thrashing about. "I think we have something here."

As they came closer they could see it was indeed a wolverine. "I hope he is caught good and not just by two toes," Monique said. "He looks awful angry."

Blair took his pack off and handed the .22 to Monique. There was no need to tell her what to do. He took out his .45, just in case and worked his way to the left. And sure enough the wolverine centered his attention on Blair, while struggling to get free and biting and chewing anything in reach. Again Blair got down on his hands and knees and this seemed to momentarily confuse the wolverine, as he stopped growling and struggling and stood erect to better see what Blair was going to do.

Monique now had a good shot at the left ear and she pulled the trigger and the wolverine collapsed. She ran up, like Blair had said, prepared to shoot again if necessary.

Blair stood up and closed in also. But the wolverine lay there rolling his eyes. "He is not dead! Shoot Monique. Shoot him again!"

She shot again and then rushed right in and put the barrel of the .22 in his ear and pulled the trigger. This time the wolverine gave his death throe and rolled. He was dead.

Blair and Monique stood there looking at each other and grinning. "He had torn this old log to pieces, fighting to get loose."

Blair released the springs and removed the trap and picked the wolverine up. "He's too heavy to carry around with us all day. I think we should skin it here."

Monique held the wolverine while Blair skun it, the same as he would a beaver, except he skun the tail and left it attached. "And this fella ain't no male. Look it's a female and there are no missing toes."

"So the other one must be the mate to this one. I hope we don't have any trouble with that other one, if this one is its mate," Monique said.

The wolverine was easy to skin and flesh. Much easier than even a beaver. There was not so much fat and sinew attached to the hide. When he finished he rolled the pelt up and put it in his pack.

"Shall we move on, my lady?" They both laughed and went to the next set, on the beaver dam.

"Well, the trap is gone," Monique said.

Blair pulled in a huge beaver and while he was skinning it Monique reset the trap and then held the beaver for Blair. The legs were cut off and rolled up in the hide, and the castors put in the pack.

Something had been on the hardwood knoll and scratched at the ground in front of the hollow log, but it had not sprung the trap. "The scratching marks look more like a cat than anything else."

The trap in the meadow where the wolverine had left two toes had been dug out and then buried.

"Well, he came back. We might as well pull this trap. He'll only keep burying it."

"Blair what if we suspend some bait above the ground and set several traps under it."

"That might work. But I only brought one extra trap. If he springs one trap he might not suspect a second one."

He had to lash a small green yellow birch tree to two other trees and with the wire in his pack he threaded three fish heads on the wire three and a half feet above the ground. Then they set the two traps beneath the bait and brushed out the ground. "I think this just might work. You're turning into quite a trapper, sweetheart," and he hugged her.

Monique was so happy she was almost in tears.

At each of the next six sets they had pine martins. They returned home by mid-afternoon. Most of the drying beaver hides were ready to take off and some of the fur pieces on the stretchers. The wolverine hide was nailed to the side of the shed and the beaver. The martin were put on wooden stretchers to dry.

"We have thirty four pieces of fur already. That is pretty good. I'd say no one has ever trapped around here before."

"How much will that be worth?"

"I'm not sure, but I think it'll be more than I use to make working for my father. And it'll more than grubstake us for another year."

"And we're having fun," Monique added.

* * *

They hiked around the trap line in the opposite direction the next day and Blair took two extra #3 traps, in case they wanted to do something different. The first set produced another martin and at the next one a bobcat and they took the time to skin it. The next two traps were untouched. The next one another martin. Then a female fisher, then a martin, otter and a beaver on the dam and a lynx at the hollow log with the beaver carcass stuffed inside. This surprised Blair. When they got back to the dam they had another beaver and they took the time to skin the lynx and the beaver. And they took the time to start a fire and roast some beaver meat. "I was wondering when you'd get hungry," Monique said.

"I was too busy I guess thinking about that lynx in the hollow log. I never expected that."

"This beaver meat is so good I could eat it all winter, I think," Monique said.

At the new pole set nothing had touched the trap. Blair smeared some castor on the fish heads.

They had another surprise at the honey log. They had the other wolverine with the missing toes. "I wouldn't have expected to catch him here."

As they were eating supper that night Blair said, "I think tomorrow we should pull all of our land sets and if we have a smaller beaver from the dam, then we pull that one also. I really hate over-trapping this area. It has been good for us this year. Maybe a few more beaver. As soon as the river freezes solid we'll go up to the oxbows after beaver."

***

The next day they went in the same direction around the loop line and they had four more martin and a male fisher. At the pole set, much to their surprise, they actually had an otter in a land set." I thought otter stayed mainly to the water," Monique said.

"They usually do. This one must have been travelling over land between water sources. Either that or he could smell the rotten smell of the fish heads."

They had another large beaver on the dam and decided to pull that trap regardless. This close to home it would be a good idea to leave some seed.

"Now that we are done with land trapping, can I get rid of the rest of these smelly heads?"

"Sure, dump them in the river."

During the evening in the light of the fire Blair would preen the fur, untangling the fur knots and combing the fur. He wanted his fur to look the best. During the day instead of lazying around and drinking coffee, he worked on next year's firewood. He worked up one tree at a time. Splitting the blocks and piling the split wood up in the woods.

For two weeks the weather was warm and then in the middle of November the temperature dropped. The river was freezing solid and Blair took the canoe out behind the cabin and put it up on stands, upside down, for the winter.

The spring brook hadn't frozen over yet and Blair wasn't sure if it would or not, since spring water usually stayed at 43°. He did dig a deep hole in the brook, so it was easier to dip water with the pail. Monique made water storage urns from clay. They each would hold about ten galloons.

There was no snow yet and this was alright with Blair. Let the river ice freeze solid first.

"How much extra firewood have you worked up out back?"

"Oh, maybe two cords."

"You know, Blair, we could use something to sit on in here, instead of the benches up to the table. We need chairs more than extra firewood now, Blair."

"Okay, I'll start this morning."

After breakfast Blair went down by the river looking for an ash tree that he could cut out the rockers from. He cut a four foot length and roughed out an inch and a half plank and he smoothed that out with his draw shave. Then he drew the outline of one rocker and worked that until he had exactly what he wanted and he smoothed the rough spots out with a rasp. Then he drew the outline of that rocker on another rough hewn plank and smoothed that out until he had two rockers exactly alike.

The fame to the rocker was easy. When he had each piece ready to assemble he cut notches to lock each piece to another. The back and seat he made from thin cedar slats. When he had finished, he sat down in it and rocked back and forth. It was comfortable to sit in and rock back and forth.

"You did a very good job, and it didn't take you long either."

"And just in time. Tomorrow we go after the beaver again."

That afternoon he cut down another ash tree and rough hewed two planks for the rockers. Then he went for a walk looking for two small hardwood saplings that he could cut down and he and Monique could use for walking sticks on the slippery ice.

* * *

The next morning for breakfast, it was that time of the month, Monique had fried thick slices of bear bacon, scrambled eggs and pan bread with hot coffee.

"We'll take our .45s today in case we get a good chance

at a moose or caribou. And dress warm. I think the wind will blow before we're back."

"If we do shoot a moose or caribou this ice will make it easy to drag back," Monique said.

Blair put another stick of wood in the fireplace, then they went outside. He gave her one of the walking sticks. She knew instinctively what they were and didn't have to ask, *Why?* The ice was pockmarked and really not that slippery and it was an easy hike to the first beaver dam on the river about half way through the oxbows. "We'll set two traps here."

They both made a trough about four feet from the center of the dam. There was a little free water along the dam. When they had finished Blair said, "It may take longer for the beaver to come down to inspect the dam than in open water. So we might as well go up to the next dam and set that up."

They walked on the dam to the river bank before stepping on ice.

They hadn't gone more than fifty feet when they heard one trap spring close. "Well, there's dinner," Monique said. Blair smiled. Monique was really getting into this trapping.

They went back and waited five minutes, from experience, before pulling it in. "It's a heavy brute."

The other trap was right behind Monique and that suddenly snapped closed and another large beaver splashed back into the water. Monique gave a little scream of surprise. "Oh my God! That jumped me."

"Don't fall in." Blair had his beaver on the dam and was removing the trap. "These two beaver are going to be too heavy to carry in the pack basket, so while you're waiting for your beaver to stop struggling, would you reset this one and I'll take this one ashore and start skinning."

As soon as Monique had the trap reset she started pulling in the other beaver. "Blair, I think this is as big and as heavy as yours."

"Do you need any help?"

"Not yet. He's just heavy." When she finally had it on the dam she couldn't believe how big it was. "Blair, I have never seen such a big beaver. Bigger than anything we have caught so far, by far."

She removed the trap and reset it. She had all she could do to lift it. "Blair, I'm going to need your help."

Blair stopped skinning to help her. When he lifted it, he said, "This weighs almost as much as you Monique. He is huge."

"You know, I think tomorrow I'll stay home. We have a lot of beaver meat and it'll spoil. So I want to can it."

"Well, there'll be more meat here when I have these two done." He was an hour skinning the two beaver, while Monique cut off the legs and tails.

The next flowage was two oxbows upstream and on a small feeder stream on the right. "I don't expect too many beaver in this one."

They set two traps like before and then moved upstream to the end of the oxbows. This colony was not as big either, but they set their two traps and headed for home. The wind was blowing some, but it was to their back.

They pulled in another beaver at the first dam. Not quite as big as the first two. With the beaver skun and the meat, tail and castors cut off Blair said, "Are you ready to head home?"

"Yes, I'm cold."

* * *

Cold weather turned the beaver hides white and the fur buyers usually paid more if the hides were white and not all blood soaked. Blair nailed those three beaver up and it was obvious the first two beaver caught were so much bigger than any of the other beaver.

There was less daylight now and Blair found he could not get as much work done each day. "Well, you need a break, Blair. Look at all you have done. You work like three men. If you want something to do, you can fill the wood boxes."

That evening after supper and washing up, Blair read a few articles in the oldest of the newspapers they had brought with them.

They went to bed early and talked for a long time in the warm glow of the firelight and listened to the logs snap and crack as they dried.

The wind stopped blowing during the night but the temperature dropped. The ice on the river was freezing and when cracks opened up the loud snap would resonate up the river valley.

In the morning the floor was cold like ice. "When we get snow I'll be able to shovel it up against the cabin and the floors won't be as cold."

"Well, I'm just as glad to stay home today and do some canning. We'll have beaver tail soup tonight."

"And how about biscuits?"

"I can do that."

The river was still making ice even in the sunshine. It was bitterly cold and it hit Blair in the face like a slap. He wore his knit hat and he pulled it down over his ears and the back of his neck. The bushes were all covered with a layer of frost. He looked up at the clear sky and said, "It'll snow or rain soon." And this made him decide to pull all of his traps. He had his .45, pack basket, axe and walking stick. As long as he was walking he was warm enough.

Both traps at the first dam had been pulled under the ice and he knew he had two beaver. Before pulling them in, he went ashore and started a fire. Then he went back and pulled one out and skun that by the fire and wrapped the legs, castors and tail up in the hide and he put it in his pack.

Then he warmed his hands before he tackled the next. When he was warm he pulled the other one in. These two were not quite as big as the two yesterday. He was a little longer skinning the second beaver. He had to keep warming his hands.

When he had finished he left the traps on the ice and would pick them up on the way back. At the next flowage he only had one adult beaver. This was okay with him. Then at the last flowage he had two more. He built another fire. After he had skun the first beaver to put some meat on to roast while he skun the last beaver. Working alone and in the cold, he worked up an appetite and ate both hind legs of one of the beaver.

He had five beaver hides, the legs, tails and castors and six traps in his pack basket, as he made his way down stream to the cabin. The sky was overcast now and the moisture in the air was freezing and turning into snowflakes. It would snow during the night; he was sure of that.

"I have five more big beaver and I picked up all of the traps. It's going to storm tonight and I didn't want to have to break-out a snowshoe trail to the head of the oxbows."

"How many beaver do we have now?"

"I think twenty-three. Counting the two summer beaver.

"I don't think it has warmed up outside at all today. The wind is beginning to blow, at least it was to my back coming back. How are we set for water?"

"We could use a couple of pail fulls. You're expecting a bad storm aren't you?"

"Yes," and he picked up the pail and headed for the spring. Monique took the mason jars out of the canner and set them on the counter to cool off.

Blair filled the one urn and went back for one more pail full that he set beside the fireplace.

Monique had been simmering a beaver tail soup all afternoon. "As soon as the biscuits are done we can eat."

"As cold as it is outside, this cabin sure does stay warm."

"Biscuits are done if you want to sit down." She filled their bowls and set the hot biscuits on the table.

"This tail soup is so good. It's a little difficult to believe a beaver tail could be this good."

They ate in silence for a few minutes and then Blair

broke the silence. "I am a little worried we haven't shot a moose or caribou yet. I would have thought we would have seen one while trapping."

"Maybe this snow will make them move or change their feeding habits," Monique said.

"I think when the snow settles after the storm we should go look for one and not wait until one happens upon us. What is it anyhow?"

She laughed a little before replying it is November 25th, and today is Sunday."

"It doesn't seem like Sunday."

"That explains the cold, but I would have thought we'd have snow before now."

"Do you want more tail soup?"

"No."

"Good, there's just enough left for breakfast tomorrow. We have hot biscuits and honey for dessert."

It began to snow about the time they were preparing for bed. They lay in bed that night talking and enjoying the soft glow of the fire as it illuminated the cabin. "Even though it storms tonight, it is still kind of a good feeling. If you know what I mean."

"I think I do," he replied. "This is our little world here. We have a comfortable cabin, a home, plenty of firewood and if we can get a moose or caribou we'll have plenty of food. If we don't, I still think we have enough. And most important, Monique, you are my wife and I love you and I have never in all my life been so happy."

"I can't explain how I feel any better than that and I love you and I am truly the happiest that I have ever been."

* * *

Blair woke up some time after midnight and put some more wood in the fireplace. There was still a good bed of coals and there was no sense in letting the fire burn itself out. He had a drink of water and crawled back in bed with Monique.

The cabin was still warm when they awoke. Monique put some wood in the fireplace then stood in front of the fireplace letting the fire warm her bare backside. Blair started a fire in the cook stove. He looked at Monique and said, "You sure do make for a pretty picture standing naked in front of the fire."

"Well you come back to bed and I'll show you how hot I am," as she dove for the bed.

It was snowing heavy and there was very little that needed to be done right away and what better way to spend a stormy day than making love to the person you loved.

* * *

It was noon before they finally got up and dressed. Breakfast now became lunch. While Monique was warming the soup, Blair opened the front door and stepped out on the porch. It was still snowing heavy and no wind. The temperature was still cold and the snow was dry and fluffy.

"How much snow is there?"

"We must have a foot of snow and it is still coming down heavy. After I eat I think I'll go out and bank the cabin with snow."

The beaver tail soup had more flavor and body to it than the night before. After his second cup of coffee, he dressed and went outside. Problem is the shovel was in the shed. The snow was almost to his knees.

It didn't take long to bank snow around the cabin. He piled snow up almost to the bottom of the windows. Of course, though, the snow would settle each day. He finished and put the shovel on the porch and since he now had a trail through the snow to the shed, he decided to work on another chair. At first he was going to make another rocker but now he changed his mind. It would be a straight leg chair and much easier to build.

By sunset he had a good start on the chair. He waded back through the snow and kicked his feet against the cabin to knock off the snow. He opened the door and asked, "Before I come in, is there anything in the root cellar you want?"

"Yes, we ought to use up the smoked deer meat before it spoils. I have a jar of cattail tops to go with it.

"How much snow is there now?"

"It was over my knees when I came in, but it is so fluffy and dry there isn't anything to it. A good wind could blow it all off."

"Well, I'm just glad you pulled all of our traps."

"Yeah, me too."

"If the weather breaks are we going to continue trapping beaver?"

"I think we have more than $1000.00 worth of fur now. That's more than enough to grub stake us for two years. If we leave what there is there'll be more next year and we won't have to travel so far."

"Then I say we don't take any more—unless we need one for food."

It stopped snowing an hour after sunset and the wind started to blow. But this was a warmer wind. Still cold but not frigid.

"Wow, listen to the wind howl."

"Be a bad night to be caught out in the cold. Let it be cold and the wind blow. I'm pretty comfortable here holding you," Blair said.

The wind howled all night, but inside the cabin they were warm and comfortable.

Come daylight they couldn't see out the front window. The wind had blown the snow around so much that the porch was full of snow, covering the window. The snow had drifted up on all sides of the cabin insulating it from the cold.

"Blair, this floor isn't cold this morning."

"Looks like I have some shoveling to do." He opened the front door to a solid wall of snow that had been packed in by the wind. "I'll have to go out the back door and wade through the snow to the porch. The shovel is on the porch."

There was only a little impacted on the back door and along the north wall of the cabin the ground had almost been swept clean. But out front was a different story. From the cabin to the river the snow had drifted in about four feet deep.

After struggling to wade through the snow he finally made it to the porch and had to almost tunnel through the snow to find the shovel. From now on he'd leave the shovel inside during a stormy night.

Once he had the shovel and had cleared a spot to stand, he wasn't long throwing all of the snow over the railing. Then he cleared out the back door; the wood shed, tool shed and root cellar. And instead of shoveling a path from the cabin to the root cellar he strapped on his snowshoes and beat down a path. And then a path to the spring hole also that was free of ice and snow. Most of the snow had blown off the roof.

He went inside for a cup of coffee. "How bad is it?" Monique asked.

"I have everything cleared and a snowshoe path to the root cellar and spring. There isn't a cloud in the sky and I could feel warm air on my face blowing in from the south. The warmer air will help to settle this snow."

"I'm glad we stopped trapping. We would have worn ourselves out just getting to the traps." Monique said.

The wind blew in warm air all night and all the next day. What little snow had been on the roof was now melted and there were many places showing bare ground where the wind had blown the snow off. For three days the temperatures stayed warm and most of the snow had melted. There was a river of water now on top of the river ice.

During this warm weather Blair worked on building more chairs. He made another rocker and another straight leg chair. He made more shelves and cupboards for Monique and when he and Monique were not working on some project they would relax with a cup of hot coffee sweetened with honey, and talk.

Towards the end of the warm spell a snow squall came through and dumped an inch of wet snow and this immediately froze to the river ice and now they had a walkable boulevard. "I think we have seen the end of the warm weather for awhile, and I think tomorrow after breakfast we should go up to the oxbows. I'd like to get a moose or caribou before we get any more snow and right now is ideal walking on the river," Blair said as he rolled over and hugged his wife.

The next morning Monique fixed a hardy breakfast of flapjacks and honey, bear bacon and honey sweetened coffee.

When they had finished eating Blair said, "I have to go out to the outhouse. When I come back we'll leave." He closed the door and walked up to the outhouse.

Monique started clearing the table and noticed movement on the river. She went to the window, there were four caribou walking up the river. Instinctively she grabbed the rifle and eased the front door open. Leaning against the door jam she sighted in just behind the head of the caribou in the lead. It was also the biggest. She squeezed the trigger and the caribou fell on the ice. The other three ran off.

Blair came running from the outhouse holding his pants up. He couldn't imagine what had happened. When he opened the back door Monique was just closing the front door. He just looked at her without saying anything.

"There were four caribou on the river. I shot one."

Blair opened the door to look out. "Well I'll-be-to-go-to-hell. Right in our own front yard. He started laughing then and said, "You are one hell of a pioneer woman, Monique Kelley." Then they both began laughing.

"Well, he hasn't moved, so he must be dead. Nothing like shooting game right in front of your own home. This will certainly save a lot of dragging and carrying. Shall we get to work?"

They put their jackets on and Monique carried two pails

down and Blair, two sharp knives. "This isn't as big as a moose and that'll be good. This meat with what we already have will more than see us through to spring."

"That sure is a big rack." They rolled the caribou on his back and Monique held the legs so Blair could start skinning. "This hide will go nice on the floor."

The hide wasn't quite as heavy as a moose's hide and it fleshed easier also. Blair worked as fast as he could. He would have to stop occasionally to warm his hands. Then Monique would skin until her hands were cold. He skinned all the way to the head. "There's a lot of meat on this neck that we'll probably have to can."

Once the hide was free, Blair cut off the backstraps and put them in a pail then he cut off the four legs and rolled the carcass onto the ice and off the hide before he went inside for the heart and liver. Monique carried the pails back to the cabin and Blair carried the four legs to the root cellar and hung them up. Then with his axe he cut off the ribs and hung those in the root cellar.

He cut the antlers off and then cut a hole in the ice and pushed the remains in the water and the head. "This will feed the trout, mink and otter all winter." The next thing he did was to nail the hide on the side of the cabin to stretch and dry. In this cold air, it wouldn't take long to freeze-dry it.

It was now noon and Monique was frying some liver in bear fat for lunch. Blair walked over and gave Monique a hug and said, "Now the work begins."

"What would you think about roasting one side of the ribs this afternoon? Is it too cold to roast?"

"As long as the fire is hot, I don't think it would matter. While you're fixing lunch, I'll start the outdoor fire pit."

Monique didn't fry up as much liver as she had first thought. Instead she wanted supper of roasted ribs. Just the thought of it was making her mouth water.

Blair was just as happy she hadn't fried up a big mess of liver. He used some of the real dry round wood that he had set aside. His father had called this biscuit wood, because of the hot quick heat it would produce. When there were an abundance of glowing hot coals he put on some split greenwood.

The smell of roasting caribou permeated the air. An otter even came out of the hole Blair had chopped in the ice for air and Blair watched the otter put his nose into the air smelling the delicious aroma. It sure hadn't taken the otter long to find the caribou remains in the river.

While the ribs were roasting Monique cleaned and peeled a squash. And she collected the seeds in an empty milk can. She decided to use up the biscuits and save the potatoes for later in the winter.

The more Blair stayed by the fire, tending to the ribs or adding more wood, the smell of the roasting meat was making him hungrier and hungrier. Once in a while he would pull off a piece of meat and sample it. It was delicious.

He went inside and asked, "What do you have that I can put the ribs in to bring them inside. They're done."

The only thing big enough was the dish pain. "This will do."

The table was already set. "Just set the pan on the table. Everything else is ready. There's biscuits and squash."

Blair separated the ribs and put one on Monique's plate and took one. "Wait until you taste this," he said.

There wasn't much said as they each enjoyed the taste of real fresh caribou meat. It was a little like moose but different. Better.

* * *

The next morning while eating breakfast Blair asked, "How much of the caribou have you canning jars for?"

"Probably enough for the neck and both front legs. As we use up the herbs we can reuse those jars also."

"Do you need to do that right away? I mean, before we

get any snow I'd like to backtrack those caribou and see where they had come from."

"Why don't you go and I'll work on canning what I can."

Blair strapped on his .45 said goodbye and walked down to the river. By the looks of the tracks in the snow where the caribou fell, it looked as if there had been several otters there during the night.

The caribou tracks were easily visible and he began to follow downstream. There was no wind but the air was cold and crisp. The dry snow under his feet squeaked. It was a nice day and he was enjoying himself.

He was puzzled by the caribou tracks. They stayed pretty much to the center of the river, never veering to either side to browse. It was almost as if they had a single purpose for being on the river and traveling upstream.

The tracks suddenly had turned to the left and through a small opening from shore. Very near the honey log. But once again the tracks seemed to have a single purpose in mind. The caribou were not browsing.

The tracks led him up the game trail and across the open meadow. He had about determined that the caribou must have come from their summer habitat area and were on their way wherever they wintered. He kept following the trail and after leaving the meadow, the caribou had crossed the south leg of his trap line on that side of the river.

He followed their trail for another hour before turning back. It would be hard to guess from where they had come. Now he wanted to see where they were heading. So rather than following his tracks back, he cut across country north of the cabin and came back to the river at the lower end of the oxbows.

Part way through the oxbows two more caribou had come out from the north side and joined the ones Blair was following. It was beginning to seem that the caribou had been spending the summer months just to the north and were now all migrating somewhere to the west.

Near where he and Monique had set the last beaver flowage several more caribou had come from the north and joined the others. There were so many tracks in this new trail, Blair was unable to determine how many there were.

He kept following the river through hardwoods, the marshy area left behind. There were beaver dams after beaver dams.

He eventually came to another series of sharp oxbows and all of the caribou left the river to the southwest. He had seen as much as he wanted and found next year's beaver trapping. He turned around and headed for home.

Clouds had blown in and he wasn't sure where the sun was. He just figured sometime after noon.

While Blair had been out following tracks and feeling happy, Monique had been spending her time salvaging the good meat off the caribou neck and the front legs and canning it. She would have enjoyed being with Blair exploring the wilderness around them; she was equally happy doing just what she was doing.

It was later than Blair had thought. The sun was beginning to set just as he came in sight of the cabin and the welcoming illumination of the lantern light. He knocked the snow off his boots on the side of the door jam before going in.

"Did you have a good walk?"

"I'll tell you all about it. First, do we need any firewood?"

"Yes, both boxes are low and no kindling."

Blair brought in enough wood to fill both firewood boxes and enough cedar kindling for three days. He took his coat, hat and gloves off and backed up to the fireplace. "The cold has worked its way through my bones.

"I made a loop around the cabin and ended up going a couple miles upstream where we last set for beaver." He told her where the caribou had come from that she had seen going up the river, and about the other caribou that had joined up and all traveling the same trail "I believe to their wintering area. I'm guessing maybe twenty or thirty in this group."

He told her all about the numerous beaver flowages he had found just beyond where they had stopped trapping and about his idea about concentrating their beaver trapping there next season a few days at a time.

"It sounds like you really enjoyed yourself today."

"I did. And there's a lot more country to explore around here. How was your day? Did you get everything done that you wanted?"

"Well, my day wasn't as exciting as yours, but I was happy doing what I was doing. Being a housewife." She hugged him then and they both laughed.

"I canned all of the neck and the front legs and had four jars left over. Then I had an idea. I hung one hind quarter outside and let it freeze. Then I hung it back in the root cellar. This should preserve the meat a little longer. I thought we'd eat from the other one when we wanted fresh steaks."

"You know, that was probably a good idea. And the hindquarter will stay frozen inside the root cellar for a long time.

"I haven't eaten since breakfast and I'm so hungry I could eat a bear."

"Well, no bear. I've been baking ribs."

* * *

There was a foot of new snow on the ground the next morning and Blair banked the cabin walls again and packed down paths with his snowshoes. The rest of the day he spent in the tool shed splitting cedar into rough planks and then using the draw shave to make boards. It was a long process to make boards; it was the only way he had. He was three days making enough boards to build a bureau with drawers to store their clothes and linen. He wanted to surprise Monique, so whenever she asked what he was doing, he would say, "Oh, just making boards for a barn next summer for the goats and chickens."

The days were cold and the nights even colder and daylight was short. Every few days there would be another foot of snow or more. Blair's snowshoe paths now resembled tunnels. And Blair had the cabin banked up to the bottom of the windows.

There was so much snow on the river the ice stopped making and the weight of it was pushing the ice down and forcing water up through cracks. No matter how cold it was outside they were always warm and comfortable inside the cabin. Even the floors had stopped being so cold.

The caribou hide was cured early. That was now beside the bed for a rug. Blair and Monique had prepared well before the cold with plenty of food and firewood and now their life was not that of survival but of leisure.

Blair had the frame work of the bureau complete and he was working on the drawers. He didn't have screws or glue so everything or most everything had to have locking joints. He was meticulous and every joint and every piece had to fit just so.

As Monique emptied canning jars she would refill them with caribou meat until both hindquarters were all canned. Once each week she made apple pie and baked bread and biscuits. She was rationing the eggs and hoped they would last until the geese returned in the spring.

Monique's caribou antlers, Blair attached to the peak of the roof above the porch roof. Blair thought about making a plaque to mount them to the fireplace, but he had no way of securing them to the clay mortar. "It was just as well," Monique said. "They are a little too big for in here. I think they look good where they are."

The middle of February brought a reprieve in the cold and windy weather and the weekly snow storms. The sun would be out bright and water would run off the roof eaves from the melting snow. The snow settled and water began collecting on the river ice. "Ah, Monique?"

"Yes what is it?"

"I need your help to carry something across the snow to the cabin."

"What is it?"

"Oh, just something I've been working on."

"Are you going to tell me what it is?'

"Nope. I want it to be a surprise." He took her hand in his and led her out to the tool shed—i.e. workshop. "I hope we can get it through the door."

It took her eyes a few moments to adjust to the lantern light and when she saw what Blair had been working all winter on she screamed with happiness and hugged him. "Oh Blair, it is so beautiful." He had rubbed the outside with a piece of slat to get a smooth finish on the cedar.

"So these are the boards you have been making for the barn."

"I wanted to get it in the cabin before you saw it, to surprise you, but it is too awkward to handle alone."

"Well you certainly surprised me. I love it.

"Where did you get the handles?"

"I carved them."

"You did a marvelous job."

* * *

For fifteen days March came in like a roaring lion. The wind blew every day and night and when it didn't snow, the temperature dropped and they would lay awake in bed listening to the river make ice. But they had nowhere to go and they still had plenty of food and firewood. The only thing they were running low on were eggs. And those that were left Monique was saving to use to cook with.

"This has been the coldest day of all winter," Monique said. "I'm just glad we don't have to go out in it."

On March 16th the cold blustery weather broke. The

daylight temperatures rose in the 40s and some days in the 50s. And seldom did they drop below freezing at night. The snow on the roof had all melted off and although the river was still iced over there was a foot of water running off on top. The snow depth that winter had been deep, but it was all dry powdery snow and in the warm weather it was settling and melting fast. "You know Monique, as fast as this snow is melting, the St. John River is apt to flood."

"I wonder why the caribou haven't come back through here."

"Maybe when they migrate back to their summer range they have to wait for the high water to drop. It'll be interesting to see if they migrate back to their winter range next year up the river."

"If they do and do so every year there's caribou meat every year and we don't even have to leave the front porch."

As they were laying in bed that night Blair said, "What you said today about the caribou migrating every year up the river, started me thinking."

"What about?"

"Well, I have never believed in coincidences. I have always believed that every event in our lives happens for a reason. I mean have you noticed that everything we have has been in a way handed to us. First we found that abandoned cabin and look what we were able to salvage from that. Look at the sight where we decided to build. It happens to have a good supply of savvy clay, a spring brook where brook trout spawn, spruce, cedar and hardwood trees in abundance. A caribou migration trail right in front of our cabin. There's food here in abundance, meat and herbs. There was slate when we needed it. Fur bearing animals to trap so we can afford to buy what we don't have. What I'm saying, Monique, everything we need is given to us."

They were both silent for a few minutes and then Monique said, "I have been thinking the same thing ever since I shot the caribou. What do you think is happening, Blair?"

"I think there is—how do I say it without sounding like an idiot?"

"There's something watching over us?" Monique said.

"Yes, exactly. Some entity. You know I came through the Civil War without a scratch. I thought then that something had been watching out over me."

"I agree with you and I wonder why."

They were quiet again and they went to sleep wondering about this entity and why.

* * *

March rolled into April and there was only a little snow left now, and the river was free of ice and its banks were full. To busy himself, Blair started clearing some ground on the step down from the cabin to the river. The soil was rich, black and full of nutrients. The dead trees that were standing, their roots were rotting and easy to pull out of the loose soil. The wood Blair chunked up for firewood.

"Blair, I need some ash to make some baskets."

"What do you need?"

"Ash logs six or eight inches through and six feet long. Aren't there some ash where you want a garden?"

"Yes. I was going to take those down anyhow."

He only had a spade to turn the sod over so the vegetables were planted in beds and not rows. While Blair spaded up the soil Monique planted the seedbeds. There were potatoes, squash, carrots, peas, beans, tomatoes and corn. There wouldn't be much to put up for winter, but during the season they would have a rich variety of vegetables, plus what herbs Monique could find.

"Next we need to build a barn for the goats and chickens. But there's a problem with just two goats and a dozen chickens in the same barn or shelter. They will not stay warm enough in the winter, to keep from freezing."

"So how do we do it?"

"The only thing I can think of is to put it underground like the root cellar. That way the coldest it would ever drop to inside would be between 38°-43°. And that would be okay for the chickens."

"Okay, where?"

"Well, the only spot with enough slope would be between the outhouse and the spring brook."

"Okay, then let's do it. The seed beds are all planted and we still have plenty of food. You have two spades. I can help."

"We'll use the cart so we can haul some of the sand away."

"When do you want to start?"

"Now?"

There was no humidity in the air yet. The temperature was comfortable at 65°, and there were no pesky insects. An ideal time to work. They first removed the top soil, which was shallow and it was used to fill in rough places in the shelf between the river and the cabin. They squared off an area to fit a 10'x12' log structure.

They were another two days digging the hole. Once Blair had the trees down and cut to length the structure went up fast. And again, the slanted roof was made up of logs lying next to each other like the floor of the cabin. The cracks between the logs were filled with moss and then covered with sand.

Blair hoped it would be big enough to store grass for the winter. He sectioned off one end for the chickens with nesting boxes and places to perch off the floor.

The morning after, the shelter was complete, with a log sided door, back filled and the front sloping off towards the river and an entrance walkway to the door. While they were enjoying a cup of coffee on the porch a flock of geese came flying up the river towards the oxbows. Blair and Monique looked at each other and both said the same thing, "Fresh eggs."

After Monique had all the vegetable seed planted, in the evenings she would strip the bark from the ash logs and using a hammer she would pound the green wood in a straight line from end to end and then using a screwdriver for a pry bar, she'd lift a thin strip of wood about an inch wide and gently pull the strip free, the length of the log. Sometimes the strip would be too thick and she would insert a knife blade across the end of the strip and pull the knife the length of the strip. Now she would have two thin strips that were very pliable. She would do this all the way around the log until she had enough strips for what she wanted to make. If the strips dried out some before she could use them she would soak them in water.

When the baskets were finished she set them in the sunshine to dry. And as the strips dried they would shrink and tighten up, making a strong durable basket.

She made two pack baskets, a basket for dirty clothes, and baskets with handles.

"These are very good, Monique. I assume you learned how to do this from your grandmother."

"Yes, she was very good and could weave a basket as fast as I could cut the strips.

"When will we leave for the farm?"

"It'll be a while yet. We need to wait until the St. John water level drops. Maybe mid-May, as long as we don't get any heavy rain.

"You know, Monique, I've been thinking about the goats and chickens."

"Oh, what about?"

"I hope I can put up enough feed for the goats to carry them through the winter. And I'm not certain about being able to feed that many chickens either."

"Well, if we can't, we can always eat them."

Another flock of geese had flown overhead and Blair could see they were coming down towards the marsh. "Do we have any eggs left?"

"Only two," Monique replied.

"I just saw another flock of geese overhead heading for

the oxbows. Maybe tomorrow we should see if they are nesting yet."

For the rest of that day Blair cleared more bushes, stumps and rocks from the shelf. He wanted to turn that into a garden spot and be able to cut winter grass for the goats. The shelf ran along the river downstream from the small spring feeder for quite a ways. If it was all cleared there'd probably be a couple of acres he could turn into grass. More than enough for two goats.

* * *

They left for the oxbows right after breakfast the next morning. The river was still high and there was no shoreline to walk, so they took the canoe. As they paddled closer they could hear what sounded like thousands of geese all honking at the same time. They had left their .45s home. Today they were after eggs.

They put ashore in the same place and crawled on top of the berm. "Look at all those geese, Blair. There must be thousands," Monique whispered.

"Let's start off here on the edge of the flock." They separated, each carrying one of Monique's baskets with a handle. This time the geese, at least some of them, didn't want to give up their nest and they had to drive the goose away. In only a half hour they had filled both baskets. "I never dreamed it would be this easy and so many geese."

For lunch that day Monique fried the last of the bear bacon and fried four eggs for Blair and two for herself, with warmed up bread and coffee.

"These goose eggs are so much better than chicken eggs. Did you count how many we have?"

"Sixty three. You know, we are all out of bear meat and I don't have any lard left."

"I'll catch some fish this afternoon and set the bait pail like last year. We can have fresh trout for supper and maybe with eggs in the morning."

"Speaking of fish. I was suppose to build a smoker wasn't I."

"That's what you said."

"Tomorrow. Right now, I've got some fish to catch."

The river was still high and the trout weren't pooling in schools. But there were enough for a couple of good feeds of fresh trout. He cut the heads and tails off and cleaned them and put everything in the old pail and hung it in the tree across the river.

* * *

The next day Blair started work on a smoker. The good thing about it, it didn't have to be anything real elaborate. He used hardwood trees and peeled, since the bark came off easy in the spring. He stood the logs on end this time, with a sloping roof towards the woods. He made it four feet wide and eight long and seven feet tall with a stone fire pit and door. He finished on the third day.

"Now all we need is a bear." And that evening as they were sitting on the porch a lone bear was standing on his hind legs trying to get at the fish bait.

Without a word Blair got his rifle and shot the bear. "Now the work begins."

It was a good thing there was a full moon because they were still taking care of the bear long after sunset. "I'll wait until tomorrow to nail this hide up to dry, but I think we'd better start smoking this bacon tonight." While Blair carried the four quarters to the root cellar Monique started a fire in the smoke shed. Then she hung up the sides of bacon.

"There's more bacon here than the bear last year, but not as much fat. I think there'll be enough though."

The next day Blair took down the bait pail and emptied it by banging the pail on the tree root. Then he nailed the bear hide to the cabin wall. Then he helped Monique cut up the bear meat for canning. "I think there'll be enough empty jars now for most of the meat."

This time of year there was a lot of sap and sugar in the maple wood and this would enhance the flavor.

Monique rubbed hemlock bark on the fleshy side of the bear hide every day and by the time it was completely dry it had a nice brown color to it. Then she washed it in the river and Blair helped her put it back on the cabin wall again to dry.

This smoke house was hotter than what they had used the year before and it didn't take as many days to cure the meat.

They still had a lot of smoked fish left, and canned caribou, two jars of beaver and the deer didn't last through December.

"How are the vegetables doing?" Blair asked.

"Everything is through the ground."

"Tomorrow, I think I'll clean out the outhouse and put that around the garden. I hope the human scent will keep the animals out while we're gone. Have you made up a list of what you want to bring back?"

"Not yet, but I'll work on it."

"I'm thinking about another smaller canoe. One that we can use here that'll be easier to handle."

"I think that would be a good idea."

"I'm thinking we could probably leave next week. What's today?"

"This is Wednesday the twelfth."

"Okay, why don't we leave bright and early Sunday morning."

Monique was all smiles. She started making a list that evening. Blair pretty much knew what he wanted, but so not to forget anything he too wrote out a list.

Before leaving in three days he decided to make some animal retardants. He had some wide pieces of cedar boards any where from two to three feet long. He then filled them with nails so the sharp ends were protruding up. He'd lay one in front of each cabin door, one on the front step and another in front of the root cellar door. He would spike all the doors closed just before leaving.

They were sitting on the porch watching the sunset and Blair was explaining why he had made the boards with the nails sticking up. "Are you expecting trouble?"

"Not expecting, but there are a lot of scents here that meat eaters would like and without us here, there is nothing to keep the bear, wolverine and big cats from breaking in. We have shot two bear across the river and trapped two wolverines less than a mile away. Just being cautious. I'd hate to come back and find a bear in the cabin or root cellar. That crap I dug out of the outhouse may help. But I know if a bear or wolverine steps on one of those boards with the nails, he'll leave and not come back."

They were quiet for a while listening to the evening sounds and the river. "I think while we are in town one day after supplies we should file for homestead here. So this will legally be ours."

"Are the pelts all ready to go?"

"I'll bundle them up tomorrow."

It was obvious that they would be away for a few days more this trip in order to get everything done, and this worried Blair. He hoped he had done everything he could.

The next morning before he bundled his fur pelts together, he brushed them thoroughly one more time.

"What do you want to do with the bear hide?"

"Has the fur dried since you washed it in the river?"

"Yes, the fur and hide are both dry."

"Well, I don't see why we can't take it off the cabin and take it inside."

This bear rug was put on Blair's side of the bed and the caribou hide went in front of the fireplace. "There, I like the looks of that."

"Do you think we can make it to the farm in one day like we did last year?"

"I don't see why not. The current will be swift and the water will be high. Coming back will be like our first trip. It might take us three days."

"It'll be a long day, so I'm going to bring some smoked fish and bread."

They had everything they were going to take with them in the cabin. "I want you to take your .45, Monique." There was no question why, nor argument.

They went to bed early that night knowing the following day would be long and tiring. Blair laid on his side with his arm around Monique. "You make me so happy, Monique." She hugged him.

Chapter 12

Blair was awake before daylight and he eased out of bed trying not to awaken Monique. It would be a long day as it was, without his rousing her early. He started a fire in the cook stove and then shaved. Then put water on for coffee.

When the water was warm he washed up and put on clean clothes. "Hey you," he touched her shoulder, "are you going to get up?"

The water was still warm and she washed up and then started preparing breakfast. Blair carried the bundle of fur pelts to the canoe, then he nailed closed the doors except for the cabin. Monique already had the pack basket packed with clothes and Blair took the leather pouch Monique had made to keep their money in from the bureau drawer, and he put that in the pack.

"I think we should open a savings account at the bank instead of keeping all our money here."

There were goose eggs and smoked fish with hot bread for breakfast. And coffee, always coffee. "It's a good thing we're going now, we are almost out of coffee."

Monique cleaned up the cabin while Blair nailed the back door and laid the nailed boards in front of each door. Lastly he nailed the front door closed. He looked at Monique grinning and said, "Are you ready?"

She hugged and kissed him and said, "Let's go."

Monique steadied the canoe while Blair worked his way to the stern and sat down. Monique then pushed off from shore and climbed in.

The river was still a little high and the current was about 5mph, but with both of them paddling with true earnest they were probably traveling about 15mph. The high water had taken out the beaver dam across the river and it was smooth sailing all the way to the St. John River at Allagash.

Here the St. John was higher than Blair would have liked, but they were both good canoeists, and besides, they were in an unusually big canoe.

The St. John's current was even swifter and Blair kept the canoe close to the right shore. There were other trappers at Pelletier's Trading Post when they canoed by. No one seemed to notice them. Blair had always sold his fur at Pierre's Furrier in Clair, New Brunswick and he would this year. He figured Monsieur Pierre had always given him a fair deal.

"Are you hungry, Blair? I am."

"Yes, toss me a trout."

While they ate the smoked fish Blair let the current take them. The brief rest felt good for their arms. "I think we have made a faster trip than last year," Monique said.

There was still so much water in the St. John River, Blayne had not put their wharf back in the water yet. Blair brought the canoe in alongside shore and steadied it with his paddle for Monique to get out. When he was out she helped him drag the canoe out of the water on to land. Blair put the bundle of fur on his back and Monique carried the pack and blankets.

No one had seen them until they were at the porch door. Then Peter was walking across the yard and hollered, "Blair and Monique! They're back! Everybody, Blair and Monique are back!"

Blayne came running out of the barn and Regina and Faye came out of the house. Everyone was so excited to see them. And Monique with her .45 and green hat. There were hugs all around and then Monique asked, "Where is my grandmother?"

Everyone was silent then and Regina spoke up. "We're sorry, Monique. Rose died last month. We went after the doctor, but before he could get here, she had passed. The doctor said it was a heart attack. We had a graveside funeral for her, Monique, and she is in our family cemetery here on the farm. I hope you don't mind."

"Certainly not and thank you."

"Come with me, Monique," Regina took her hand and led her into the house.

"Sit down, Monique. Blayne was needing another cook to help out Fred at the lumber camp. Rose overheard us talking and she asked to go out there. We told her she didn't have to do that; she could stay here with us. But she insisted. She and Fred really hit it off and the crews all loved her. She said after the camps were closed for the season that she had never felt more needed than she had felt at the camps. She was very happy, Monique. While we waited for the doctor she told me just before her body died that she was so happy for you and that she loved you. Those were her last words, Monique."

Regina's eyes were filled with tears and Monique was crying. Something she seldom had done in her life and even now she was not crying for herself, but instead she could feel the love of her grandmother, Rose Lamoureax, and of the Kelley family.

"You can put your fur in the barn, son," Blayne said.

"No Dad, I think the porch. These furs represent our income for the year and I'd hate for them to be chewed by mice."

They all went inside and Faye had made a big pot of coffee. Faye had tears in her eyes also.

They all sat around the table and Blair said, "Monique shot a big caribou on the river in front of the cabin. There were four migrating to their winter range. The next day I backtracked them to a well used migration trail and then up river where several more had joined the group. Monique is quite the hunter and trapper." And then he told them about Monique's first beaver when she fell backwards in the mud.

"What do you have for fur, Blair?" Peter asked.

"Beaver, bobcat, lynx, two wolverines, otter."

"Wolverines!?"

Monique told them about the honey log and how the wolverine had torn the log apart to get the rest of the honeycomb and they had set a trap there. And about the one that had lost two toes.

"Being that close to home we thought it a good idea to get rid of them."

"I have heard stories of wolverines being in this part of the state, but I have never seen any," Blayne said.

"What do you eat out there, Monique?" Faye asked.

"Well, besides the caribou, I shot a deer and we smoked it, we eat beaver, bear and we smoked a hundred brook trout. They spawn in a spring brook next to the cabin—and many different herbs. We roast geese and eat goose eggs. And Blair made smoked bacon from bear and we like it better than pig bacon. We don't go hungry. And much of what we do is either hunting or gathering food."

"I don't know if I would live like that," Faye said.

After supper Monique said, "Blair, will you show me the family cemetery. I'd like to say goodbye to my grandmother."

"Certainly."

Blayne and Regina watched as they walked off holding each other's hand. "They are certainly well matched, aren't they Regina." Blayne said.

"Yes, they each have so much love for the other."

"Have you noticed when either one of them is talking, it is never *I* did this or did that. It is always *we* did it."

"Yes, I noticed that also. They are never putting themselves above the other. I'm real proud of our son, Blayne."

"Me too. And I think they live an exciting life together."

"I think it is so wonderful, Blair, that your Mom and Dad would bury my grandmother here in their family cemetery."

"They must have accepted Rose as family."

"She has an Indian name, although she never liked to be called it. *Little Moon.*"

"That's a pretty name, I wonder why."

Monique knelt down on the grass and closed her eyes and talked with her grandmother on the inner soul.

"You know, Blair," Monique said as they walked back to the house, "I'm so glad grandmother came to live and work here with your family. Even if it was only for a short while, I believe she was really happy. Something that she never had much of in her life. I think she was at home here."

Faye made some more coffee and they sat out on the porch for a long time talking. Everyone had so many questions.

"Is the ferry to Clair, New Brunswick in service?" Blair asked.

"Yes, they started up again two days ago."

"Can we take a horse and wagon to town tomorrow?"

"Certainly."

"After we sell our fur, I want to go to the land office and file for homestead. Set up a bank account, and buy a smaller canoe we can use to trap and hunt with on the Little Black. And we have a lot of supplies to pick up. What about the two goats and a dozen chickens. Can we buy them from you?"

"Certainly. But where will you keep them?" Blayne asked.

"This spring we built a barn underground, thinking they would stay warmer."

"Did the river flood this year?"

"No, the banks were full but it never came over the top. A lot of people in town were worried though, because we had so much snow. Thank goodness it was dry snow and not much water content to it."

"You and Monique really enjoy your life out there on the Little Black, don't you?"

"Yes, Dad, we both do. It's as close to being in Heaven as we are apt to come in the physical world. We have talked about this before, Monique and I, and neither one of us would want to be anywhere else."

"I'm glad for you, son."

Regina, Faye and Monique had gone inside earlier. Leaving the men to talk amongst themselves.

Faye had difficulty understanding why Monique enjoyed so much, living alone with her husband in the big woods and never seeing another person until they took a trip back to the farm.

Regina was older and she understood what it was like to love someone the way Monique loved Blair and Blair loved her. She understood that with love like this, you really didn't need to be around other people.

"Do you think you'll have any trouble going back with the river as high as it is, and towing a canoe?"

"It'll be slower, there's no question about that, but I don't think there'll be any trouble."

"How long are you planning on staying?"

"Well, it could be four days."

"Dad, why don't you and Mom come visit us this summer. There's always some slow time before harvest begins."

"I'll talk it over with Regina and let you know for sure before you leave."

The air was getting cool and the men went inside to join the women.

They had an evening snack of hot coffee and cake and they talked almost to midnight.

* * *

The next morning before leaving for town Blair said, "I think maybe you should leave your .45 here, Monique. We have to talk with people in the bank and at the land office. A gun might make them nervous."

"No problem, as long as I am with you, Blair, I feel safe.

"If we take the wagon, Blair, how do we cross the river?"

"Dad said the ferry was operating."

"I'm surprised with this high water."

It was still early and they met no one on the road. St. Simon's ferry was just coming across the river when they arrived at the terminal. They waited until the one wagon drove off. "Good morning, Simon."

"Oh good morning, Mr. Kelley. You going across?"

"Yes."

Simon had a steam powered winch that he used to pull the ferry back and forth across the river. With the river so high and the strong current there is no way he could operate without the powered winch.

"That's $1.00 for the horse and wagon and 10 cents apiece per person."

"Has your ferry ever broke loose, Simon?"

"Once, you were away in the war then. It was in the spring and like now the water was high. Had me quite a ride before we washed up in a lagoon down stream about a mile. Never lost my passengers or cargo though. But getting my ferry back up here cost me a fortune. I use stronger ropes now. Maybe someday someone will find a way to put a bridge across here that won't wash away every time the river comes up."

"Thank you, Simon," and Blair drove the team off and up the ramp to the road and then to Pierre's Furrier on the hill.

"Ah bonjour, Mr. Kelley. And who is this beautiful Madame?"

"Pierre—my wife, Monique."

"Hello, Mrs. Kelley."

"Good morning, Pierre."

"What have you for me, my friend?"

"We have some beautiful fur, Pierre," and he picked the bundle up and carried it inside.

Instead of wandering around looking at things in the trading post, Monique watched as Pierre looked over the pelts. She was just as interested as Blair.

"These are nice looking pelts. You take good care of them."

Blair handed him a list of each specie. "No small beaver, this is good. Twenty-one super blankets and two large blankets." Pierre was especially taken with the two wolverine pelts. He ran his hand through the fur many times. "These are colored good. Nice fur."

Pierre was an hour and a half before he could give a price. "You have the castors too. This is good. The fur market is good this year. I give to you $1200.00 for fur and d'castors."

When he said $1200.00 Monique tightened her grip on Blair's arm. Blair knew never to accept the first offer. "You give us $1300.00, Pierre. U.S. dollars."

Monique's grip tightened. "Okay, just for Mr. Kelley. I give you what you wish—and U.S. dollars."

As they were on the ferry back across the river Monique said, "That is a lot of money, Blair."

"It is. And now we go to the land office to file for a homestead."

"What can I do for you this morning?"

"Good morning, this is my wife Monique and I am Blair Kelley and we would like to file for a homestead."

"Certainly. Oh, my name is Henry Abbott. Here sit down. Now where is it you wish to homestead?"

"Do you have a map?"

"Yes, on the wall behind you." Blair and Monique stepped over to the map and Blair pointed to the Little Black River.

"Here just below the oxbows."

"When do you plan to build?"

"We already have. Last year."

"Okay, I'll date this, July 1st last year then. Now you have seven years to show improvements and come back in and I'll then make you out a deed for your property. How many acres are you wanting? Usually here in this state homestead lots are forty-three acres. What are your intentions with the property?"

"We already have a cabin, a barn, root cellar, woodshed, tool shed and we have started clearing two acres for feed. We have goats and chickens and a garden."

"And we trap," Monique added.

"Since you two have already done this much work to the property I'll change the seven years to five, effective since last July 1st. So four years from this June 1st, if you are still on the property, I'll give you a deed for it. There is a $17.00 filing fee due now."

Mr. Abbott wrote out a receipt and a temporary homestead deed to the property. "Now you will have to mark off forty-three acres before you come back."

"Thank you Mr. Abbott."

"I can't believe our luck, Blair. First the $1300.00 and now we own our property. Where to now?"

"Let's do our shopping and then go to the bank."

First they needed a canoe and there was only one place in town that sold canoes. There was a trading post just east of town overlooking the river.

"Good morning, folks. How may I help you?" Mr. Sirway said.

"We are wanting a sixteen foot canoe and paddles."

"I have something new that might fit your needs. It's sixteen feet, a wood and canvas canoe built by Evan Gerrish. Would you like to look at it?"

"Yes."

"It's over here in the front of the store."

Both Blair and Monique liked the looks of it and it was no where as heavy as their twenty-four foot canoe. "Is canvas coating something new?" Blair asked.

"Yes it is."

"How much for the canoe and two paddles?"

"$63.00 and I'll throw in the paddles."

Sirway helped Blair load it into the wagon and gave him enough rope to secure it. Then Blair gave him the $63.00.

"Thank you, Mr. Sirway."

"Okay now Ouelette's General Store."

"While you are picking up things here, Monique, I'm going next door to the hardware store."

"Can I help you?"

"Yes, here is a list of things I need" and Blair gave him the list.

"We have everything except books. What are you looking for in a window?"

"It's for the front wall of a log cabin."

"I have one that is all encased three feet by three feet. Anything larger has to be special ordered."

"That'll do. Is it possible to have one master key to open all three different locks?"

"You can buy a set of four with a master key."

"Okay." He picked out an assortment of screws.

"The screen is for what?"

"To make two screen doors."

"Okay, not a problem."

"The shotgun you'll have to get at Ouelette's."

"Okay."

"Two rolls of chicken wire."

"Is there anything else?"

"I think that should do it." Blair paid him and then loaded everything into the wagon with the canoe.

Monique was almost done. "I thought we'd only get fifty pounds of flour for now, since we'll have a load. We can pick up another fifty pounds when we come out in the fall. I still have ten or fifteen pounds left from the hundred pounds we bought last year," Monique said.

"Okay. I'm going to get a shotgun also. A double barrel .12 gauge and a box of #4 birdshot."

"I bought us some clothes, Blair. Underwear, socks, shirts, pants and a dress."

"Is it a pretty dress?"

"Yes."

Everything was put inside the canoe. The weight would help keep it from bouncing. "How much of that $1300.00 is there left Blair?"

"A little more than $1000.00 left, plus we still have the three thousand. So let's go to the bank."

* * *

The McQuale brothers saw Blair and Monique go into the bank. "Well looky-there, Blair and his cute little wife," Burl said.

"Ain't she a pretty one though, Burl," Burk said.

"Come on fellas, you know what he said he would do to us if we bothered her again. Come on, let's get out of here. And remember what Pa said if we were ever to bother her or him again."

"Just be still Boydie, we ain't gonna do anything, now that is. But all three of us owe him for what he did to us. None of us has been fully right since that beating he gave us. And people are always staring at me with these damned scratches scaring my face that she did."

"Pa and Ma always leave on July 1st for ten days in Presque Isle right? Well, that's when we find where their cabin is and we go get Blair and shoot him and then we'll have all the time with that pretty wife of his."

"Yeah, but we don't know where they are, Burl," Burk said.

"I overheard his sister Faye tell someone they are living on the Little Black River. It shouldn't be too hard to find their cabin. We know now which river to look on. Yes sir, Blair Kelley, first of July we are coming for you."

"Hello I'm Robert Jones, how may I help you?"
"We would like to set up a savings account?"
"Certainly, in whose name?"
"Blair and Monique Kelley."
"And how much do you wish to deposit?"

Blair counted the money and said to Monique, "We should keep—what, maybe $300.00?"

"That should be enough."

"Here's $3700.00 Mr. Jones."

"You already have an account here Mr. Kelley, do you want me to add this deposit to the same account?"

"No. A new account in both of our names. The old account I signed over to my father last year. Apparently he hasn't withdrawn the money and closed the account. I will talk with him."

As they were walking out of the bank, Monique said, "What about the kerosene and another lantern?"

"Oh yes. I forgot. We'll have to go back to the hardware store. I should have remembered to bring in the two kerosene cans. I'll get a five gallon can."

"Are you hungry, Blair? I am."

"Let's go eat." They found a good restaurant and went inside and sat down.

"I think I'll have a big piece of beef steak," Monique said.

"That sounds good, and baked potato and green beans."

While they were waiting for the meal Monique said, "You know, we were so busy this spring we forgot to look for fiddleheads."

"I never gave it a thought. Next year. Did you get a calendar?"

"Yes."

The McQuale boys were in an alley across the street from the restaurant watching Blair and Monique eat their lunch sitting in the big window out front. "Look at that wagonload of supplies. I'm saying when we take care of Blair in July, we take apart his cabin and we just might find his money," Burl said.

"Come on, Burl, Pa will be looking for us," Burk said.

"That beef steak was good. If cows weren't so much trouble to take care of, I'd get one," Blair said.

It was mid-afternoon when they returned to the farm. Blair drove the team and wagon in the barn so the supplies would be protected from the weather and he unhitched the horse and fed it some grain before turning it loose in the corral. Monique put the case of eggs in the root cellar where they would stay cool.

"Did you take care of everything, son?"

"Yes. Dad, last summer I signed my bank account over to you for the $4000.00 you gave us. I expected you would withdraw it and put it in your account."

"I guess I just forgot about it. You sure you don't need it son?"

"I'm sure Dad, Monique and I do very well with our trapping."

"Okay, next time I'm in town. Now what do you and Monique need from the farm?"

"Maybe a bushel of potatoes. We can get more when we come out in the fall."

Monique surprised everyone including Blair when she put on her new dress for supper. Faye was the first to say anything. "Monique, you are so pretty."

"Yes you certainly are, Monique," Regina said.

The men, including Blair, were still staring at her. The dress was white with green swirls and flowery plants.

* * *

For three days Blair and Monique were once again a part

of the Kelleys on the farm, "But I miss our home, Blair. Our log cabin has a special meaning for me."

"Me too, Monique."

At the supper table that evening Blair told his family they would be leaving in the morning. "We need to get home."

After supper Blair paid his Dad $5.00 each for the goats and $1.00 a piece for the twelve chickens. The chickens were only chicks and the twelve fit in a small open crate. The two goats were only kids and Blair would have to tie their legs together to keep them from jumping out of the canoe or running off when they made camp.

After everything was settled Monique went by herself to visit her grandmother's grave.

Tomorrow would be another long day and Blair and Monique went to bed early.

They and the entire family were up when the sun rose over the hills. Instead of feeling sorrow for leaving, they were excited about going home. They ate a good breakfast of ham and eggs and then Blayne and Peter helped to load both canoes. The goats with their legs tied together were put in the smaller canoe to be towed along with the crate of chickens. The two rolls of chicken wire were put in the smaller canoe also along with the stove pipe. Some ballast was needed to keep the canoe from swaying.

The food supplies, clothes, etc. and the window were loaded into the big canoe and covered over with the piece of canvas they had brought with them.

Regina had put up another basket of food for the trip home. "We'll try to be there, Blair, on August 1st. If we're a day late don't get concerned."

Monique hugged and kissed everyone and said, "I'm so grateful for you taking in my grandmother. You all were so good to her. It really means a lot to me."

"We were glad to have her, Monique," Regina said.

"You be careful of this high water."

"We will, Dad, see you August 1st. Peter, Faye it is always good to see you."

Peter and Blayne held the canoe while Blair and Monique got seated and then they pushed them away from shore. "Have a good trip," Peter said.

"Goodbye," Faye said.

They stood there on the shore of the river watching until Blair and Monique were out of sight.

"They make a good team don't they," Peter said. He was a little envious of his big brother, but he was enjoying his new status on the farm and lumbering business. Blayne was allowing him to assume more and more decision making. And Blayne approved and was happy with his son's assertiveness.

* * *

"You know towing the other canoe isn't as bad as I thought it might be. It's not swaying and I can't feel the extra weight. I think, though, when we start up the Little Black we might have to shorten the tow rope."

They were able to make their usual camp site that first day, but after fighting the strong current all day they both were tired. And they had to untie the goats and let them stretch and feed, but tied to a leash. The chickens were kept in the crate, but put on the grass. They would eat just enough grass to give them what moisture they needed.

When they turned south on the Allagash away from the St. Francis River, the river current was not as strong. "Must be the St. Francis is the reason for the high water downstream from Allagash," Blair said. "Maybe there was more snow along the St. Francis watershed."

Although the current in the Little Black was not as strong they were having more difficulty with towing the canoe. Because of the numerous sharp bends the current would sweep the towed canoe sideways. They were a day longer on the Little Black.

"Boy, will I be glad to get home. This has been a real chore towing this canoe on this river."

The goats and chickens were making a noisy racket. The goats were probably tired of being hog-tied and the chickens were probably hungry and thirsty. Blair and Monique were both tired also. When Monique saw the cabin she said, "Home at last."

Before they could unload the canoe, the two goats were staked out to graze and the chickens were taken to the barn and turned loose. Monique brought out a dish of water. They were all thirsty. Once they were used to the barn and their pen, Blair would turn them out in the day to feed. Chickens seemed to always know; by dark they would wander back to the pen or coop.

Blair pulled the nails securing the doors and put the nail boards in the workshop. Then he took some cured trout and broke it up and fed the chickens. They were ravenous. "I didn't know chickens would eat meat or fish."

"They'll eat almost anything."

For now the food supplies, clothes and such were taken inside and the hardware supplies to the toolshed. It was becoming obvious he should have built the toolshed (workshop) bigger. And most surprising of the whole trip was that the window was still intact. That would have to wait for now. He needed to fence in an area for the chickens. The goats would be okay to stake out each morning. The shotgun of course went inside and in the corner with the rifle. Monique took her .45 off and hung it on the peg with Blair's.

The last two days had been tiring, fighting the tight turns in the Little Black. After supper they sat on the porch and watched the goats eat and play, until it was time for them to sleep also. Blair put them in the barn and closed the door.

* * *

The next morning while Monique was preparing breakfast Blair staked the goats out to feed and where they could get to water. He picked handfuls of clover and sorrel and gave it to the chickens.

"Breakfast is ready, Farmer Blair," Monique hollered out the back door.

"I sure do like these goose eggs. You know it's too bad they wouldn't lay eggs regular like a hen does. We'd have us a bunch of geese."

"Well we have enough goose eggs now to last until August anyhow."

"What are you going to work on first, Blair?"

"Fence in an enclosure for the chickens, so we can turn them out. Then I'm going to make two screen doors before the bugs get bad."

"I'm going to take care of the food supplies and put away our new clothes."

Blair went out back to cut enough cedar trees for fence posts for the enclosure. He couldn't fence off in front of the barn, because they still would have to have that open for spring water. So he made a walk way leading out behind the barn and where there was some shade.

The fence posts went into the sandy soil easily. Then he began stringing the fencing.

While he was doing that Monique was busy putting curtains around the cabin windows. She hadn't said anything to Blair about curtains and she now wanted to surprise him. She hoped he would like them.

Monique brought lunch out to the porch. She wasn't yet done with the curtains and she so wanted to surprise him. "It's such a nice day and not much to speak of yet for bugs. I'm fixing a boiled supper tonight."

"Oh boy, I'll be hungry too."

"Only, there aren't any mushrooms yet."

Before going back to work they walked down to see the goats. "What shall we name them?"

"Well one is male and the other is female."

"I'll name the female Nanny."

"Okay, and the other one will be Billy."

After the shock of being tied up for three days Billy and Nanny now were friendly. "You know it'll still be awhile before we get any milk from Nanny. She'll have to be bred first."

"I never thought of that. I was so hoping for milk this winter. I don't think either one have stopped eating all morning."

They each went back to work. It was obvious before Blair had the little pasture completely fenced in there would be some fencing left over.

He put a gate in on top and another one at the entrance to the barn. Once he had the fencing up and secured he made wooden pegs to hold the bottom of the fencing tight to the ground, to keep predator animals from looking for an easy meal. When he was done he tested the fence and each fence post, making sure everything was tight.

He put his tools away and went inside to wash up. Monique didn't say anything, she stood to one side waiting for his reaction.

Blair stood in the back doorway and his first thought was he was in the wrong cabin. Then he looked around and saw Monique standing there watching and waiting for his reaction.

He looked at the curtains again and then at Monique. She was still waiting. When he began to grin, she exhaled and started breathing normally. "They really dress things up, don't they."

"Do you like them?"

"Yes, they make the cabin—well, homey is the only word I can find."

She tossed him a towel and soap and said, "Go wash up in the river, would you?"

When the goats saw Blair coming down from the cabin they started bleating and stretched to the end of their ropes. He walked over and patted them both. They had eaten almost everything in a circle around them as far as their rope would reach. Even the small bushes and bark off the trees. He decided to put the goats in the barn, since no one would be outside and their bellies were full.

Monique had everything on the table. "We have canned bear meat, potatoes, cabbage and onions and a fresh batch of biscuits."

"It all smells so good." He took a bite of the meat. "This is so tender. What did you do different?"

"I let it simmer all day with an onion, salt and pepper. I think letting it simmer all day is what made it tender."

"Well it's good. I don't suppose you had time to make an apple pie? Just joking."

"I plan to make one tomorrow. In the morning though I'm going up to the oxbows and get us a goose to roast and look for herbs. I may not be back in time for lunch. But I will to make the pie. The goose will be for the next day."

After supper Blair carried the big canoe out back and put it on the cross supports that he had used for the winter storage.

The next day he went out to the grove of cedar trees and found two about five inches through. Monique put the small canoe in the river and her .45 and pack basket. The shorter canoe was handling just fine in the river and around the sharp oxbows. She pulled up in the usual spot and crawled over the river berm and there were two geese not nesting. They were probably males. She shot the closest one and retrieved it and put it in the canoe and then pushed the canoe to the other shore and tied it off and took her pack basket and went in search of edibles.

Cattails were just sticking above the water and even though they were short she took a good bunch of them for the white stalk near the root. She found a lot of woods sorrel but no mushrooms. She did find some onion grass, but they already had onions. In under the softwood canopy the ground was covered with t-berry plants. When the leaves were dry they made for an excellent tea. She finished filling her pack basket and headed for the canoe and then home.

Blair had all the rough stock he would need and cut to

length and he'd be another two days making enough boards to build two doors. There was no rush and besides he liked working with wood.

He was so busy making boards he didn't know Monique was back. He had never made boards the length he needed for the doors and it was time consuming.

Monique made the pie and put it in the oven then she took care of the herbs. She kept a few of the cattail stalks for supper and everything else she took to the root cellar. Then she opened the door to the workshop and asked Blair, "Would you have time to pluck a goose? I have a pie in the oven."

"Sure, I was needing a break from making boards."

"How is it going?"

"It's a lot of slow work. For two doors, I need eight, seven foot boards."

He took the goose out back and to one side to pluck the feathers. There were thousands of feathers and he didn't want them around the cabin. It was slow work removing all the feathers and the tiny pin-feathers, but eventually he had a smooth-skin goose.

He took it in the barn and wanted to watch the chickens as he gave the innards to them. He gave them the heart and liver first and they gobbled them down. Then the lungs and all of it. He twisted the neck and gave them the head to peck away at.

He washed the goose out in the river and then took it to the root cellar.

For supper they finished up the boiled dinner from the day before and apple pie for dessert.

* * *

Two days later Blair had all the boards he would need and by the end of the third day the two screen doors were built and hung. He attached the springs and opened and closed them several times. "Just like a fancy house," he said.

"And just in time, the blackflies are here."

"Tomorrow I'm going to put the new window in so we may get a few flies in here. Maybe you could get some of that tansy weed and make a smudge in the outside fire pit."

It only took him a day to install the new window. "Look how much more light there is inside Blair. What are you going to do with the one you just took out?"

"I don't know. Would you like another window over your counter here?"

"That would be nice."

"Okay."

The next day he put that window in. Then for something to do he started clearing more trees and brush from what he was now referring to as the field. He would have to keep the goats out of this so there would be grass to put up for the winter.

It was nice to be able to leave both doors open with the new screen doors, without the cabin filling with blackflies and mosquitos. They were really bad this year. It seemed that any winter when there was a lot of snow the bugs were worse.

Everyday, just about, Monique would go off with her basket and harvest herbs. She wanted to can more this year. She went down to the meadow and filled her basket with pennycress while she picked the plant she would eat some raw.

When the cattail flower was out she picked a basket full of those. She would try canning these also.

The chickens were growing bigger and Blair figured they were accustomed now to their new surroundings, so he turned them loose in the fenced in pen. Instinctively they knew what to do and they started scratching and feeding.

One morning while they were eating breakfast Blair asked, "What's the date?"

"June 25th. And it's Friday."

"Hum, summer is going by fast."

"Maybe, but you sure have accomplished a lot."

The two goats were fast becoming more like pets than

farm animals. They had very easily accepted Blair and Monique and when they were let loose, they would fellow them around. Even inside the cabin, until one day Nanny deposited a pile of droppings on the floor. "That's enough of that," and she opened the screen door and shoed them out. "No more inside."

The chickens were growing fast, faster now that they were able to go outside and forage. But Blair and Monique would pick a hand full of clover or other weeds and throw it inside the pen. Their yellow downy feathers were being replaced with brown feathers.

Blair began working on two more chairs and one of them being another rocker. He was thinking of his folks when they came, so they all could sit out on the porch.

* * *

Bouchard McQuale had shut his sawmill down like he always did on the last day of June for the summer. And he and his wife Thea would take a ten day trip to Presque Isle. The three boys were left behind to clean the sawdust out of the mill and from in and around the machinery.

They were on the log deck cleaning out the old bark and dirt. Burl said, "Ma and Pa are leaving early in the morning for Presque Isle and they'll be gone for ten days like they always do. As soon as they leave we put the canoe in and go after Blair and his wife Monique."

"I don't know, Burl," Burk whined, "You know what he did to us last time. And what if Pa comes back and finds we haven't finished cleaning the mill?"

"First I don't intend to let Blair near enough to do anything to us. We're taking Pa's double barrel shotgun and we'll shoot Mr. Kelley. Give him what he deserves for what he did to us. Then we can take our time with Monique. And as far as this mill and Pa, we'll be back and have it cleaned out before he gets back."

"Yeah, but Burl, we don't even know where their cabin is," Boydie added.

"We know it is on the Little Black River. We keep canoeing upstream until we see a cabin."

"Who's gonna shoot Blair? I don't want to kill him," Boydie said.

"If you're not man enough after what he did to you, I will. Gladly. Now, I don't want to hear any more whining. Here comes Pa."

* * *

Blair decided to build the rocker first since it would be the most difficult. He had the ash boards already cut out and standing in the corner of his workshop. There was no doubt about it, he should have made the toolshed, workshop bigger. "Maybe when I don't have anything else to do."

"I'm going to catch some trout today, so we can have fresh brook trout for supper," Monique said.

* * *

The three brothers stood in the yard as their parents were boarding the early east bound stage from Allagash. As soon as the stage was out of sight they began loading their canoe with blankets, shotgun and shells and some food and a fifth of Bouchard's whiskey. "Let's go." Burl was in the stern, Burk in the bow and Boydie sitting in the middle.

"I sure hope we get back before Pa," Boydie said.

"It shouldn't take us, at the most, two and a half days to find the cabin. We probably could make it back in a day and a half—two, tops. A day to finish cleaning the mill, that's five and a half days. That gives us at least four days to have our fun with Monique. Stop your damned worrying, Boydie," Burl said.

"Alright, alright, now that you have put it like that."

The brothers' canoe was not as long as Blair's and with three men in it, it didn't ride on top of the water and their progress was slower. In one day that hadn't quite reached where Blair and Monique would make camp when they were transporting a heavy load.

The next morning the three brothers stopped at Pelletier's Trading Post and asked, "Do you know where the Kelley's cabin is?"

"No, Monsieur. The Kelleys, they stop here a year ago in d'spring, have not seen the Kelleys since then."

They left Pelletier's and continued up river. "This is the Allagash River, I don't think they are on it. We should find the Little Black soon," Burl said.

It was almost noon when they found the mouth of the Little Black River. "From now on, fellas, we must be quiet. I have no idea how far we'll have to go and I certainly don't want them to hear us coming."

Their progress was slow and they had only gone maybe two or three miles when they decided to make camp. "It's warm enough, fellas, so no fires. If they smell smoke they might come to investigate. And I don't know how close we are."

They slept pitifully. The mosquitoes were terrible. They would cover their head with their blanket, but they were still bothered by the almost constant buzzing.

Just before dawn the mosquitoes disappeared, and the bothers did get a couple of hours of restful sleep. And they were late getting started.

"We are getting closer. So no talking," Burl said in a low voice.

* * *

When Monique had her early morning chores done, she took the goats out and staked them in some new browse and started fishing. She caught several small ones and threw them back. She wanted two that they could really sink their teeth in. After a while, about mid-morning, she caught two about two pounds each. This was all she wanted and she took them up to the cabin and set the pail in the corner on the porch and took the trout inside. She cut the heads off and cleaned them and took that out to the chicken pen. As she walked through the back door she saw movement on the river and went to the other door to see.

She gasped when she recognized the McQuale brothers. She strapped on her gun belt and unholstered her .45 and from the cabin porch she put a bullet through the bow of their canoe. She jumped down off the porch and ran down toward them. About thirty feet away Burk had his paddle straight up in the air and she fired again and broke the paddle just above his hands. "That shot was to show you that the first shot was no accident." She turned her attention now on Burl who had been reaching for the shotgun.

Blair was in his workshop and he stepped out and hollered, "What did you get, Monique?"

Still pointing her .45 at Burl she hollered back, "You'd better come down here, Blair, I have three dirty pigs!"

He couldn't imagine what she was talking about until he saw the McQuale brothers in the canoe.

"Yeah, I'd say you caught three dirty pigs alright. That's exactly what you three are. Dirty pigs. Do you remember what I said I'd do if you ever came after us?" When no one replied Blair said in an even tone, "I said I'd beat the living hell out of you."

Monique was swinging her .45 back and forth. Pointing at Burl, then Boydie and then Burk and back again at Burl. "Can I shoot them, Blair?" and she turned her head towards Blair and winked.

Blair decided to play along, "Not just yet, Monique. Let's have us some fun first." Now all three of the brothers were scared and worried. Boydie was almost in tears.

Blair walked down to the shore and said, "Bring your canoe in," and again he didn't raise his voice.

Without hesitating Burl swung the canoe and brought the bow in to shore. Blair reached down and grabbed the bow and turned it over dumping all three in the river. Burk hardly got wet at all, so Blair spun him around facing the river and grabbed him by his shirt collar and his pants and in the same motion lifted him off the ground and threw him over his brothers heads into the river.

He saw the shotgun spill into the water, "Boydie, hand me that shotgun. Monique, if he points it at me, shoot him." Boydie's eyes got as big as silver dollars and he was crying now and shaking as he handed the shotgun to Blair butt first.

"You three sit down in the water. All I want to see above the water is your heads."

They slowly obeyed until Monique cocked the .45 and pointed it at Burl.

"This is a real nice shotgun. Fancy scroll work on both sides of the barrels." He broke it open and removed the two 00buck shells, "I guess it's obvious what you intended to do with these. You came here to kill us. How does that set with you, Monique?"

"We would be legally within our rights, if you let me shoot them now."

"Nah, we don't have to hurry about this. I want these little boys to understand their mistake first."

Boydie was real scared now and crying, "I told you, Burl, we shouldn't come. I told you I didn't want to kill nobody."

"Boydie," Blair seemed real sympathetic now, "Boydie, you were going to shoot me weren't you, Boydie."

"No, Mr. Kelley, not me. It was all Burl's idea. He said he would shoot you."

"And what were you going to do with my wife, Monique, Boydie?

"Boydie, what were you going to do with Monique? Don't make me have to ask you again." And Monique aimed her .45 at Boydie's head.

"Okay, okay, I'll tell you! Just don't let her shoot me!" He howled.

"Shut up, Boydie!" Burl shouted.

Monique now turned her gun at Burl and said, "I don't want to hear another word from you, Burl, or I'll put a bullet in your eye," she said in a low voice.

"Burl said after we shot you, we could all have at Monique. Have fun doing her for four days."

"Burk, you've been awful quiet. How come you haven't anything to say?" Monique asked.

"What do you expect me to say. It was just as Boydie said. But I surely don't want to die."

"I have an idea, Monique. You keep your .45 trained on them and if they try to get out shoot 'em. I'm going up to the workshop. I'll be right back."

Monique started walking back and forth on shore in front of the brothers, and this seemed to make them even more nervous.

Blair came back with some wire and pliers. He pulled their canoe up out of the water and hit the center thwart with his fist breaking it. Then he picked up their shotgun and while looking it over and admiring it, he said, "This must be your old man's; you boys couldn't afford anything this nice. Must have cost a lot of money." Then he took it by the barrel and swung it against a rock breaking the barrels off. Then he wired the barrels across the broken thwart and twisted the ends of the wire so tight together he knew they would never be able to undo the wire and remove the barrels. If they did then the canoe wouldn't hold together. Then he snapped pieces off the paddle so all that remained was a narrow stick.

"I'm going to let you boys go. With no paddles you'll have to pole your way home and by then your old man should be back and what do you think he'll do when he sees you broke his nice shotgun to repair the broken canoe. He'll probably also ask about the bullet hole in the bow. You see boys, I'm figuring your old man will do more to you than we will. He has an awful nasty temper." And he tossed the other half of the shotgun into the canoe.

"Now take this warning to heart. If we ever see you, any of you after us again, we'll shoot you on sight, is that understood?"

They all nodded their heads yes.

"If we see you on the river when we are on it, we will come after you and ram you with our big canoe. Do you understand this?"

They nodded their heads again.

"I want to hear you say you understand, not just your heads moving."

Together the three said, "Yes, I understand."

"Then come out of the water." They all three were shivering from the cold.

Monique walked up to Burl and without saying a word she brought her .45 down across his nose breaking it and cuts on both cheeks. He screamed and fell to his knees. Then she did the same thing to Burk and Boydie. Boydie screaming the most and the loudest. "That was for you trying to rape me," she said.

"Now get out of here and don't let either of us ever see you again."

The front of each of them was red with their own blood from their broken noses. They didn't waste any time poling out of there.

"I'm surprised you didn't beat them."

"Oh, I wanted to and thought more than once about beating them. But I have to watch about losing my temper and getting angry. I have never hit anyone with my closed fist. Not even in war. If I hit anyone in the head with my fist I'd kill them."

Blair understood why Monique had hit them with her .45 and there was no need to ask her about it. And he knew the brothers also understood. "Now their worst punishment will come when they return home. Bouchard loses his temper over nothing."

Monique holstered her .45 and picked up a rock about the size of a goose egg and threw it at them. It hit the canoe beside Boydie. He turned to look back just as Monique was picking up another rock. "Faster, Burl!" Boydie howled. "She's throwing rocks at us now."

Monique threw that rock and hit Boydie on his right shoulder, drawing blood. Boydie screamed and started crying, "Damn it, Burl!" He hollered in between sobs. "She hit me that time and my shoulder is bleeding and running down my back! Get us out of here, Burl! Damn it! Now!"

Monique threw another rock and hit Burl in the back this time. He wasn't crying or screaming like Boydie, but he was just as scared. Blair put his arm around Monique. They stood there watching until the McQuale brothers were out of sight.

"I left the two big trout on the counter. The whole cabin probably smells like fish now. Are you hungry?"

"Yeah, I am," and they both laughed and walked arm in arm up to the cabin.

Neither of them wanted to say it, but they each found relief as the McQuale brothers disappeared. They each knew this day would come some time. It had come and they had faced it down and were the stronger for it.

* * *

The McQuale brothers visit was forgotten and Blair and Monique both believed that that would be the last they would ever hear of them again. So their lives went back to normal. Monique continued gathering herbs and processing them for winter.

Blair finished the two chairs and finished clearing the pasture–field on the shelf next to the river. It would be a few years before all of the stumps and roots rotted away. But the soil would grow grass. He now had a good start on next year's winter firewood. It was split and piled beside the woodshed.

"Have you thought where we'll sleep when the folks get here?" Blair asked.

"I thought about it, but didn't come up with an answer."

"Well, we could put a piece of canvas up behind the cabin and sleep on the ground. It'd only be for a couple of nights."

"That sounds okay to me. Let's put the canvas up, then I can gather moss and sprills for a bed. They'll be here in a couple of days."

"Okay, after breakfast I'll find a spot and put it up.

"You know, I was thinking about treating the folks to one of your special beaver tail soups."

"We'd have to go get a beaver tomorrow."

"We could do that."

Nothing more was ever said about the McQuale brothers. The memory of that day would stay with each of them though.

"You might want to take your .45, Monique, but I want to set a trap for the beaver."

"Alright. Are we going to eat beaver for lunch up there?"

"To have enough tail soup for four people we probably ought to have two beaver. That way there'll be enough meat for a meal for the folks."

"I was planning on roast goose with my special stuffing."

"That sounds even better. Maybe we'd better bring the shotgun too, just in case."

As they canoed out of sight the two goats began blatting. Monique laughed and said, "Our kids miss us." Blair laughed too.

They canoed up to the head of the oxbows and set a trap on the first dam, and then they went ashore to wait. "This is where I'd like to trap this fall. There are many more beaver upstream."

"Wouldn't that make for a long day, this far from home?"

"What if we made a temporary shelter here to spend a couple of days at a time? It's something to think about."

The trap snapped and the beaver took off for deep water.

They waited an extra five minutes to make sure the beaver had drowned before pulling it in.

"He's a big one, isn't he?" Monique gasped.

They reset the trap and Blair said, "Let's go get our goose or two."

They canoed back to their favorite goose hunting berm and crawled to the top. "Two geese," Monique whispered.

"You take the one on the left, Monique. When you fire then I'll take the other one."

Monique hit her goose in the head and before the other one could even out stretch its wings, Blair shot that one in the head.

When they returned to the beaver dam the trap was still there so they went ashore to wait and roast beaver. "Do you want to skin this one Monique? And I'll get the fire going."

"Sure," and she went at it like a seasoned expert. While watching her Blair concluded there wasn't much she couldn't do.

"Have I ever told you I think you are one hell of a woman."

"I like to hear that."

By the time Monique was done skinning, the fire was hot coals. Blair had cut two roasting sticks and they began roasting meat. "Oh, I'd forgotten just how good fresh roasted beaver is."

They had eaten all they wanted before the trap snapped again. "I'll skin this one at home so we can give the remains to the chickens."

"How old does a chicken have to be before it starts laying eggs?" Monique asked.

"Usually, six to seven months."

"That will be in January."

On the way back they were in no particular hurry, so they drifted with the current. Paddling only enough to keep out of the bushes. "You know what would go good now?"

"What?"

"A cup of coffee."

"When we get home, while you're skinning I'll make a pot."

As they drifted ashore in front of the cabin the mouth of spring brook was black with brook trout. "They must be gathering for the cold spring water."

"You know those trout tasted awful good two nights ago," That's all that had to be said.

"I'll get right on it, but you might have to do all the plucking."

"That's a good trade off."

He had the beaver skun in short order and the castor cut out. He nailed the hides to the large pine tree so the hides would dry in the shade. Then he cut off the meat from the beaver and put that in a covered dish in the root cellar. What was left of the carcass he cut up and gave to the chickens. He even opened the stomach and they went after the contents first. Then he started plucking the two geese. He had just finished one when Monique called him into eat a mid-afternoon dinner/supper.

While he was finishing the other goose, Monique went in search of moss she could use for their bed while the folks were here. It was easy to find and she brought back enough for two beds. As long as the canvas was up, it didn't matter if it rained or not.

When Blair pulled the innards out of the geese he was careful to save the makings for giblet gravy. Monique would start the stuffing in the morning, counting on the folks to arrive by noon.

"Are you all done work for the day?"

"Yes, everything is taken care of."

"Okay, we need to take a bath in the river this evening, before your folks arrive tomorrow."

There wasn't any point arguing with her. He was sweaty and dirty and he had goose-down feathers all over him.

She had already taken her clothes off inside and now she

walked down to the river with soap and a towel. "Do you suppose it would be alright to let the kids go? I don't think they'll run off."

"Sure, go ahead. They pretty much follow us everywhere we go."

She put the towel in the canoe and then waded in the river out to Blair. "The kids are right behind you."

"Oh, my word, they aren't a bit afraid of the water." Monique leaned back against Blair as they watched the antics of their kids. After a while they tired of the water and ran ashore and rolled over and over in the sand and then went back to eating.

Blair washed Monique's back and then she did his back and by now they were beginning to feel chilled by the cold spring water.

Chapter 13

Monique was out of bed before Blair and she quietly started the fire, enough so she could fix breakfast. Both doors were already open so the heat from the stove would go out. She made a pot of coffee and started frying thick slices of bear bacon, with goose eggs and hot stovetop bread.

Blair awoke to the smell of coffee and when he distinguished the smell of bacon, he was out of bed and dressed. "You're up early today."

"Well, I wanted to get an early start with the giblet gravy and stuffing and I want to sweep the floor before the folks get here."

"Well, I can sweep now," and he started at the back door. And he was surprised how much sand and softwood needles he was accumulating. "Do you always get this much sand when you sweep?"

"Close to it."

"Hum, I never realized before."

"Everything is ready."

"Boy, does this make for a good breakfast."

"It sure does."

When they had finished eating Monique said, "Now you busy yourself outside and don't keep coming in here and tracking more dirt in."

"Yes, dear."

He went out and turned the chickens loose and gave them some fresh water. They were still pecking away at the beaver and goose innards. He staked the goats out where they could forage on bushes and weeds. Goats will eat almost anything.

The green beans in the garden patch would be ready to pick soon. There were four tomatoes that he picked and took up to the back door. "Monique if you take these I won't have to come in."

"Why don't you put them in the root cellar for now. I am planning to have a nature meal."

Blair didn't know what to do with himself. He was bursting with nervous energy, waiting for his folks to show. After all the work Monique was going through he certainly hoped they would come today.

With nothing else to do he sat on the porch in one of the rocking chairs. Monique heard him and stepped out and said, "Can't find anything to do?"

"There's plenty I can do but I'd get all sweaty and dirty again. I forgot to get any books on our trip out."

"I'm making a list so I'll add that, okay?"

"Okay, I think I'll just sit here and watch the kids." Monique went back inside.

He sat on the porch watching the goats for a half hour and he just had to get up and walk around. He went out and watched the chickens for a few minutes. Then he tried out the moss bed Monique had made, and it was very comfortable.

He went back to sit on the porch. It was a beautiful day even though it was hot. He was in the shade, though, under the porch roof.

"Monique?"

"Don't bother me, I'm busy."

"Monique."

"Okay, what?"

"They're here."

She came running out onto the porch with flour on her hands and face. "They just came around that dog-leg sharp corner and they're coming up the straight away."

They walked down to the river to wait for them. Monique was as excited about their arrival as Blair. Blayne waved his paddle above his head and he was smiling. "Blayne!" Regina said excitedly, "look at all this. I never expected to see this. I imagined a small dingy log cabin. And look at that field."

Blair pulled the bow in and said, "Hang on, Mom," and he picked the bow up, clear of the water and brought it ashore, "Now you can step out."

Blayne was laughing and said, "I have forgotten how strong you are, son."

Monique hugged and kissed them and said, "I'm so glad you could come. I have been cooking all day." Then she looked at her hands and noticed the flour. "Oh my word, I'm a mess."

"No you're not, Monique. A little flour doesn't make you a mess."

They carried everything up to the cabin. The goats were bleating their welcome also.

When Blair tried to explain to his father how they had constructed the floor last year, he thought he understood. But now looking at it, "It's a wondrous piece of engineering, son. This whole cabin is a marvel. I just find it difficult to understanding taking the time to do all this, and it must have taken a lot of time, and to trap, hunt, fish, smoke-cure meat. I don't see how only two of you could have accomplished so much."

Monique answered Blayne, "We help each other, Dad."

"What smells so good?" Regina asked.

"I have two geese and an apple pie roasting. They should be done shortly."

Blayne was taken by how they had constructed the fireplace, using clay as a cement. "And you used the clay to fill in the cracks in the floor. I would have thought it would flake off."

"Well, there is no spring to the floor, so maybe that helps. I only know it works."

"Your goats look good. Have we time to see the barn before supper?"

"Just don't be long," Monique said.

"Where is the barn? I haven't seen it," Blayne said.

"It's over here, Dad. We dug out a hole in the bank and put it underground, so the goats and chickens will be protected from the cold."

"Ingenious, I must say. Your chickens look good too."

Blair showed his Dad the woodshed, workshop and root cellar.

"Mom, will you holler to the men supper is ready."

"Blayne, Blair! Supper is ready. Is this the cook stove you found in the other cabin?"

"Yes."

"I'm surprised it is in such good shape."

Everything was on the table and while Blair was carving the goose Monique was filling their plates.

"What is all this food Monique? I'm not familiar with some of it," Regina said.

"The tea is teaberry. This is cattail flower tops and stalks, this is raw pennycress."

"It all looks and smells so delicious."

After Blair had given everyone some meat Regina tasted the stuffing. "My, is this good. Try some Blayne. It has a completely new and different taste. What is it, Monique?"

"Bread crumbs, sorrel roots and tops, pennycress, a little bear fat, a little giblet gravy and ground hazelnuts."

"I would never have believed that concoction would taste so good, if I hadn't eaten it myself."

"The cattail tops actually taste like corn and the sorrel roots like potato," Blayne said. "Marvelous, simply marvelous, Monique, you are indeed a surprising cook."

"Thank you."

"And this stuffing flavors the goose so well," Regina said.

Blayne and Regina kept going on and on about how much they enjoyed their supper and how good a cook Monique was.

The mosquitos had been bad so Blair started the outside fire and put on some tansy weed to make it smoke.

"There, let's bring our chairs out and sit on the porch."

Blayne had assumed that Blair had made a smudge for insects the same way he had always done, until he realized there were absolutely no bugs at all flying round. "What was that green weed you put on to make a smudge? There are absolutely no bugs flying around."

Monique answered, "It is tansy and it is a natural bug repellant. My grandparents had been using it for as long as I can remember. You can also rub the green leaves on your skin and the bugs won't even fly around you."

"Boy, I'll have to remember that."

"I bet you have some growing on your farm. Grandmother and I use to get it along the river, about this time of year."

"I guess you're never too old to learn something new."

"What is that path I see across the river?"

"We put up a fish bait for bear. We have shot two so far there and Monique has shot two bobcats."

Monique said, "The first cat came on this side of the river when we were smoking fish. We saw its tracks all around here."

"That's when we decided to build a smoke house, to keep the animals out," Blair added.

"These chairs are very comfortable. I never knew you were this clever, Blair." Regina said.

"Out here, Mom, we pretty much have to make everything."

Blair and his Dad left the women on the porch talking and they went to put the goats in. It was almost dark and the chickens had already returned to their coop. Then they returned to the porch with Regina and Monique.

"I don't think you'll have to worry about the McQuale brothers any longer." He left it at that and waited.

Blair and Monique waited to see how much they knew. "Yeah, they have come up missing."

Blair and Monique's first thought was that the boys had drowned on the way back. Still they were silent.

"Some folks say that Bouchard kicked them out for good with the understanding they never could come back. There was something about a broken shotgun, too. The boys were seen at the stage depot one morning and I hear tell how they each had been hit with something across their nose and cut their cheeks. A lot of people are glad they aren't around anymore."

Still Blair and Monique kept silent. Not wanting to dredge up old memories. So they all sat there for a long time enjoying the warm evening and listening to the sounds of nature.

"Where are you two going to sleep?" Regina asked.

"We have set up a bed behind the cabin with a piece of canvas over us, in case it rains," Monique said.

"Well, I for one am ready for sleep," Regina said.

* * *

Monique and Blair were awake before the folks were and they tended to the chickens and the goats then they sat on the sandy shore, just the two of them talking like young lovers.

Blayne rolled over in bed and looked out the new larger window and said, "Regina look at this," and he pointed towards the river.

"They are still acting like teenage lovers. You know, Blayne, living out here has really been good for the both of them, and they are so much in love."

"I think this life out here where they have to depend on each other has brought them so close together," Blayne said.

Blair made a pot of coffee while Monique made breakfast of bear bacon, goose eggs, and hot bread. But she didn't tell Blayne and Regina what the bacon was.

"Wow, look at those eggs," Blayne said. The coffee poured, everyone sat down to eat.

Blayne tried the bacon and then took another bite, "This

is very good, and seasoned well, but I can't identify the meat."

"It's bear," Monique said. Regina looked skeptical at Blayne.

"Try it, you'll like it," and she did.

"Do you two always eat like this?" Blayne asked.

Blair and Monique looked at each other and they both said, "Yes."

After they had finished eating, Blair and his father poured another cup of coffee and went out on the porch.

Blair wanted to know all about the farm and the lumbering business. "People are moving in all the time and I have a difficult time keeping up with timber sales and the crops are completely sold. Everything is sold. Peter has to clear a couple of more acres to put into more potatoes and wheat. I expect next spring we will put some of the winter crews to work clearing more land."

"Peter has really changed. It took him time to understand and accept the fact that you were not coming back. Now he is shouldering more responsibility and is running the timber crews. He is doing a real good job. I'm proud of him."

"I'm glad he has a real interest in the business and can take over for you.

"What about Faye?"

"Right after you and Monique were home last May, she signed up for nursing training in Presque Isle. There is a new medical center being built in Madawaska and it will be completed this winter. Faye has been guaranteed a job once she finishes her training. I'm real proud of her. You know I'm proud of all four of you, Monique included."

Monique and Regina came out to join them. "It's a beautiful day isn't it," Regina said.

"It sure is in more ways than one."

"How would you like to go for a hike this morning; to our special place?" Blair knew what she was talking about.

"Blair would you get some smoked trout from the root cellar to take with us? I'll put up some bread."

It was a nice day for a walk. "We call this the honey log. Monique found honey bees using it," Blair said.

"Yeah, we both got stung pretty bad trying to get all the honey. We were able to get at most of it, but the bee stings were getting the best of us. When we got home we put some of the savvy clay on the stings and the swelling reduced and the pain was gone," Monique said.

"It was an awful ordeal and I'm not sure if I'd want to do it again or not. Maybe if we were dressed properly."

"I use honey in the apple pie for a sweetener."

"I thought I could taste honey, but I wasn't sure," Regina said.

"A wolverine actually finished ripping this apart and later we baited it with some honeycomb and caught it."

They continued on to the top of the ledge lookout. There was a nice westerly cooling breeze. Regina inhaled deeply and said, "The air smells so good here."

"Yes, we like the smell and we come up here sometimes to watch the sunset."

They ate their lunch of smoked fish and bread and talked in between mouthfuls. Blayne and Regina wanted to know everything about their life here in the big woods. And at times Blayne seemed to be a bit envious of his son's lifestyle.

"We need to be leaving so I can start preparing our supper. Don't ask, because I want it to be a surprise," Monique said.

On their way back Monique picked a lot of wood sorrel. But what surprised Regina was that she was taking roots and all. "Try some of the tops Mom. They are very good," and she ate some.

Regina didn't want to disappoint her so she tried some. "It has a tangy, lemony flavor. And probably good for your digestive system."

Back at the cabin Blair restarted the fire in the cook stove and put a pot of coffee on to boil.

"Do you have any more of that smoked fish? I'd like some more and bread with my coffee. That hike made me hungry."

"Certainly," and Blair went out to the root cellar and brought back several smoked fish for them all.

When the coffee was ready they went out on the porch to eat lunch. "This evening, Dad, I'll take you fishing so we'll have fresh trout with eggs in the morning."

When they had finished eating Regina said, "You hiking in the fresh air—well I could use a nap. What about you, Blayne?"

"No. I'm alright."

"Would you like to go for a walk out back, Dad?" Blair asked.

"Yes, I would."

"While you take a nap, Mom, I'll start fixing supper. I'll be quiet."

Blayne spotted Blair's huge wheelbarrow behind the woodshed, "So this is what you wanted the iron wheels for. How does it work with two wheels instead of one?"

"It's more stable, of course I take a big load of wood. But it saves a lot of trips back and forth."

"I see you already have some wood worked up."

"Yes, most of that is from the clearing by the river. I have another two cord piled up in the woods, too."

Blayne wanted to ask Blair about the McQuale brothers. But he respected him enough so he didn't intrude. For whatever reason he and Monique didn't want to talk about it. But he also thought there was more to the story.

"These are nice cedar trees, tall, straight and the grain doesn't twist."

They circled around to the left and in an open meadow they saw a huge bull moose with his antlers in velvet. "We haven't seen many moose around. More caribou. Which is alright. I like caribou meat better than moose."

They found a huge stand of rock maple trees and this gave Blair an idea for a spring project. Tap some of these trees and make some syrup and sugar. They would need to get some buckets.

It was the middle of the afternoon when they had circled back to the cabin. Monique and Regina were on the porch. "Did you two have a nice walk?" Regina asked.

"Saw some awful pretty timber. I'd like to have me a sawmill set up here. Only there's no way of getting anything out of here except by canoe. Someday, someone will figure out a way."

"After supper, Dad, we'll catch a few brook trout for breakfast tomorrow."

"Would you two like some fresh coffee?" Monique asked.

While they sipped their coffee Blair said to Monique," I have me an idea that I like."

"What's that?"

"Next spring we could tap a few maple trees and make maple syrup and maple sugar. That way we won't have to fight with the honeybees again. All we need is a pan to boil the sap in and a few buckets. I can make the hollow taps from willow bushes. Just hollow out the pithy centers."

"Sounds good to me," Monique said.

"How's supper coming?" Blair asked.

"It's almost ready," and she went inside to check on the soup.

Monique cut up a few cattail stalks to eat raw along with the soup and she sliced the four tomatoes that Blair had picked the other day. By the time the bread was sliced the soup was ready. She filled the four bowls and set them on the table. "Supper is ready. This is wilderness soup, except for a few potatoes. Not many though."

"It is delicious," Regina said, "but I can't place the ingredients. I can taste potato and corn, but that's it."

"Dad?" Monique asked.

"I haven't a clue. It is delicious though."

"Well there is sorrel roots which taste similar to potato, cattail flowers which taste a little like corn, onions, chopped cattail stalks and beaver tail."

"Beaver tail? I would never in all my life assume a beaver tail would be any good to eat. But this certainly is. Son, if you don't keep busy living out here, you're going to get fat."

"Did you learn to cook like this, Monique, from your grandmother?" Regina asked.

"Mostly, yes."

"Then it's no wonder the wood crews all liked her cooking."

"I think we should be leaving in the morning. By the time we get home, we'll have been gone a week. I told Peter we wouldn't be over a week. And I'm a little anxious to get back. This is the first time Peter has been alone on the farm."

"Well, we'll send you off with a basket of food."

"Now, son, how about those brook trout." All they had for a fish pole was an alder branch with a line tied to the end. But when the fishing is good, you really don't need much more. And Blayne was having the time of his life. He would never have guessed that fishing would be so good almost in front of the cabin. He caught enough for breakfast and they cleaned them there at the river and put some green grass in with the trout to keep them fresh until morning and then Blair put them in the root cellar.

Monique had put up a jar of caribou meat, some smoked fish, some goose eggs, some cattail stalks, two ripe tomatoes and some bread dough for stick bread. She put everything in one of the baskets she had made.

The lightning bugs came out as the sun was disappearing and so too were the mosquitos. Blair and Blayne made a smudge with tansy and then went back on the porch. There was only a slight breeze which helped to keep the bugs away. The sky was clear and the stars were shining so bright it was almost as if you could reach up and touch them.

"You two certainly have a good life here." Then he added, "When will you come out again?"

"It'll probably be early in September. We want to get an earlier start to trapping this year."

The smudge fire had burned out and everyone was ready for sleep.

* * *

"I don't know when I have eaten sweeter tasting brook trout. I don't know how or why, but Blair and Monique you somehow have found your garden of Eden. Everything—practically, that you need is here. You are very fortunate."

"That Dad—" Monique said. "Blair and I have often thought and talked about the same thing. And that's why I know we are where we are suppose to be."

They ate in silence for a while; enjoying the goose eggs with the trout. "I like your curtains Monique. They dress up your home," Regina said.

They all had another cup of coffee on the porch. "In a way I hate to leave, but I know it is time for us to go home. Peter might be needing my help," Blayne said and emptied his coffee cup.

Regina finished hers also and took them inside. Monique went in also. "Don't worry about clearing up, Mom. I'll do that."

Regina hugged Monique and her eyes were filled with tears. "I'm just so happy for you, Monique and Blair." Monique hugged her back.

"I'm happy to be part of your family."

Even though Blayne and Regina had enjoyed their visit, they, like Blair and Monique, knew when it was time to leave and they were looking forward to returning to their home.

"Dad, don't try to do the trip in one day like we can do it. We have the advantage with the larger canoe and double ended paddles. Plus the current isn't as swift right now."

"We'll be careful and plan to camp out on the St. John River tonight."

They pushed off from shore and Blair and Monique stood on the shore watching until they had disappeared. "I guess I'd better tend to the kids and chickens," Blair said.

* * *

Both Blair and Monique were extremely happy to see their folks. There was as strong of a bond between Blayne, Regina and Monique, as there was between Blair and his Mom and Dad. And they were also happy to be by themselves again.

Blair went to work installing the window he had removed from the front wall, to the side wall by the kitchen counter. This way Monique would have more light.

Monique went after edible herbs every day that weather allowed. She canned what she could. When the garden was ready to harvest she canned everything except for one meal of green beans. The potatoes, squash and cabbage of course would keep in the root cellar.

She began venturing further from home and this didn't bother Blair. By now he understood that Monique had as good an understanding of the wilderness and as capable as he. But he still insisted that she take her .45, matches and compass.

When the window was finished, he worked on winter firewood. The shed was now full of wood he had cut and piled last year and now he was working on next year's supply. Plus making sure they had enough dry cedar kindling.

September seemed to come early. Maybe because the two had been so busy preparing for winter. Blair had finally remembered to install the padlocks and he hung one key next to the fireplace and he hid one outside on a nail on the backside of a spruce tree away from the cabin. "Why so far away Blair?"

"If by chance someone should come when we're not here they probably wouldn't think to look for a key so far away."

"Good thinking."

There had been several days off and on of rain and the river was flowing good and they decided now to take their trip out to the farm and purchase the last of their supplies for the winter. They brought the two empty one gallon kerosene cans to fill, potatoes, eggs, onion, flour, salt, sugar, mason jars and everything they would need. The big canoe even still would be loaded light. Blair even bought a sack of hen feed, just in case.

They stayed at the farm an extra day. Monique was picking apples and Blair helped with the wheat. The day when Blair and Peter were off by themselves Blair said, "Peter, I'm happy to see how you have taken to the business here. You're a natural and you'll do fine. And I'm proud of you, Peter, for taking on so much responsibility."

"Thank you, Blair. I really like the farm and almost as much as you did in the winter running the timber crews. I'm staying on the farm."

And this trip they both remembered to get plenty of reading material. All while they were out, no one mentioned the McQuale brothers and Blair and Monique had forgotten about them.

As light as they were loaded the trip back was a fast one. They had seen enough of the settlements and town life and were happy to be back in the wilderness. They had left extra feed and water for the goats and chickens and now that they were almost home, they began wondering if the kids and chickens had been okay.

The kids heard them pull the canoe ashore and started a steady chorus of bleating. And this disturbed the chickens. He let the goats run free, for a little, he knew as long as he and Monique were around the kids wouldn't run off. The chickens seemed glad to get out also, as they went right to digging and scratching for bugs or anything edible.

* * *

The only herbs left to gather were mushrooms and onion grass. Blair had the hay cut with the scythe from the two acre field and stored under canvas. Monique had caught and smoke cured all the fish they would need and one day a bear arrived across the river where the bear bait was usually hung. Monique saw the bear and decided to shoot it before it ran off. This was a bigger bear and the sides of bacon were bigger. And most of the meat was smoked and hung up in the root cellar. Monique wanted to save the mason jars for caribou meat.

With all other chores now taken care of before cold weather set in, Blair decided to start trapping. From what he had seen last year the guard hairs had filled in before they had started trapping.

They made a makeshift lean-to and stayed out the first night. They had four super large beaver that first day. The next day at a different colony they had four more. The third day they stayed home and finished skinning and stretching.

If they found a natural covey near one of the dams they would set a trap for a land animal.

By the time the river iced over they had thirty beaver, four otter, four mink, twenty pine martin, four bobcats, four lynx, and six fisher. They could have kept trapping but, they had what they would need and neither one of them wanted to over trap the area when there was no need to.

A heavy snowstorm blew in the third week of November and the river had not frozen over yet. Then a week later a cold front came down from the north and artic cold settled over the Little Black River.

By the first week of December the river had frozen solid. And on cue, the group of caribou were moving upstream to their winter range. And for a week they worked on canning and smoking the meat.

The chickens by now had their adult brown feathers, but were not yet laying eggs. The goats were still being staked out, only to feed so they would not freeze, so he would not have to use the harvested hay yet.

That winter, like their first winter, was snowy and stormy, and like the previous year the snow was dry and fluffy.

Much of his time in that winter of 1868 he worked on making a cedar chest for Monique and a stand-tall cabinet for her dishes. She was complaining about running out of room, so he began planning to build an addition for their bedroom.

The floor was constructed in the same manner and a window in each wall. These windows were double hung so they could be opened and with an outside screen.

Another year Monique asked. "Blair, I would like a sink in the kitchen. Is that possible?"

"Not only that, but I've been thinking about installing a hand pump so we no longer have to haul water from the spring brook."

Feeding the chickens wild carcasses, the chickens were actually producing more eggs than they could eat. So in the fall some of the old eggs, that had a harsh smell were used for trapping bait. Because it was a new smell in the woods they actually worked very well.

They were still milking the goats, while old billy was killed and eaten by a family of bobcats one spring. The two milking goats provided all the milk and cream they could use. Turning much of that into butter and cheese.

They were making maple syrup and candy and sugar now and no longer did they worry about the honeybees.

About every other year they would trap a huge male wolverine. The price of all furs went up a little each year and the Kelley's were making $2500.00 a year now from their fur pelts. Each year they bought the necessary supplies for home and banked the remaining.

Blair, with Monique's help, measured off forty-three acres, which included the ledge hill with the view. They drove steel pipes in the four corners and with his compass, he and Monique cleared their property lines and scarfed the trees.

When they went to the land office Mr. Abbott was quite impressed with how much they had accomplished. They were given a deed to the property and it was filed properly in the registry of deeds.

"Now nobody can ever take away our home. We own it legally and everything is registered. I think maybe we should buy a couple of bottles of wine to take back with us to celebrate."

"That sounds like a good idea."

Blayne and Regina were getting older and Peter and his wife Angela were now living in the farmhouse and had taken over most of the responsibilities for the business.

Faye was also married and working as a nurse in Madawaska.

* * *

Five more years had passed, Blair was now thirty-four years old and Monique was twenty-nine. Their love for each other never settled at a flateau and then with waning years disappear, their love for each other grew stronger and more adoring. They were seldom apart and Monique still enjoyed showing off her beautiful body in attractive and enticing ways.

There was more than enough hay from the two acre field for the goats, so each year they made their garden a little bigger. They no longer had to bring back vegetables from town. What they couldn't grow in the garden, Monique would substitute with wild herbs.

The old cook stove they had found in the abandoned cabin ten years ago finally had to be replaced with a new one. Blair and Monique had worked together to disassemble the new one so they would know how to put it back together. They had made a special trip out just for the stove and transported it back in the canoe. They were several days putting it back together. Just when they thought parts were in the right place, they would have to unbolt it and reposition it. But they succeeded. This new stove had a wider cooking surface and there was an oven thermometer on the door. The fire box was larger and often times, even in the winter this would be all the heat they would need.

The Canadian geese kept nesting each year in the marsh in the oxbows and with their own eggs they only took a couple of geese each year to stuff and roast.

Some of Monique's apple cores that she had thrown out had taken root and now each year they had a few of their own apples.

In the spring 1880 they had decided to make a spring trip out to visit family. There was no hurry so they waited until the third week in May. The water level had dropped, but there was still a good current. There was no rush to get to the farm, but Blair and Monique were still young and feeling good and they arrived at the farm before supper. Actually it had been about twelve hours of paddling.

Tragedy happened as Blayne and Regina excitedly came running across the yard toward them when Blayne collapsed to the ground from a massive heart attack. He had actually died before he fell.

Blayne's passing sent a terrible shock through the entire family. A telegram was sent to Faye and her husband in Madawaska and they hired a special coach to take them to the Kelley farm that night.

Because of Blair and Monique's need to return to their home the funeral was held at the Kelley farmhouse two days later. Peter was so torn up about his father's passing Blair and Monique had to do most of the chores and dig the grave alongside Rose, Monique's grandmother.

Regina welcomed her children home, but she, like Peter, was beside herself with grief and loneliness. Blayne had always been her rock that she could lean against for support. He had never raised his voice to her or their children.

Blair and Monique had to say their good-byes and leave. As much as they both would have wanted to stay a couple of days longer, it wasn't possible.

"We won't be out again, Peter, until next spring," Blair said.

"I was surprised to see you and Monique this spring. You have only been coming in late summer for the last few years," Peter said.

On their way upstream on the Little Black River Monique said, "I really feel bad for Mom, Blair. But at least she has Peter and his family there to help her."

* * *

Changes were coming fast. That year in 1880 the state legislature had formed a new department called Game Warden Service, to prevent the over harvest of the state's wildlife. One of the first changes was to stop the commercial hunting of moose and deer.

That didn't really affect Blair and Monique, but they both could see changes coming. While they were at the farm they had heard rumors that in the near future timber companies would start driving logs down the St. John River to sawmills downstream. But no one seemed to know when the log drives would start.

On October 1st that fall Regina also passed away. She had never been able to get over the anguish of losing Blayne. Dr. O'Neil said, "She simply died of a broken heart. I could find nothing physically wrong with her." It wouldn't be until months later before Blair and Monique would know of their Mom's passing.

As they laid in bed that first night home Blair said, "You know, Hon, as much as I'll miss Dad, I'm glad he went fast like that."

"I don't think he was ever aware he was dying. It came on him so suddenly. I will miss him also, my husband."

That fall was extremely cold and Blair and Monique

got an early start to trapping. Apparently the animals were all expecting an early and cold winter because everything was coming easily to the bait in the trap sets and the beaver had the most fat on them that Blair had ever seen. Even the bear they shot in September had two inches of fat on his back. His sides made for some excellent bacon.

The animals were coming so easily to their sets, they were afraid of over trapping. So they pulled their land sets and already they had more pieces than in any other year. They did take a few more beaver, and they pulled the last sets before the river froze over solid.

To keep himself busy during the cold winters, Blair made furniture for the cabin and he whittled out wooden spoons for Monique. Monique learned to knit and she made sweaters, hats, mittens, and scarves. Their bedroom was now completely covered with bear rugs and a caribou rug in front of the fireplace and one in front of the large window.

He already had enough firewood worked up and piled in the woods to last for two more winters. But some days he just needed something physical to do. Besides there was little snow all winter.

* * *

Five more years had passed since the passing of Blayne and Regina and to both Blair and Monique their now yearly visits to the Kelley farm did not seem to them to be as warm and loving. They felt like they were an intrusion in the lives of Peter and his family.

On one trip they had decided to stay in town at the popular hotel after selling their furs. "Blair, there is actually running water in the bathroom and a tub and you can actually go to the bathroom and flush it away. No outhouses or commodes."

"What will they think of next?" Blair said in total disbelief.

"I don't know about you, but I'm going to take a hot bath."

"Is that tub big enough for us both?"

"I don't see why not."

Later they found the fanciest restaurant in town and enjoyed a beefsteak dinner. Afterwards they deposited that years fur trapping money in the bank. After nineteen years of living and trapping in the wilderness they now had $24,543.10 in their account. In any circle of people in the town of Fort Kent they would be considered well off. But for Monique and Blair their simple, happy lifestyle was more important to them than how much money they had.

The rumors Blair had heard five years earlier of timber companies using the rivers to drive their logs to markets apparently were just that. Rumors. Blair had seen no evidence of log drives on the rivers. Although, he knew the day would come. *The forests are thick with valuable spruce and pine trees.*

At home on the Little Black River when they didn't have anything else to do, they would spend a lot of time at their special place on the ledges overlooking the river. And on many occasions they would make love there and lay nude on the thick moss, in the sunshine.

Neither one of them ever forgot that there was some special entity that was watching out over them. They could feel the touch of each other's skin. "Perhaps, sweetheart, this is to even out the debt or the ugliness I experienced in war and for you, to make up for your hard life."

"I have been sure of this, my love, for a long time now. I think that as long as we do not over trap and take too many animals, that this entity will continue to watch over us."

* * *

Another five years had passed and one day in September Blair said, "What would you think, Monique, if we only trapped for beaver. We use the meat and tail for food, where the other animal carcasses are thrown away. I mean we now have more than $30,000.00 in our account. It isn't like we need the money. If we see predator tracks around home then *yes*, we set traps."

In the early mornings as daylight was beginning to make an appearance and then again just before dark, deer would come to the green two acre field to feed. Now instead of caribou meat they would shoot two stag deer each fall. The caribou herd was shrinking. Though each year they still migrated upstream and joined up with other herds in the winter range, but there were noticeably fewer animals. The caribou were moving out and the deer were moving in.

Blair kept the two acre field like a golf course. Each spring he would fill in ruts and holes and he pulled new seedling trees and bushes out by the roots.

The old Nanny goat had seen her best years and they brought back another young Billy to breed with the young Nanny. Mice were becoming a problem so on this same trip when they stopped at the farm Peter was happy to get rid of two cats. There were at last count twenty cats on the farm. These two were tiger gray males and small enough so Monique carried them both on the inside of her shirt.

They became very interested with the chickens but soon learned they were off limits. From an early age they began catching mice and Monique never saw another mouse inside the cabin.

By 1895 they had a virtual heaven there on the Little Black River in the wilderness of T18-R11, and the only residents in that township.

That year Blair and Monique trapped twenty beaver and two foxes and a bobcat that were after the chickens. They sold the fur pelts for more money than the total of sixty pieces of fur in 1867. The fur trade and market had changed that much.

Through the years they had bought so many books Blair had to build a bookcase to keep them in.

There were rumors circulating around town again about log drives on the St. John River. When they stopped at the farm on their way back, Peter told them that the Bangor and Aroostook Railroad would be coming to Fort Kent from Ashland and a spur line to St. Francis and the railroad was coming across the farm near the river. "This will be a great opportunity to ship more potatoes and sawn lumber. I'll be able to reach markets to the south now. It has already put many people to work surveying the right of way.

"I have already started clearing more of the brush land to put into potatoes and I'm making plans to start buying logs."

"This all sounds good for you, Peter. I'm happy for you."

While in town that year they ordered a new canoe, to be built during the winter. "How long do you want this, Mr. Kelley?" Sirway asked.

"Twenty-four feet long, five feet wide at mid-section and seats bow and stern."

"I could have this done for you in two months."

"But we won't be back in town until next year."

"I'll have to have $50.00 down payment."

"Certainly," Blair replied.

The old canoe was showing too much wear and Blair didn't want to have to use the shorter canoe on the big river.

* * *

The next year when they started the trip to town Monique said, "We are getting the new canoe just in time. This old girl is beginning to leak." Nothing serious, but water was seeping through some of the old cedar slats.

Before leaving town Blair picked up the day's newspaper and as many back issues as were available. On the front page of the current issue were headlines of the B&A Railroad being built north of Oakfield and that the right of way had already been cleared as far north as Soldier Pond and expected to have it all cleared to Fort Kent by year's end.

"The railroad will surely be good for people living at the top of the state. Transportation to the south from here, and farmers will be able to get their wheat and potatoes to the Boston and New York markets. Sawmills will start operating full time, not just during the winter. It'll put people to work in the woods supplying timber to the mills. And some day the timber crews will be cutting next to our land."

"I hope I'm not around when they do," Monique said. "It would destroy our way of life."

"I hear ya there, sweetheart," Blair replied.

They stayed an extra day in town in that spring of 1896. "Blair, we need new clothes and boots," Monique said. "I'm not mending our old clothes anymore."

"Okay," was all he said. Their list of supplies seemed to be less with each passing year.

Blair was surprised how easy this new canoe went over the water. It was somewhat heavier and he had naturally assumed it would be slower.

The deer that came out to feed in the field were growing less and less skittish of Monique and Blair and often times they would come to feed during the day or lay down on the edge of the field. At one time Monique had counted twenty deer in the early morning. Later in the season when they would shoot a deer apiece, it would always be a buck.

They had made several trips downstream out to town and Blair discovered he liked how well this canoe handled compared to the one he and his father had made.

In the spring of 1900 when they reached the mouth of the river where it joined with the Allagash and the St. John River there were spruce saw logs in the river. The current was swift and they had to be careful not to collide with one. At times it seemed like a slalom course, trying to dodge the logs.

When they canoed passed St. Francis there was even more wood in the river. They were okay here as long as they stayed to the right and close to shore. Their progress had been slower and that first night they stayed at the farm with Peter and his family.

Peter told them, "The B&A Railroad have started to lay tracks from town to St. Francis and they are building a stationhouse in town now, a turntable and rail yard. Supposedly in 1902, in two years, the tracks from Ashland to Fort Kent will be completed. People all around are excited about it. Just think, we'll be able to travel from Fort Kent to Bangor in one day instead of a week by coach."

"Yes, it'll surely help people around here, providing jobs."

Through the years Peter and Blair had sort of grown apart. They were not as close as they had been. Perhaps because there was so much more responsibility now with year round crews and farming more acreage. But both were pleasant.

On the way back there was even more wood in the river and Blair had to depend more on Monique to steer clear of the wood. By the time they were home they were exhausted and for two days they just sat on the porch and watched the goats. Blair was fifty eight and could still do the work of four men. Monique was fifty-three and she was still as slender, fine-skinned and as beautiful as ever. They each had streaks of graying hair, but to look at either one of them, it would be difficult to judge their true age.

That fall after beaver trapping and the river had frozen solid, the caribou never passed through. One morning after breakfast Blair said, "Do you want to go for a hike today?"

"Sure, where and why?"

"The caribou didn't go by here this year. I'd like to hike up above the oxbows and see if there is any sign of them up there."

Blair took his pack basket with food and a pot to heat up water for some t-berry tea.

Just above the oxbows where another group of caribou would come down the stream to join the one on the river and continue north, there were no sign or tracks there, either. They continued on to where the caribou would leave the river to the left for their winter range and again there were no tracks or sign that they had been there.

"What do you suppose, Blair? We never shot that many."

"No and we have never heard any gunfire at all, so they were not hunted off. The only thing I can think of is the forest, their habitat has changed enough to make them leave. Look how wide their antlers are and look how thick the woods are. They would need open marshland or tundra I think, than thick forest."

"Well, we have the deer now, which supports our needs even better."

"I know what you are saying, Monique, but it also is a sign that things are changing. To me it's a drastic change. But I agree with you, I'd rather have the deer."

They made a fire and boiled some tea and warmed up their lunch.

* * *

The following year and thereafter they waited until the middle of June before making their trip to town. Even then there was some wood in the river, but not as much.

When they canoed out in June of 1902 they saw the B&A train just leaving St. Francis for Fort Kent. A siding had been made at the farm for empty flat cars so Peter's crews could load them with sawn lumber. He had a good market in Boston now.

The McQuale sawmill closed its doors. Bouchard had refused to make changes and soon after, he died. No one ever heard from the three brothers again.

Before leaving town for home they stopped at the butcher shop and bought two sides of pork bacon and two ham legs, all maple-smoke cured. The butcher wrapped them in butcher cloth to keep the air and bugs out. Monique carried the two sides of bacon and Blair the two legs. They had all the canned bear meat they would need and very little bear bacon left. "This ham will be a good treat," Monique said.

When they came out in 1906 they bought two more sides of pork bacon and ham legs.

Some of the hens were too old to lay more eggs and occasionally Blair would kill one and Monique would roast it with stuffing and gravy.

That fall on their first run upstream to the oxbows to trap beaver at the second flowage, Monique slipped while walking across the top of the dam. Her mid-section landed on the dam so she didn't get too wet. Her ribs and right arm were bruised, but nothing was broken.

"What happened, sweetheart?"

"I don't know, all of a sudden I got dizzy and slipped."

"Are you alright?"

"I think so, I wrenched my right arm and bruised my right side."

"Are you going to be okay?"

"Yes, yes, but I think I'll go ashore and sit down," Monique said.

After he had finished setting the trap he went to see how Monique was. She was looking pale, but other than that she was looking fine. "How are you now?"

"I think I'd better go back home. I feel kinda jittery on the inside."

"Yeah, I agree." The trap just snapped. "I'll bring in this beaver and then we head back. We pick up the other traps too."

Blair didn't bother to skin the beaver. He put it and the traps in the canoe and helped Monique get in. "Let me do the paddling."

At the next flowage they had another beaver and he put that in the canoe and pulled both traps. Monique stayed in the canoe.

Blair was really worried about Monique and he kept asking her if she was okay. "Yes, I'll be okay, Blair. I think I need to lay down for a while."

He paddled for home as quick as he could. Not wanting for Monique to step out and pull the canoe up on shore, Blair got out in the water and pulled it up and helped Monique to get out. He held his arm around her as they walked up to the cabin, and lifted her up over the steps.

Once inside he helped her out of her heavy clothes and boots and she lay down on the bed and pulled a blanket up around her. Their two cats, Mike and Fred, jumped up and lay down with her.

Blair started the fire in the fireplace and put water on to heat on the stovetop.

"Are you going to be okay, Monique? I need to take care of things."

"I'll be fine."

He skun the two beaver as quick as he could. And being in a hurry he cut two holes through each hide. He cut the legs off and left them in a pan on the shelf in the root cellar for now.

Then he put the goats and chickens in and gave them some water.

When he went in to check on Monique. She was asleep.

He fried up some fresh beaver meat with fried potato and green beans. He kept checking on Monique and she was still sleeping. He finally decided if she was sleeping this soundly then she must need it. So he let her sleep and he ate supper.

Afterwards he checked in on her again and she seemed fine, just asleep. He sat in the other room reading a back-issue newspaper.

It was dark out and he was getting sleepy.

Monique hadn't moved since she lay down. Very gently he pulled the blanket back and removed her clothes and managed to get her under the covers without waking her.

He felt of her forehead and she wasn't hot, her skin wasn't clammy. He snuggled up close to her and put his arm around her and remained like that all night.

At daylight, rain and wind woke him. When he moved, Monique woke up and turned over and held onto Blair. "You had me scared yesterday, sweetheart. How do you feel now?" He was still concerned but tried not to show it.

"Is this tomorrow?" she asked.

He laughed and understanding what she wanted to know he said, "Yes, this is tomorrow. You have been asleep for fourteen hours."

"Wow, I feel good now. Maybe all I needed was sleep."

When she started to get out of bed Blair tried to help her. "I'm fine, Blair. I can get out of bed on my own."

He stepped back and watched. She rolled out of bed like she did every morning and dressed. "I am hungry, though."

"I'll start the stove," Blair said.

"Are we going out to trap beaver today?"

"I don't think so. We don't need the money and I want to be sure about you before we go anywhere."

So he busied himself between the cabin, the goats and chickens and stretching the two beaver hides with holes in them. The two cats wouldn't leave her side.

For the next two weeks she was okay. Blair watched her closely for anymore dizzy spells. Then one morning while she was cleaning the kitchen after breakfast she felt the jitters or whatever it was that was making her feel unsettled. But not dizziness this time, whatever it was passed in a half hour and she decided not to say anything to Blair about it. But it was on her mind constantly. She was also afraid that Blair would become so concerned and worried, he would insist they go out to a doctor or hospital. If they went out now, they would not get back before freeze-up.

She started slowing down and pacing herself to see if being too active had anything to do about these awful feelings of trepidation. These feelings were nothing like she had ever experienced before. Her nervous system seemed to be short circuiting from her head to her feet.

She was doing well hiding these minor attacks from Blair until the end of November. And this time it was bothering her walking and she fell. Blair picked her up and lay her on the bed.

"What's going on, Monique? Why did you fall?"

"I don't know, Blair. All of a sudden my legs felt like rubber."

"Can you feel anything touching your legs?" and Blair started touching her legs all over.

"I can feel all that."

"Does anything hurt?"

"I don't feel any pain anywhere. Maybe something pinched a nerve."

"Maybe, I don't know, but I think I need to get you to a hospital."

"No, Blair, please no," she was almost in tears.

"What is it sweetheart? Is there something you aren't telling me?"

"Just I feel if I go to a hospital I'll never come out. People go there to die and I don't want to die there. If I'm not better come spring then I'll go."

She'd lain in bed for what seemed like hours and she was tired of laying on her back. She eased out of bed on wobbly legs, she walked out and sat in her rocking chair near the fireplace. Blair came in and was surprised to see her.

She saw the questioning look on his face and said, "I couldn't stand lying down anymore. My legs were wobbly, but I made it this far," trying to be cheery.

But she was so unsteady. Neither one of them had been sick a day since they started upon this wilderness living forty-one years ago. She felt like her whole nervous system was trying to respond at the same time. She was shaking on the inside and once in a while she noticed her hands trembling. She was scared—because she didn't know what was happening to her.

Blair waited on her hand and foot. He made a cane to help

her keep her balance when she walked. He was no longer aware of anything outside of the cabin walls, except for tending the goats and chickens and carrying in firewood. His whole world was Monique and he would do everything he could to help her. He was doing all of the cooking and cleaning. He dressed and undressed her, he bathed her and sometimes when her hands were too shaky, he fed her. Every morning and every night he brushed her hair.

They would sit by the fireplace and he would read from their books for her. For her sake he tried not to show his sadness when he was around her, but on his inside he was crumbing also. He wanted to sit down and cry. Their whole world was crumbling down around them.

About February of 1907 she began repeating herself a lot. There would be one subject each day that she would repeat over and over all day. Then the next day it would be something else. And Blair never lost his patience with her.

He wasn't sure now if she would live long enough for him to get her to a hospital in the spring after ice out. Monique also knew she was declining and although she hadn't said anything to Blair yet, she knew she would never see another canoe trip down the river. She knew she was dying and there was no place she'd rather be at the end than in her own home.

The whole month of March was unusually warm and no wind. On bright sunny days Blair would carry her out on the porch and set her in her rocking chair. She responded to the touch of warm sunshine on her face and she would smile. There was even times when she could carry on a conversation with Blair. He'd wrap a blanket around her so she could stay on the porch as long as she could without getting cold. For Monique, this time on the porch was a glorious time. When they weren't talking, she was reliving her thoughts of their life together. A life with some entity that had always been watching over them.

By April the snow was gone but there was still ice in the river. Monique wasn't sure if Blair understood she was failing, but she knew. She wasn't eating solid food any longer. Blair would make a broth and feed her a spoonful at a time.

Even though the days were warm, the ice had frozen so thick because of the extreme cold that winter, that the river was not clear of ice until the first week of May. The two acre field was turning green, the sweet smell of Balm of Gilead was in the air. The night after the ice had cleared while they were laying together in bed Monique said, "Do not bury me in the ground, Blair. Take me to our special place and leave me sitting up against the tree. I have taken a lot from this land. Let the animals take nourishment from this body as my gift back to them."

"I will, sweetheart. And when it is my time I will join you there on the ledge knoll."

"I have always loved you so much, my husband."

* * *

Monique's body died during the night and Blair was not aware of this until morning when he put his arm around her to hold her close.

He stayed there holding her in his arms for a long time. He knew what he had to do. He finally got up, dressed and then dressed Monique in one of her spring flowery dresses, washed her face and brushed her hair.

Then he set her in her chair on the porch and opened the gate and the barn door to turn the goats and chickens loose.

He came back and picked Monique up in his arms, to fulfill Monique's last request. All along the way he talked constantly to her. Even laughing as they passed the old honey log. He was now sixty-five and Monique, sixty. Although he was still as strong and tough as a bull, he began tiring on the hike up to the top. His breathing was raspy and shallow and he could feel a pain in his chest. But then again there had been a pain there all winter. Pain of a broken, lonesome heart. But this time it was more. And the truth be known, he didn't care. In fact he started climbing faster, making sure to get to the top before the big one came.

Finally he was at the top and the pain in his chest was excruciating. But he stood tall and straight and holding Monique lovingly in his arms he turned so they could see the view and smell the sweet scent.

He couldn't stand anymore; he sat down with his back leaning against the tree with Monique still in his arms.

When the big one did happen, Blair was never aware of it. He had already joined Monique and they were traveling in another world.

Epilogue

When John finished talking there were tears of sadness in his eyes. Even Dr. Morneau had to blow his nose and wipe the tears from his eyes. Ann was silently crying.

"That was some story, John. I don't think I have ever heard of anyone experiencing a past life with so much detail. You said earlier, John, that you have very clear memories of this past life, are there other things you remember when you said you seem to be far away?"

"I don't understand; what story are you talking about?"

"The story you just told us of your past life with Monique?"

John went very quiet then. He pulled back staring straight and not moving his eyes. "There, Dr. Morneau, this is the blank stare I was speaking of. He is somewhere else now."

"John," Dr. Morneau said, "John, John." He took John's hand in his and squeezed his hand slightly. John squeezed back. "John, are you back here with us again?"

John smiled and said, "Hi." That's all.

"John, do you recognize this woman beside you?"

John turned and looked squarely at Ann. "Yes, I recognize her."

"Who is she John?"

There was a moment of hesitation and Ann took his hand in hers and squeezed like Dr. Morneau had done and John squeezed her hand.

John smiled at Ann and said, "Yes, you are my wife."

"What's my name?" Ann asked.

This seemed to confuse John and the blank stare started to come back when Ann squeezed his hand again. John smiled at her.

"Ann," Dr. Morneau said," there is no doubt in my mind he has advanced Alzheimer's disease. But John's ability to see so clearly a past life is truly amazing. I can give him a prescription for Alzheimer's which will, for a time, help him to be more cognitive, but that will only help for a short time. One will be for a patch, that'll give him a continuous small dose all day. And another that he is to take every morning.

"My recommendation is a nursing home."

Ann was crying now and shaking her head no. "No, Ed. I can't do that. You heard him tell us about taking care of Monique to the end. Ed—the sweet scent on the ledge knoll was Balm of Gilead, the tree was spruce, the moss was six inches deep. I remember that smell, Ed, I don't see that past life as clearly as John does—but I do remember the smell of Balm of Gilead, how every spring the air would be filled with the sweet smell. I remember the cabin, the goats, the two cats, Mike and Fred. Ed, I was Monique. I'm as sure of that as I am sure I am in your office."

"No, Ed. I will not put John in a nursing home. He took care of me when I was Monique—I will take care of him now." She squeezed John's hand again and this brought another smile to his face.

"Let's go home, John."

The End

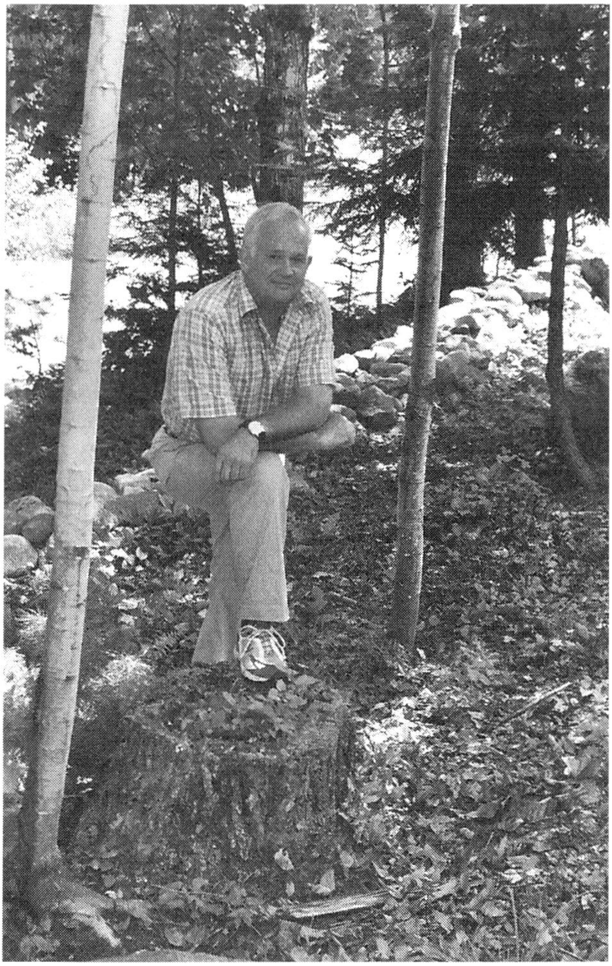

About the Author

Randall Probert lived and was raised in Strong, a small town in the western mountains of Maine. Six months after graduating from high school, he left the small town behind for Baltimore, Maryland, and a Marine Engineering school, situated downtown near what was then called "The Block". Because of bad weather, the flight from Portland to New York was canceled and this made him late for the connecting flight to Baltimore. A young kid, alone, from the backwoods of Maine, finally found his way to Washington, D.C., and boarded a bus from there to Baltimore. After leaving the Merchant Marines, he went to an aviation school in Lexington, Massachusetts.

During his interview for Maine Game Warden, he was asked, "You have gone from the high seas to the air. . .are you sure you want to be a game warden?"

Mr. Probert retired from Warden Service in 1997 and started writing historical novels about the history in the areas where he patrolled as a game warden, with his own experiences as a game warden as those of the wardens in his books. Mr. Probert has since expanded his purview and has written two science fiction books, *Paradigm* and *Paradigm II*, and has written two mystical adventures, *An Esoteric Journey*, and *Ekani's Journey.*

Made in the USA
Columbia, SC
27 February 2025